Gears of Wonderland

JASON G. ANDERSON

ISBN: 1466420251
ISBN-13: 978-1466420250

DEDICATION

To Marina, for putting up with all my weird ideas, and my parents, for planting and watering the seeds of those ideas.

ACKNOWLEDGMENTS

Many thanks to Lynn O'Dell, for all the hard work she put into editing *Gears of Wonderland*, along with Irene Steiger and Misti Wolanski for their careful proofreading. Thanks also to Keith C. Blackmore, for his invaluable feedback and suggestions on the manuscript as it was taking shape.

CHAPTER 1

For what felt like the hundredth time, James glanced at the clock on the far wall of the office. The grinning Cheshire Cat plushy sitting on top of his monitor appeared to mock him as he again confirmed it was past seven o'clock.

He cursed his luck as he typed. Officially, he'd started his vacation two hours ago. Three hours ago, if you counted his plan to leave work early so he could be home in time to finish packing. But as he had shut down his computer, his boss, Ian, had dumped a pile of work on him, work that he'd quickly discovered were reports Ian should have completed.

The thought of leaving them undone and making his boss do his own work had been tempting, but he'd quickly pushed the idea aside. He didn't want to cause any trouble.

James worked frantically, the clatter of the keyboard echoing throughout the empty office. Forty-five minutes later, he typed the final words on the last report and hit 'Send.' He sighed with relief. They weren't perfect, but they would do. He'd been afraid he was going to be stuck in the office until midnight. At least he was going to have time to finish packing.

As he threw his few personal items into his bag, he glanced at the calendar on the rear wall of his cubicle. Seeing the next two weeks blocked out with 'Holiday' gave him a feeling of comfort. His fiancée had been pushing for the trip for months, and his agreement had changed their conversations from how much she wanted to go, to what they should do when they went—a much more pleasant topic. Then, he noticed the note he'd scrawled on the calendar for today.

'Parcel.'

His heart leapt into his throat. The parcel! He'd forgotten all about it in the mad rush of the afternoon. The other reason he'd planned to leave early was to intercept it before Laura got home.

The bus ride seemed to take forever. A glance at his phone as he got off the bus confirmed that it was almost eight thirty. He hoped Laura had gone out with her friends for after-work drinks when he'd messaged her that he would be late. It was the only way he would get home before she did.

Rounding the corner onto his street, he breathed a sigh of relief. The lights in the small flat they shared were off. He was safe. Then, he realized he was looking at the wrong flat. His heart sank when he saw the lights of his own flat. Laura was home.

James climbed the stairs to the front door with trepidation. Outside the door, he took a deep breath, forcing himself to relax. Maybe the parcel hadn't arrived. Maybe Laura had ignored it, seeing that it was addressed to him. Maybe everything would be all right. He opened the door, and stepped inside.

The open box on the floor of the lounge room told him it wasn't going to be all right. Laura was sitting on the edge of the sofa, still dressed in her work clothes. She had a calm expression on her face, although she sat stiffly. His purchase rested on the coffee table in front of her.

He forced a smile and tried to keep his voice light and happy. "Hey. Sorry I'm late, Ian gave me some—"

She pointed to the box on the table. "What's this?" Her voice had a hard edge to it.

"It's nothing, really. Just something I bought for—"

"When we talked about it last time, you promised you would give it up. For me. For us. That you'd get rid of your childish habits and stop playing silly games. You agreed that you would put it behind you."

He looked at the boxed chess set. He had paid a lot of money for it. The pieces were Swarovski crystal with flecks of red or white marble in the tops, and the board was made of etched glass with intricate patterns around the outside. He had stumbled across it online by accident and been captivated by its beauty. The plan had been to keep it hidden at work, so she wouldn't find out about it.

So much for that plan.

"I'm sorry. I didn't buy it to play, I swear. I thought the set looked pretty, so I got it to—"

"James, it's still a chess set!"

He stared at his feet. "I'm sorry."

"How many times do I have to tell you, James? We've been over this before. Chess is a game. Only children and pathetic no-hopers play games." Laura stood and put her hand gently on his cheek, her voice softening. "You're twenty-four now, an adult, soon to be married to a wonderful woman who wants only the best for you. It's time to grow up and act your age. I know growing up can be hard sometimes, and we have to give up the things we loved when we were kids, but as an adult, we get lots of new fun things to do. You'll do this little thing for your fiancée, won't you?"

James sighed internally. His inner voice wanted him to stand up for himself and argue with her, tell her that it was his chess set, and he'd keep it if he wanted. But he knew that if he did, the fight would go on for hours. And he'd ultimately give in, anyway. He always did.

He put on an apologetic smile to satisfy Laura. "Of course I will. I'm sorry I upset you."

"I know you're weak, James." She gave him a peck on his cheek. "That's why you have me to be strong for you." She picked up the chess set and walked toward the door. "I'll put this in my car and dispose of it in the morning before we leave. We don't want to keep it in the flat, do we?"

"I could always send it back and get a refund," said James hopefully.

Laura shook her head. "No, the only way you'll become strong enough to resist your urges is by learning that if you waste your money on things like this, it's gone for good. You need to learn your lesson properly. It's best for both of us if I get rid of it." She flashed him another smile, then stepped outside.

James sighed. It had been a wonderful chess set. He would miss it. And he hadn't even had a chance to study it.

His cell phone rang. He glanced at the number before answering. It was his boss, just the person he didn't want to talk to.

"Hey, Ian. Don't worry; I got your reports done. And I've left documentation with Al, so if you have any questions while I'm away, he should have the answers."

"Ah, James, I'm glad I caught you before I left. Listen, I'm going to be away next week. Something's come up, and I have to leave for

Hawaii immediately. I need you to come in next week and cover for me."

"What? But Laura and I are going to France tomorrow. I've had this vacation booked for months. The hotel is paid for, and I had to make a reservation six months in advance for the restaurant Laura's been dying to try. I can't cancel it."

"Sorry, James, but you'll have to put your holiday on hold. I need you to manage the Henderson project while I'm gone. Al knows the details, but I need you to provide the guidance. He can't see the big picture like you can. I'm counting on you."

"Ian, come on, please. Be reasonable about this–"

Ian cut him off, a hard note audible in his voice. "It's a simple choice, James. Either you come in to work next week, or you don't bother coming in to work at all." Then, his voice softened. "You don't want to be looking for work in an economy like this, especially with a wedding coming up."

James gripped the phone tightly, then bowed his head. "Okay, I'll get the files from Susan on Monday morning and get the project finished."

Ian coughed. "Actually, Susan has had to take an emergency vacation. Something about a sick mother to look after. Good luck, James." Ian hung up.

He stared at his cell phone. Susan didn't have a mother. At least, not one who was alive. He remembered talking with Susan once about their parents, and she had told him her mother had passed away when she was very young, and she had grown up with only her dad. The lying son-of-a—

Laura returned to the flat. "Who was that?"

Trying to ignore the falling sensation in his stomach, James cleared his throat. "It was Ian. We need to talk…"

* * *

After the incident with the chess set, he had expected Laura to blow her top with the news he couldn't go to France. Instead, she had icily informed him to find somewhere else to stay the night and think carefully about the choices he had made over the past few days.

He quickly realized that one of the choices he had made was to leave his wallet in his bag and, in the drama of being kicked out of his own flat, he had forgotten to pick it up. That made his destination options rather limited.

He decided to walk to Melvin's house. Laura didn't approve of Melvin—she didn't approve of much anything James had done or enjoyed before she met him—therefore, he hadn't seen a lot of Melvin over the past eighteen months, even though Melvin was his oldest friend. Despite the circumstances, he was happy at the chance to see Melvin again for more than a few stolen minutes during his lunch break.

The only downside was that Melvin lived some distance away, and James had little option but to walk. He was thankful the weather was reasonable—crisp, but not too cold, and with no sign of rain.

After an hour and a half of trudging, Melvin's building finally came into view. His tiny flat was above an old bicycle shop. Melvin had lived there ever since James had known him, for reasons he couldn't fathom. The place was a dump. Cold in winter, hot in summer, it had water pipes that spat brown-colored water, and an electrical system he was sure would cause a fire at some point. But Melvin loved the place. He claimed it had 'character.'

"Excuse me, do you have the time?"

James jumped. He hadn't noticed the man standing on the corner. He wore a white suit, with a wide-brimmed hat that obscured his face with shadow. His voice had a strange accent to it that James couldn't place. To James's bemusement, the man was looking at some sort of pocket watch.

"Er, sure." James fumbled for his phone. "It's just after ten. Ten-oh-eight, according to this."

"Excellent; I'm not late. Thank you." The man adjusted his watch slightly, then flipped the lid shut and put it back into his pocket. He gave James a faint smile, his mouth the only part of his face visible beneath the hat, and leaned back against the building.

"Yeah. No problem. Have a good one."

Chuckling to himself, James crossed the street. The outfit the guy wore was unusual, even for London. It almost looked like a cross between what a nineteen twenties gangster would wear and a suit from Victorian times. And who used a pocket watch in modern society?

He put his thoughts about the man aside when he reached the building with Melvin's flat and climbed the rusty stairs leading to the front door. He knocked loudly, trying to make himself heard over the loud sounds of the TV coming from within. After a few moments, the volume lowered, and he heard shuffling movements. The door opened slightly, a security chain stopping it from opening far.

"Who's there?"

"It's me. Sorry for the late hour, but I need somewhere to crash."

"James!" Melvin closed the door to undo the chain, then opened it fully to let him enter. "I wasn't expecting to see you. Come in, come in. What's happened? Is everything all right?"

"Not really." He entered the flat. "Laura and I had a fight."

Melvin sighed, shaking his head, as he motioned for James to take a seat. "Was it a real fight, or did she just tell you the latest thing she thought you had done wrong?"

"Hey, it's not like that. I broke a promise, and she was upset. Then, my boss called and said I had to go into work next week or I'd lose my job, even though we'd already booked a trip to France. So she's mad about that, and mad that I ordered a chess set after I promised her I would give it up. She wanted to be alone this evening."

Melvin sighed again. "You need to learn to stick up for what you want, James. One day, it will be very important that you do."

"I know, I know. I shouldn't have let my boss browbeat me into going to work next week."

"That's not what I meant. But you already knew that."

James looked away uncomfortably, then stood. "If you don't mind, I have to use the bathroom."

Melvin waved his hand. "You know where it is. I'll make us some coffee. I have a feeling this is going to be a long night."

James stepped into the small bathroom and closed the door. After he had finished relieving himself, he flushed the toilet and washed his hands, drying them on the threadbare hand towel. He was about to go back out into the living area when a loud crash startled him. It sounded as if something had smashed through the front door.

"You!" Melvin's voice held a combination of surprise and fear. James opened the bathroom door a crack to see what was happening. A giant of a man, almost seven feet tall, stood inside the broken door. A tarnished metal mask covered the man's face, and he wore black leather gloves and a long brown leather coat with the Ace of Spades symbol clearly embossed on the lapel.

His heart skipped a beat when he saw what the intruder held in his hands—two large knives, almost eighteen inches long with the blades curving up slightly to end in a lethal point. They weren't blades intended for decoration. They were blades designed to kill.

Before James could react, the man slashed several times at Melvin's neck and torso. Blood exploded from Melvin's body, and he let out a sickening gurgle as he slumped to the ground. The murderer stared at Melvin's collapsed form for several moments.

James stood frozen in fear. His hand slipped on the door handle where he had been holding it after opening the door, and the handle flicked back with an audible noise.

The killer raised his head and stared directly at him.

James took one look at the man who had killed his best friend and did the only thing he could think of. He slammed the bathroom door, flung open the window, and threw himself onto the fire escape. The intruder crashed through the bathroom door, but James was already halfway down the fire escape and running for his life.

He'd hoped the killer would let him escape. After all, as he wore a mask, James couldn't possibly identify him. But as he reached the bottom of the fire escape, the killer began to follow.

For the second time that evening, James cursed the fact that Melvin lived in such a remote area of the city. Anywhere else, there would have been other people around, forcing the murderer to leave him alone. But the deserted street offered no chance of safety. He knew if he went to one of the surrounding houses to get help, he would be dead before anyone could answer the door. That was if they even answered the door.

His legs hadn't had a chance to recover from the long walk to Melvin's place, and his leg muscles almost immediately burned from the exertion. With no option left, he fled down the street, hoping to reach a busier area with traffic and people before the killer caught up to him.

He spied a narrow lane he remembered Melvin leading him through once. They had used the shortcut after going out to grab some takeout food. He risked looking behind him. The murderer was fewer than twenty yards behind and closing in fast. He could see the glint of the knives in the moonlight and knew if the killer caught up with him, he would be as dead as Melvin. He threw himself around the corner into the lane.

He nearly lost his footing as he realized the man in the white suit from earlier stood around the corner. Almost casually, the man lunged forward and tackled him.

"I'm sorry for this," the man said. "But I need to keep a promise to an old friend."

James braced himself to hit the ground, but the ground seemed to disappear beneath him. He felt as if he had been knocked into a deep hole. Or off a cliff. The man pushed him away, then disappeared in a bright flash of light.

After a moment of shock, James screamed as he fell. Thoughts flashed through his mind, all the hopes and dreams he had held for his life.

It took him a few seconds to realize he hadn't hit the bottom of the hole. He stopped screaming and began to take notice of his surroundings. Then, he blinked a few times, trying to make sense of what he saw.

Cupboards and bookshelves lined the walls of the hole he was falling down, along with pictures of places, people, and maps hanging on short pegs. Most of the cupboards and shelves were empty, but a few contained various small items—jars, books, even a few dolls and other stuffed toys.

The thought that he was dead and having his final hallucinations crossed his mind.

He noticed a bright light far below him. Focusing on it, he realized with a sinking feeling that the bottom of the hole was fast approaching. He couldn't make out what he would hit at the bottom. Not that it mattered. He wouldn't survive landing on anything after falling such a long way.

For the second time, James screamed.

CHAPTER 2

James landed heavily, the fall knocking the wind out of him. The overpowering smell of rotten food and other things he didn't want to think about assaulted his nose. The sound of indignant squeaks and lots of creatures scurrying away told him he wasn't the only occupant of whatever he had landed in. He opened his eyes, unable to believe he was still alive after such a fall, then blinked in confusion.

He lay in an alleyway in the middle of a huge pile of rotten garbage. Unfamiliar buildings loomed on either side, and past them, he could see the night sky, with no sign of the hole he had fallen down.

"Must have been dreaming," muttered James. He suddenly remembered the events before the imagined fall and looked around urgently for the killer or the man in white, but saw no trace of either one of them.

"Cops. Gotta get the cops." He hauled himself out of the garbage pile and shook off the few items clung to his clothes. He pulled out his phone. No service.

He cursed the phone—the only place it ever had a reliable signal was inside his flat—and put it away. Figuring there would be a pay phone nearby, or maybe an open store, he hurried toward the end of the alley.

Reaching the street, he almost collided with a woman crossing the entrance to the alley. He managed to stop himself in time.

The woman seemed as surprised to see him as he was to see her. She wore a costume that looked vaguely Victorian, dark blue, with a full skirt but tight bodice. Her long black hair and slim figure suited the costume, but the thick leather belt around her waist with the large leather pouch attached didn't match the rest of the outfit. But it was probably the perfect place to keep her money and phone.

His brain finally caught up with the idea that she might have a phone.

"Please, I need to use your phone. My friend's been attacked, and I need to call the cops. An ambulance, too. He might still be alive."

The woman looked at him as if he were mad. "Phone? Cops? What are you talking about?" She looked him up and down. "And who the bloody hell are you, anyway?"

He stared at her in disbelief. She was either drunk—although she didn't sound drunk—or stupid. He was going to have to find someone else to help him.

A loud noise interrupted his thoughts. It sounded like a steam train coming down the road. He turned to see a strange sight. Four lights, nothing like the lights of a car, hurtled toward him.

The girl grabbed him and pulled him back. "Quick! Into the alley, you idiot."

The cry of annoyance James had been about to loose died on his lips as the source of the noise became visible. The vehicle was like nothing he'd ever seen. The shape was similar to a horse-drawn carriage, but instead of the usual wood finishes on the side, the carriage was made from a weird lattice of metal bars meshed together in a way that suggested function, instead of comfort or design, had been the overriding theme. No horses pulled the contraption. Instead, the vehicle had a huge engine on the back, with a smoke stack billowing a noxious black cloud. His nose burned as the smoke reached him. The lights he had seen were lanterns, and they illuminated the carriage enough for him to see the man sitting in the driver's seat—a man who appeared to be wearing a 'red coat' British soldier's uniform from the 19th century.

As James tried to take in the strange carriage, he began to notice other details of his surroundings. The street on which he had emerged looked nothing like the main street he expected. The light level was low, with only a handful of street lamps visible, and the street lamps had been replaced with old-style gas lamps more fitting in a museum. They created just enough illumination to make out several of the buildings opposite. Unlike the shops and flats he knew, the buildings were small Victorian terraces. No, that wasn't right. Paying closer attention, he realized that the details were wrong. They looked more like someone's idea of what a Victorian terrace house *should* look like.

"Thanks for almost getting me caught, idiot." The woman fixed him with a contemptuous gaze. "You know there's a curfew in this section of the city. The guard can execute us on the spot."

"Curfew? Guard?" It was his turn to repeat words as he struggled to come to terms with the odd view.

The woman rolled her eyes. "You really are a moron, aren't you? I should have guessed from your clothes. What are you? Some village idiot who's come to the big city to try and make his fortune?"

"Hey, you're the one in the fancy costume." He'd only just met the woman, but she was already beginning to get on his nerves.

The woman opened her mouth to respond, then closed it. She stared fixedly at his left arm.

Suddenly, she grabbed his arm, and before he could react, she pulled on the sleeve near his bicep. The shirt ripped without effort. Her grip on his arm became vice-like.

He finally regained his wits. "Hey, let go!" He managed to wrestle his arm away from her. "Do you have any idea how much this shirt cost?" He looked at the sleeve to assess the damage. She had almost torn it off.

The woman said nothing. Instead, she reached for the pouch on her belt, and pulled out a gun unlike anything he'd ever seen in magazines or movies. It looked like it belonged in some sort of sci-fi TV show, but it was unmistakably a gun.

James quickly raised his hands. "Hey, now, let's calm down here. There's no need to get violent. We're both adults. I'm sure we can work something out. I don't have any money, but I have a phone. It's the latest model. Did you want my phone? It's all yours."

"Who are you?"

He couldn't interpret the strange tone the woman's voice had taken. "James. James Riggs."

"Not your name." The woman waved the gun slightly. "*Who* are you?"

"I don't know what you mean."

The woman stared at him, then motioned with the gun back to the street. "You're coming with me to see my father."

"Now, look, I'm sorry I called what you're wearing a fancy costume." He took a step back. "It's really nice. There's no need for any of this. I'll just be on my—"

The woman's voice was hard. "You're coming with me to see my father right now. If you try to run, I will shoot you. Any more complaining, and I might shoot you anyway. Understand?"

He looked at the woman, at the gun, and back to the woman. "Yes ma'am."

* * *

Lahire sat back in the throne, thoughtful as he looked over the dimly lit room. Even in the limited light, the extravagance and splendor of the throne room was obvious. Marble floors and columns, gilding, huge and complex tapestries, and more than a few inlaid gems combined to create a throne room both impressive and fitting for someone of his status. It had brought him a sense of great satisfaction when the new throne room had finally been complete, allowing him to demolish the old room where his mother had held court for the two centuries of her reign. But the joy he normally felt from sitting on his throne and looking out over his creation had faded that evening. He'd expected Taxard to return from the errand an hour ago, and he didn't like to be kept waiting.

Finally, the door to the throne room opened, and a figure moved into the room. The light from the hallway silhouetted the figure's tall frame before the closing door removed the light source.

The newcomer moved smoothly across the throne room floor, stopping several yards from Lahire and kneeling with a bow. "Your Majesty."

"You're late. I trust everything went to plan."

Taxard straightened. "The target is dead, as you ordered." He paused. "However, there was a complication."

"What sort of complication?" He leaned forward in annoyance. He didn't like complications. Complications disrupted the neat order of the society he had forged.

"A witness. A native of the world. He managed to escape."

"You're slipping. You've never left any survivors before." He waved his hand. "It doesn't matter. The authorities in that world can do nothing. They may even believe the witness was the one responsible for the murder."

Taxard shifted slightly. Lahire recognized the movement. He had seen it many times from subordinates bringing him bad news. But he had never seen it from Taxard.

Lahire narrowed his eyes. "What is it you're not telling me?"

"The witness. When he escaped… he escaped to Wonderland."

"What?" Lahire was on his feet in an instant. "Explain yourself!"

"The witness, a male, passed through a portal. It closed before I could get a precise fix on its destination, but I managed to track him as far as this city."

"You're sure that it was a native of the Otherworld, and not another fugitive?"

"Yes, Your Majesty. He had the aura of a native. There was no mistake."

"You allowed an outsider to come here? You fool! Find this man. Find him at once. Mobilize the entire guard and have them do a house-to-house search. This outsider is a threat to the society I have built, and I will not tolerate it. The last thing I need is for the rebels to find him and use him as a symbol to rally behind. Or worse."

Taxard bowed low. "I will do as you command."

He fixed Taxard with a steely gaze. "See that you do. Go."

Taxard bowed again and swiftly departed the throne room. Lahire glowered after him for a moment, then turned and left the throne room via his private entrance. Taxard had made a mistake, but he knew of another who had some explaining to do.

He moved quickly through the castle's hallways. The sounds of the Heart Guards' frantic activity filled the castle as they carried out his orders. He was confident the outsider would be found. As long as the outsider hadn't made contact with the terrorists, everything would be fine. The executioner would do his job, and order in Wonderland would be maintained.

At least, that was what he told himself.

He reached his destination and descended the stairs to the lab area he had first created, and since expanded many times, over a century ago. The stairs opened out at the bottom into a huge cavernous room, filled with all manner of devices and sounds. The room was hot, but for once the air wasn't filled with steam or smoke. Electricity crackled to his left; however, he walked toward the voice straight ahead.

"No, you imbeciles! I told you to connect the dilator to the converter, not the convector. Are you trying to kill us all?" A whip cracked loudly, followed by a whimper. "Take it apart and do it again."

Lahire strode past the tables and half-built frames of various creations to the open central area. The thin and hunched form of Dr. Keron stood in front of a large engine of some kind, while two round little men frantically worked on it. Like all of his creations, it looked like a jumbled collection of parts jammed together in the middle of a large metal frame.

He had to admit the doctor had produced results over the years. He had designed all the war machines in Lahire's army, and his creations had been instrumental in the final war. But lately, his work had not been to the same standard. The terrorists had created a number of devices recently that had surprised and confused the doctor. Lahire was beginning to suspect that soon he would have to find a new head of research. Perhaps even the one currently working for the terrorists.

"Keron!"

The doctor stopped berating his two assistants and turned to face him. "Your Majesty! You come at a fortuitous time. In a few more minutes, I will be ready to demonstrate—"

"I thought you told me no one could travel to the Otherworld anymore. That it was now sealed off?"

"That's correct, Your Majesty. Travel there is now impossible."

"Then, how do you explain an outsider arriving in Wonderland?"

"An outsider? Impossible. The only way they could have come through is if another brought them while the barrier was down."

"What do you mean, 'while the barrier was down'?"

"Well, obviously you still require Taxard to travel to the Otherworld. While he is gone, the barrier is disabled. Otherwise, he wouldn't be able to return."

"You never mentioned this to me!"

"I thought it obvious."

One of the assistants let out a sudden cry of surprise. A loud screeching noise filled the air.

"Take cover!" Despite his apparent frailty, Dr Keron moved at lightening speed to dive behind a large rock slab covered in scorch marks. Lahire, no stranger to the doctor's mishaps, was right behind him.

A loud explosion caused the ground floor to shake. Smoke filled the air, causing him to cough. The doctor, apparently unaffected by the smoke, stood and moved toward what had become twisted wreckage. His two assistants lay on the ground nearby, their clothes scorched and burnt in places.

The first one sat up, apparently unharmed despite the damage to his clothes. "I told you to turn the fitting clockwise. You turned it the wrong way!"

The second one rose, staring furiously at the first. "Nohow! I was standing opposite to you, so obviously I had to turn it counter-clockwise. Besides, you gave me a wrench when I specifically asked for a spanner."

"A wrench is much better than a spanner! It doesn't repeat any letters in its name."

"Contrariwise, spanner is much easier to spell. Imagine if I had to write what I wanted, instead of speak it, and you—"

Dr Keron removed a whip from beneath his coat, and flicked it at the two men. They cringed back from the loud crack.

"Enough! Another word from either of you, and I'll cut your food rations. Get this mess cleared up."

The two men leapt to their feet and rushed over to the wreckage. Lahire managed to get his coughing fit under control. The doctor, seemingly unconcerned, took a notebook out of his pocket and made some notes. Lahire crossed to where he stood.

Dr Keron looked up. "My apologies for the inconvenience, Your Majesty. Tweedles aren't too bright, but as you just witnessed, their resilience to physical damage does mean they have their advantages."

Lahire stabbed a finger at Dr Keron's face. "I should have you executed for your recklessness. I could have been killed!"

"And yet, you weren't, Your Majesty. You are still safe and sound. And more importantly, I have some new data that should improve the speed of our latest fliers by fifteen percent."

Lahire stopped, impressed at the news despite his anger. "How soon can you have the improvements out to the navy?"

"The first fliers will be modified before the end of the night. The rest of the fleet can be upgraded over the next three weeks."

He nodded. "Do it." His mind returned to the original reason he had come down there, but continuing the topic with Dr. Keron was pointless. He had learned everything he needed to know.

Someone had known the schedule for when Taxard left for the Otherworld, which meant a spy was present in the castle.

CHAPTER 3

James walked the strange streets. The woman never wavered in pointing the gun at him, offering him no chance of escape. His few questions went unanswered. She spoke only to give him directions.

To his eyes, it looked as though he had walked onto a movie set for a Victorian film. The streets were rough cobblestone, while the houses and shops looked like something from a Dickens novel. And the smell.... The pile of rubbish he had fallen into was nothing compared to some of the places they walked past on the way to their unknown destination.

The woman directed him down a narrow alley. "Stop. This door here." A well-worn sign hung above the door, though in the low light, he couldn't read it. At the woman's urging, he opened the door and stepped inside.

The room beyond proved to be a small shop. It was well lit by gas lights on the walls, and much warmer than the city outside. It was also full of hats. All types of hats, from the sensible to the ridiculous. Next to a fashionable top hat was a strange piece shaped in a way that could only be described as a whale hat, while behind both sat a hat that at least ten peacocks had sacrificed their tails to create.

At the counter in the rear of the store sat an old man looking sad as he sipped from a china cup. However, when James stepped into the room, the man's face lit up.

"Yes! Yes! Of course! You're the one! You're the one I've been waiting for my entire life." The man leapt from behind the counter to be at James's side in an instant. "I can't believe I've finally found you. All these years of waiting, and now you're here in my shop."

"I'm sorry?" Despite having a crazy woman with a gun behind him, the old man's reaction had thrown him completely.

"You're the one! My savior!" The man turned to a shelf nearby, grabbed the most hideous hat James had ever seen, and turned back. "You're the one this hat was made for. I knew it the moment you walked into my shop. You've saved my shop, my business, and my reputation."

"Father!" The woman closed the door, but she stood next to it with her gun pointed at James.

"Not now, Kara." The man glanced at the woman before turning his attention back to James. "Can't you see I'm with a customer?"

"Father, this isn't a customer. It's nighttime. The shop closes at night, remember?"

The man looked from Kara to James. "You're not a customer?"

James, amused despite himself, shook his head. "Sorry, no. Your crazy daughter decided to kidnap me at gunpoint."

The man gave Kara a disapproving stare. "What have I told you about threatening people with guns, young lady? That's no way to make friends."

Kara pointed at James. "Look at his arm."

The man looked at James's right arm. "Well, yes, I suppose it is a nice shirt. The material is rather strange, though, and a little dirty." The man poked at James's arm. "It has a bit of muscle mass, but not much." He turned back to Kara. "It seems like a perfectly normal arm to me, my dear."

The woman rolled her eyes, crossed over to where James stood, and painfully grabbed his left arm again. She ripped away the final threads of the sleeve and lifted the arm up to her father's face. "Here. See?"

The man looked at the arm, then at James, then back at the arm. He went pale and became shaky on his feet.

"Father!" The woman let go of James and moved to steady the man. Seeing his chance, James leapt for the door.

He found himself lying on his back a yard from the door, the loud crackle of electricity ringing in his ears. His entire arm ached from where the electricity had struck him.

"I wouldn't try that again if I were you." Kara helped her father back to his seat. "I made the security system, and it's quite good, even if I do say so myself. Getting hit by that much electricity isn't healthy for you. It could kill you if you're not too careful."

He painfully got to his feet. "Who are you people? Why are you doing this to me?"

Kara's father had recovered slightly. He waved James over to sit at the counter. "The question, young man, is who are *you*?"

"I told your daughter before, my name is James. James Riggs."

"Not your name, young man."

"I don't understand."

"Your mark on your arm," said Kara with exasperation.

"My... what, my tattoo?" James held out his left arm. The tattoo of the crossed red and white knight chess pieces was clearly visible with the sleeve torn away. "What about it? I got it after a won a chess competition two years ago. What's the big deal?"

"Chess competition?" asked Kara.

"Yeah. Chess competition. Up in Manchester. Big national affair, not that you'd know it from the number of people there. I managed to knock over the reigning champion against all expectations. I got drunk that night and woke up with a new tattoo. So what? It's not like tattoos are illegal or anything."

Kara and her father looked at each other. The father spoke again. "This Manchester you speak of. Where is it?"

"What do you mean, where is it? North of London, of course. You mean you've never been there? Didn't you learn any geography in school?"

Kara and her father exchanged another look.

"Look, what's the big secret here? You abduct me at gunpoint, make a big deal about my tattoo, and now you're carrying on like Manchester is some kind of special place. Spit it out."

"You're not in your own country anymore," replied the old man.

"Obviously. It looks like I've ended up in a backwater European town somewhere, no offense meant. I have no idea how I got here, and I guess it's lucky that you two speak English. If you're thinking of trying to ransom me off, you're out of luck. And if you're planning on harvesting my organs for the black market, I won't go down without a fight."

The old man waved a hand in annoyance. "No, no, no, you misunderstand. You're not in your own country anymore because you're not in your world anymore."

"Huh?"

"You're in Wonderland, young man."

"Wonderla... okay, I've had about enough of this." Angry, James stood to leave. "I may not be the brightest cookie around, but Wonderland? You seriously expect me to believe that? You people are crazier than I thought. Now, either let me go, or do whatever it is you're planning to do. I'm not going to listen to your crap any longer."

"He's telling the truth," said Kara calmly, ignoring his outburst.

He stared at the two. They stared back impassively. He knew it was ridiculous, but a gnawing feeling at the back of his mind told him that they were telling him the truth.

He pushed the feeling away. Wonderland was a place in a kid's story, albeit a kid's story that he had read many times and bought every book and movie that mentioned it. It wasn't real, though. Those two were obviously crazy. Or he'd hit his head running away from the killer, and he was in a dream because of his interest in Wonderland. Either way, his only choice at the moment seemed to be to play along.

He sat back down heavily. "Let's pretend for a moment that I believe you. Two questions. First, how exactly did I get here? It's not like I fell down a rabbit..." His voice trailed off as he remembered his crazy falling dream.

"What do you remember?" asked the old man gently.

James composed himself. "I was being chased by this crazy guy. He'd busted into Melvin's flat and sliced him up without any warning. I managed to escape out the fire escape and was heading for the main road when I took a shortcut down a side alley. Next thing I know, some guy in a white suit tackles me. I woke up in a rubbish pile, and then ran into your gun-nut daughter here. I figured I had hit my head."

Kara looked shocked at the mention of the man in the white suit. "You met White Rabbit?"

James looked at her in surprise. "What, like Alice and the White Rabbit?"

The old man studied James intently. "How did you know about Alice?"

"You know, from the book. *Alice in Wonderland.*"

"No, I don't know." The old man sighed. "People from your world coming here has always been rare, but it's not unheard-of. We haven't had any visitors here for a hundred and fifty years. Not since the king shut down the gateways and made it almost impossible to get to your world. The last visitor to Wonderland was a girl named Alice. Very pretty, although rather rude."

"You talk as if you met her."

"Of course, I met her! She decided to intrude on a private tea party I was having with friends. She drank our tea, ate our food, then left without so much as a thank you."

James thought of the description of Alice meeting the Mad Hatter in *Alice in Wonderland*. True, Alice had sat down uninvited at the table with the Mad Hatter, Dormouse, and the March Hare. But she didn't eat or drink anything. And the others had been rather rude to her during their brief meeting.

"That's not *quite* how it's described in the book." Something occurred to him. "Hang on a second. You're the Mad Hatter from the book? But that's impossible. You said Alice came here a hundred and fifty years ago. You can't be that old."

"Mad? Mad?" Hatter leapt to his feet and looked as if he was about to start an angry tirade at James. Then, he stopped and looked thoughtful. "Well, yes. I suppose my mind does have its little fancies now and then." He sat back down. "It's rude to ask a person's age, don't you know. But if you must know, I am three hundred twelve years, two months, and nineteen days old."

James stared at him in surprise, then waved at Kara. "I suppose next you're going to tell me she's a hundred."

Kara rolled her eyes. "Don't be stupid. I'm twenty-two."

"Wonderlanders age differently than those of your world," said Hatter dismissively. "What was your second question?"

James stared blankly at the old man for a moment, then remembered. "The tattoo. Why are you acting all weird about it?"

Hatter nodded, an uneasy expression on his face. "Ah, yes, the tattoo. I think I will leave that to someone better suited to answer your questions on the matter. It won't take you long to get there. But before you go, why don't we have a nice cup of tea? Kara, if you would?"

"Actually, I'd prefer a coffee, if that's okay."

Hatter leapt to his feet again. "Coffee! Coffee! You *dare* ask for *coffee* in *my* house?"

"Father, Father, calm down. It's all right." Kara put her hands gently on her father's shoulders and sat him back down. She threw a dirty look toward James. "He's just stupid and doesn't know any better."

Her words calmed Hatter slightly, although he continued muttering, "Coffee?" under his breath.

James said nothing, not wanting to upset the old man further. Kara reached under the counter and brought out several well-used teacups.

She took them through a door at the back of the shop, leaving him alone with the old man. They were silent for several seconds.

"So... you're a hatter, then?" asked James.

"Why, yes. Yes, I am." Hatter's face lit up at the new subject. "I've been making them all my life. The finest hat maker in Wonderland, some say."

"Who say?"

Hatter's expression fell. "Well, mainly Kara, these days. Most of my friends have gone now. March moved to the Diamond Kingdom, and Dormouse—poor, sweet, innocent Dormouse—is... sleeping."

"I'm sorry to hear that," said James quietly. "How did it... happen?" With Hatter's blank expression, he added, "You know, how did he die?"

"Die? Oh, he isn't dead." Hatter laughed. "He's asleep, as I said."

"How long has he been asleep, then?"

Hatter pulled a pocket watch out of his waistcoat and opened it to look at the face. He tapped it against the desk a few times, then checked at it again. "Ninety-seven years, seven months, and five days."

James shook his head. It had to all be a dream. The feeling at the back of his mind that it was real returned, but he pushed it away again.

Kara returned carrying a tray with a pot, three teacups, and a plate of biscuits on it. She set it down on the counter. "Here you go, Father." She put a cup in front of him and poured some tea into it. Then, she did the same for herself. She made no move to pour a cup of tea for James.

With a sigh, he took the remaining cup and filled it. "You said March was in the Diamond Kingdom?" he asked Hatter. "What does that mean? Where are we?"

"We're in the Heart Kingdom," replied Hatter. "There are, or were, six kingdoms in Wonderland—Heart, Diamond, Club, Spade, Red and White."

"So, the playing card suits and the two chess piece colors from the books?"

"Do you mind not interrupting, young man? Now, I've lost my train of thought. What was I talking about, Kara, dear?"

"The kingdoms, Father."

"Oh, yes, the kingdoms. There were six in all, all happily coexisting as they had for thousands of years. Well, aside from the Red and White kingdoms, which were always at war, but even that had became routine, something they did out of habit more than anything else. Wonderful fruit buns, they made in the Red Kingdom. You wouldn't think a group of people who were always at war could bake so well, but could they ever! And the pickled carrots from the White Kingdom? Absolutely mouth-watering. One year, when March and I—"

Kara interrupted gently. "Father, you're getting off topic."

"Hmm? I am?"

"You were talking about the six kingdoms," offered James. "You said things changed somehow? In what way? What happened?"

Hatter paused. A faint noise rang outside, like some sort of chimes being struck. Kara and Hatter stiffened in their seats.

"What's that?" asked James.

Hatter and Kara shared a look, then turned to him. "That's the city guard being put on full alert," said Hatter. "They're going to be doing a house-to-house search of the city soon."

"Does that happen often?"

Hatter shook his head. "No. The last time was two years ago, when someone from the Red Kingdom tried to assassinate King Lahire. This time, I suspect the target is you."

"Me? Why would they be searching for me? How would anyone even know I'm here? The only people I've seen are you two, and your daughter marched me here at gunpoint before I could talk to anyone else."

Kara looked thoughtful. "You said you were running away from someone who had killed your friend. Did you get a look at who did it?"

James was somber as he replayed the memory of the murder. "I'll never forget it. The guy was massively tall, probably seven feet, and wearing a long leather coat with an Ace of Spades symbol on it. I didn't see his face, as he had some sort of theater mask on. He wore black leather gloves and carried two huge knives, really long ones. He knew how to use them. Melvin... Melvin didn't stand a chance."

Hatter and Kara looked at each other again with concern. He let out a frustrated sigh. "Now what?"

"The man you saw. He wasn't a man," replied Hatter after a moment.

"What?"

"The thing that killed your friend is a... construct, I suppose, is the best description. A machine made to look like a man. No one knows where it came from, but it has been by the king's side ever since Lahire took the throne. It bears the mark of the Spade Kingdom, but without any rank. It goes by the name Taxard."

"Hang on. So you're saying that this… this *construct*… was sent by your King Lahire to my world to kill Melvin?"

"So it would seem."

"But why? He was just a crazy old guy who was obsessed with murder-mystery shows. Everyone loved him. He didn't have any enemies. Certainly no one who would want to kill him."

Kara looked as if she wanted to say something, but Hatter cut her off. "Lahire does things that no one can explain."

Before he could ask anything further, a loud thump from outside interrupted the conversation.

"They're close," said Kara.

"Yes, yes." Hatter stood slowly. "You'd best get him out. Gryphon will want to meet him, and he can explain everything else to James."

Kara put a hand on Hatter's arm. "You'll be all right here alone?"

"Don't worry about me, dear." Hatter patted her hand kindly. "I'll be fine."

Kara gave him a quick peck on the cheek, then turned to James. "This way," she said without any hint of explanation.

"What, no gun this time?"

"There can be if you're going to cause trouble."

He raised his hands in mock surrender. "Fine, fine, lead the way."

CHAPTER 4

Kara led him through the door at the back of the shop. It opened into a cramped room where, James assumed, Hatter made his hats. Two benches with various bits and pieces of hats, feathers, thread, fabric, and other materials filled the majority of the room. In the corner sat a small stove, currently heating the space to a comfortable temperature. At the back, a steep set of stairs led to the next floor.

A hat stand stood next to the door. Kara took a large traveling cloak from it and threw it at him.

"Put this on. It'll cover your clothes well enough in the night light if anyone sees us." Kara grabbed a large leather satchel off the wall and put on a smaller traveling cloak of her own.

After making sure he was covered, she led him to a cupboard beneath the stairs. Kara opened the door and, crouching down, climbed inside.

"Where exactly are we going?"

She stopped, turned back to him, and rolled her eyes. "We're going to see Gryphon. He's a great man and the leader of the rebels in the Heart Kingdom."

"Don't tell me, he has a friend called *Mock Turtle*." James chuckled slightly at his joke, remembering the scene with Gryphon and Mock Turtle in the original Alice story.

Kara's face took on a look of fury, causing him to take a half-step back. "Don't you dare say a bad word about Mock. He gave his life to save the rest of us when Lahire attacked. He was a hundred times the man you could ever be." A tear formed in the corner of one of her eyes. She stared at him angrily for a moment longer before returning back inside the cupboard without another word. With little choice, he followed.

She opened some sort of smaller hidden door at the back of the cupboard. Suddenly, someone banged loudly on the door of the shop.

"Quick, get through!" hissed Kara, motioning for him to move past.

Hatter called out a mumbled, "Just a minute there. I'm not as young as I used to be." James wasted no time sliding past Kara and through the open hatch.

Standing up, he found himself in a narrow space, a yard wide where he stood but quickly narrowing to become barely wide enough to fit him sideways. Kara poked him in the leg. "Move to your right. Keep going until you don't have enough head room." She closed the hatch, and the dim light filtering into the area disappeared.

Following her instructions, he carefully felt along the wall and shuffled as quietly as he could to the right. He lost track of how far he moved, but finally, after what seemed like hours but was probably only a few minutes, he felt the change in height levels. Moments later, Kara was next to him.

"Now what?" he whispered.

Kara said nothing, but crouched down. Dim light entered the area as she removed a section of the wall.

"Mind the rubbish and rubble," whispered Kara, as she climbed out. "We don't want to make a loud racket and draw the guards here."

James carefully knelt down and managed to squeeze through the opening behind her. He emerged in what looked like a burned-out house. From the rubbish lying around, he thought it had been abandoned for some time. Looking around, he realized that several houses on either side had also been destroyed by fire.

Kara leaned down behind him and moved the wood planks that covered the hole back into position.

"How come these places haven't been rebuilt?"

"Lahire ordered that they be left as they are. The families who lived here were all convicted of crimes against the kingdom, and after the families had been executed, their houses and all the belongings were burned. They're supposed to be an example to everyone of what happens to traitors. Lucky for us, they're also a handy secret passage to and from the shop."

"Now where?"

"We've got some distance to cover through the city. With all the patrols out looking for you, we're going to have to take it slow. I know a few hidden paths in the city, so we should be safe. You'd better not be afraid of heights. Keep your mouth shut and try not to make any noise when you move."

He did as he was told, following Kara out of the house and onto the streets. True to her word, Kara led him on a twisting route through many narrow paths and between many houses and buildings. A few times, the sounds of the searching guards echoed in the distance, either on patrol around the city or forcing their way into houses to search, but each time Kara ensured they were well hidden.

After almost half an hour of sneaking through the streets, Kara led him to the base of a flimsy metal ladder hanging from a tall building.

"We need to get up high for the next section, so we'll be moving along the rooftops. Keep low and watch your footing. It can get slippery up there."

"Isn't there another way?"

Kara shook her head. "We need to move past their main search lines. The Heart Guard aren't particularly bright. So as long as we stay quiet, they shouldn't have any reason to look up and spot us."

James nodded, not liking the idea of climbing on the roofs of the buildings, but in no position to argue. It wasn't that he was afraid of heights; it was more that he was afraid of the landing if he fell. The ladder shook uncomfortably in his hands as he ascended, but to his relief it was stronger than it looked.

Once on the roof, he had his first chance to look around at the strange city. Most of the city reminded him of pictures he had seen of Victorian London, but one structure stood out in complete contrast to its surroundings.

In the distance, a strange framework of metal rose over two hundred yards into the air. A large number of lights were attached all over the structure, illuminating it and reminding him of a giant Christmas tree. Large shapes, vaguely similar in outline to airships or blimps, were attached to the framework at various points. He was too far away to make out any details, but the sight was amazing.

He turned to Kara as she joined him on the roof. "What's that?" He pointed at the structure.

She glanced in that direction, then turned back. Once again, the expression on her face indicated she thought he was an idiot. "The port. Why?"

"Port for what?"

"Skyships, of course. What did you think it was a port for?"

"Skyships?"

"If all you're going to do is repeat words back at me, you can forget about asking more questions."

James looked back at the structure. "Sorry." He wanted to ask more about the skyships, but it wasn't exactly the right place or time to do so.

Kara again took the lead. The roof was slippery as Kara had warned him, and though they moved by straddling the ridge cap, he felt his heart skip a beat every time his foot slipped slightly.

It was slow progress, but after climbing up and down a handful of roofs, he began to get the hang of it. The trick was how his weight was distributed as he put his feet down. He was almost beginning to enjoy being high up on the roofs, and several times he risked glances toward the port and the strange skyships that piqued his curiosity.

A skyship became his undoing. One of them detached from the port and moved away, slowly picking up speed. He was so fascinated in watching it move that he stopped paying attention to how he was stepping.

James let out a cry of surprise as his foot slid away from him. He tried to reach for the ridge cap as he fell but he landed hard, winding himself. Before he realized what was happening, he was sliding.

He scrambled to get a purchase on the slate as he slid, but found nothing to grasp. The edge of the roof approached at a terrifying rate. He desperately grabbed for the edge as his body left the roof.

He managed to gain purchase with his fingers on the edge of the roof. His momentum stopped, but as his body swung around, he felt his fingers slip. He fell. James tried to twist himself around so he would land feet-first, hoping against hope that he would survive falling two stories.

He landed heavily in a large, dying bush of some kind. His foot twisted on the uneven surface, and the sudden sharp pain caused him to cry out a second time.

"Are you hurt?" hissed Kara from the roof ridge. She had moved back to be level with him.

He tried to stand, but crumpled when he put weight on his ankle. "I've done something to my ankle."

Several shouts came from nearby, as searching guards who had heard his cry moved closer.

"Damn it!" Kara looked around. "Stay there. I'll draw them away, then double back to get you."

"Wait!" But Kara was already moving away, making noise and being obvious about her movements. James carefully slid so he was against the wall of the house, then slipped into the slightly darkened alcove offered by the back door. He leaned against the solid wood and tried to ignore the pain in his ankle.

He was so focused on the pain that he was taken by complete surprise when the door opened without warning. He toppled over, before everything went dark as some sort of bag or cloth was thrown over his head. Large hands clamped themselves on his shoulders, and he was dragged inside.

* * *

The door closed, and someone hauled James to his feet. He stumbled as he instinctively put weight on both feet, but the hands holding him didn't let him fall. Transferring his weight to his good foot, he stood as best he could. He heard the door lock.

"Uncover him," said a rough voice.

The cover over his head was removed, and he found himself in a kitchen. It was warmed by a wood stove, where a pot of something unrecognizable, but foul smelling, bubbled away on top. A basic wooden table and chairs took up most of the room, but left enough space for the three rough-looking men staring intently at him.

A muscular man on his right held his shoulders in a vice-like grip, while a tall but round man stood by the door. A short, stocky, and rough-looking thug stood in front of him. He had short black hair and a small mustache, and was dressed in rough trousers with a plain white vest. His well-defined arms were thick with the tattoo of a Three of Hearts clearly visible on his left bicep.

The man regarded him with some thought. "Well, well, well, what do we have here?"

He recognized the rough voice from earlier but said nothing, scared at the situation he found himself in.

"Hmmm, cat got your tongue, huh? Come on, tell us your name."

"James." His voice was unsteady.

"So, tell me, James. Why do the Heart Guard want you?"

"I don't know what you mean," replied James, trying to sound confident. The quavering in his voice ruined the effort.

The short man nodded to his companion by the door, who hit James on the back of the head. He would have been knocked to the ground if the other one hadn't held him. As it was, the blow left his head spinning.

"That was for lying to me. I know they're after you. You wouldn't have been running across my roof if they weren't. So, tell me why they were after you. Who knows? We might even be able to help you."

The two men standing either side of James chuckled menacingly.

"I don't know! I just arrived here!"

The man stared at him. "It doesn't matter why the Heart Guard want you. I'm sure if they're desperate enough to mount a full city search to find you, the reward for handing you over must be impressive." He turned back to the man who had hit James. "Harry, go to the nearest guard station and let them know we have their fugitive cornered. Deal with Connor; he'll make sure we get a reward."

"Sure thing, boss." The man moved toward the door out of the kitchen.

James's heart sank. Even if Kara returned in time, she didn't know where he was. She'd probably think he'd run off. And when the guards arrived to collect him, he was done for.

"Wait!" The man stopped, appearing uncertain. James looked at the leader. "I'm an outsider. That's why the guards are after me. Some people were going to help me get out of the city. Please, let me go. I'm not worth anything."

The stocky one beamed. "Not worth anything? On the contrary, you're worth a fortune! The reward for turning in an outsider is huge. And someone who can identify one or more terrorists in the city is worth even more. Boys, it looks like we hit the jackpot tonight. Harry, get to the guard station double-time and make sure you deal only with Connor. We don't want some bureaucrat trying to cheat us out of our money."

Harry nodded and left. A few moments later, the front door opened and closed.

A wave of hopelessness washed over him. That was it. It was all over. His journey in Wonderland was going to end before it had barely begun.

The front door of the house opened and closed again. The stocky man got an annoyed look on his face. "Harry, what the hell are you doing?" He crossed to the entrance of the kitchen. "I told you to go to the guard—"

The man's sentence was cut off by a muffled thud. He staggered backward, gurgling as he reached for the blade handle embedded in his throat. With a final gasp, he collapsed to the floor.

The man holding James threw him aside, as if he were no more than a sack of potatoes. He crashed into the wall, striking his head. He hadn't recovered from the earlier hit the thugs had given him, and the second blow only made things worse. The world seemed to swim and go out of focus as he tried to see what was happening.

The muscular man strode toward the door, then staggered back, clutching at his chest. He collapsed, several knife handles sticking out of his chest. A new figure appeared in the entryway. James recognized him from his white suit.

White Rabbit.

The suited figure moved quickly to kneel beside him. "Can you hear me? Are you hurt?" The man's voice was filled with unexpected concern. His hat had been knocked off, and James realized he looked much younger than he had originally thought him to be—in his mid-thirties at the most, with short blond hair and a kind face.

James tried to say something, but blackness came crashing down.

CHAPTER 5

James floated without a care in the world. Strange images flashed through his mind's eye, images of caterpillars and white rabbits, tall mushrooms and a huge house of playing cards. Then, a terrible smell invaded his world, an odor that could not be ignored. The images fell away from him—or did he fall away from them?—and he blinked in confusion.

"You're not dead, then." White Rabbit was kneeling in front of him. He took away the bottle he had been holding under James's nose and put it in his jacket pocket. James caught a glimpse of several knife handles sticking out from the jacket lining.

Recognition kicked in. "You!" James tried to sit up, then quickly changed his mind as his head felt as if it were about to explode.

"Careful. You've taken a few nasty knocks to your head over the past few minutes, with the fall off the roof and everything. You should rest for a few minutes before you try to get up. I imagine Kara will be back by then."

James fought through the fogginess in his brain. He sat up and put his hands on his temples. "You know about her?" He processed what White Rabbit had said. "Wait, you know I fell off the roof? How?"

"I've been following you since you arrived. I needed to make sure you made it to Gryphon safely. Unfortunately, you chose to make that difficult."

White Rabbit moved to stand, but James grabbed his arm. "You brought me here. Why? Why kidnap me?"

White Rabbit effortlessly shook off his grip and stood. "I made a promise many years ago to an old friend. One that I have now kept. The rest you'll have to discover on your own. Get to Gryphon. He'll fill you in on what's happened here."

White Rabbit turned and moved to the other door of the kitchen. He stopped, looked back at James, then put his hat back on his head. "For what it's worth, I am truly sorry. It was the only way." He then opened the back door, stepped outside, and closed the door behind him.

Trying to ignore his pounding head, James struggled to his feet. Unexpected stiffness in his ankle made him look down. His ankle had been wrapped with a plain piece of white cloth, making a tight bandage. He knew enough about first aid to tell that a pretty good job had been done. He tested his ankle. It hurt when he put weight on it, but it was manageable. He could walk again.

He took a quick look around the kitchen, then stepped back in horror. The leader and the muscular one who had held him lay dead on the floor. Blood pooled out from their bodies, although the knives that had killed them were gone. He'd never seen a dead body up close before, and although he'd seen plenty of images on television, the thought of being in a room with two dead people overwhelmed him.

He turned and fled the house.

James closed the door and sat down heavily against it, closing his eyes and trying to ignore the pain in his head and ankle. He wanted to do nothing more than sleep, but he knew that wouldn't be possible until he had met the Gryphon guy everyone had insisted he see.

Maybe then he would get some answers about what was going on.

Just as he drifted off, Kara's whisper awakened him.

"James? Are you there?"

"I'm here." He pushed himself to his feet and stepped out of the alcove.

Kara was above him, leaning over the roof cap. "We need to move. I'm not sure how long it will take them to realize I've doubled back. You're going to have to go through the next ten backyards along this row of terraces. Once you get through those, there's a narrow lane where you can get back onto the streets."

"I can go through this house if it's easier," offered James after a moment. "The occupants won't mind."

"What?"

"I'll explain later. Is it safe if I come out the front of the house?"

Kara glanced at the street, then gave an all clear signal. He steeled himself. "All right, see you in the lane in a couple of minutes."

He opened the kitchen door and quickly moved through the house. He did his best to ignore the two bodies in the kitchen as he stepped around the pools of blood. He found the third man, dead like the others, in the front room. He hurriedly walked past and out the front door.

Glancing up at the roof line, he saw Kara moving with cat-like grace along the roof ridge. Walking carefully so he didn't put too much stress on his ankle, he followed along in the street. By the time he reached the lane Kara had mentioned, she was already on the ground and waiting for him impatiently.

She eyed his gait. "How's the ankle?"

"Not as bad as it was. It's been wrapped." He lifted his leg to emphasize the point.

"Can you walk far?"

"As long as we don't have to do much running, I should be fine. My head feels like it's about to fall off, though."

"You hit your head in the fall?"

"That happened while you were gone."

"Tell me later. We need to move."

James motioned for her to lead the way.

* * *

He wasn't sure if Kara had taken pity on him, but their path for the next fifteen minutes was much easier. She moved them at a slower pace, and their path wasn't as torturous as it had been before the roof climbing. Not that he was complaining. Even with the wrapping, his ankle ached badly. He knew he needed to properly treat it, but that wasn't going to happen any time soon. Unlike before, the noise of the guards' searching sounded much more active, and they had to stop repeatedly to hide from passing patrols.

Kara had led them to the end of an alleyway between two houses when she stopped suddenly, causing him to almost run into her. She paused for several seconds to look around the corner, then motioned that they needed to retreat.

Once away from the street, she whispered, "They've stationed guards ahead."

"Can't we go around them, like the others?"

Kara shook her head. "It'll take too long. The guards I led off earlier are starting to come back to search this area more thoroughly. The longer we stay above ground, the greater the risk of being caught. We need to get through them now."

"So, what are we going to do?"

In answer, Kara took the satchel from her shoulder and opened the top. She withdrew a gun that looked like a larger version of the one she had threatened him with and a set of goggles.

James stared in shock. "You're going to shoot them?"

Kara nodded as she put on the goggles. "It's the only way. We can't risk them calling for backup."

"So, you want to kill them instead?"

"Who said anything about killing them? This will knock them out for an hour or two. Now shut up a moment, I need to concentrate." Kara fiddled with several dials on the side of the gun, then flicked a switch on top. With a final press of a button, a faint whine emanated from the pistol, as if it might be building up some sort of charge.

"Wait here." Kara crept back to the end of the alleyway. She took her time lining up her shot, then a blinding light and the crackle of electricity filled the night air. Kara let out a quiet "Yes!" in triumph. Almost simultaneously, someone cried an alarm from the direction they had left.

"Bugger!" hissed Kara. "Run!" James limped forward quickly as Kara rummaged in her satchel again. As he drew next to her, she took something out of the bag and threw it down the street in the opposite direction of the guards she had shot. She then ran toward the fallen guards.

As he hobbled after her, he could finally see the guards up close. Like the driver he had seen on the back of the strange coach, they wore tight red coats reminiscent of the English Redcoats from history. Their weapons even looked like muskets. He wanted to stop and have a closer look, but the sound of fast-approaching footsteps suggested that wouldn't be the smartest move.

Kara motioned him down an alley a few yards beyond the fallen guards, then ducked into it herself. She was standing a yard back from the entrance when he finally joined her. "We'll wait here a few moments."

"But what about the guards?"

"You'll see," was her cryptic reply.

James did as he was told, trying to hold his breath so the approaching guards wouldn't hear him. He heard them exit the path he and Kara had used, then shout when they noticed their fallen companions.

Without warning, several bright flashes appeared from the direction Kara had thrown the strange object. The guards shouted in surprise, reacting as if they were being attacked, yelling for assistance as the sound of their musket fire reverberated down the street. The guards began running again, away from where James and Kara were hiding.

"That should buy us a minute or two." Kara glanced around the corner. "Yep, they bought it. Quick, but quietly."

They moved back out onto the street, keeping close to the edge so they were in partial shadow. He risked a glance back the way they had come. A group of four guards were running the other way. Kara set off at a quick trot, while he followed as best he could.

Once the sounds of the guards had faded, Kara slowed her pace to a walk.

"What was that?" asked James through gritted teeth. His ankle throbbed.

"A little toy I've been playing with. It's like a thrown version of the gun, but with a time delay. They'll think we ran the other way and fired a few shots toward them. There may be a lot of Heart Guard, but they're not known for their brains."

James said nothing, impressed by her inventions and obvious skill at creating such things.

Kara directed him down a narrow alleyway, then stopped at an unmarked door and knocked with a sequence that was obviously some sort of code.

An answering sequence was rapped on the other side, then an old woman unlocked and opened the door. Without a word, she moved aside to allow them to enter.

Kara led him to the back room of the house and lifted a rug to reveal a trap door. Raising the trap door, she motioned for him to enter.

He began to climb down the narrow shaft into the darkness below.

* * *

Walking briskly as he flexed his hands, Lahire made his way through the dark castle. So far, the reports from the guards had all been negative. There had been an early sighting of the outsider climbing across the rooftops, but he had managed to evade the chasing guards. Lahire had also received reports that two guards had been attacked by an unknown sniper.

It was obvious to him that the outsider had somehow managed to make contact with the terrorists. Perhaps it had even been the terrorists who had brought the outsider to Wonderland. What they planned to do next he wasn't sure, but he was sure it would be bad for the stability of the kingdom.

Damn them! It had taken decades to build up everything. To unite the people of Wonderland under a single ruler. To eliminate the corrupt and useless rulers of the past, and improve the life of the common law-abiding citizen. He wasn't going to let a bunch of thugs destroy that!

"Troubles this evening, Your Majesty?" asked a deep voice from the shadows.

Lahire stopped walking. No matter how many times he heard the voice, it unsettled him and, truth be told, filled him with a small measure of dread. The way the voice emanated from the shadows, with no source he could focus on, only added to his unease.

He looked to the area he thought the voice had come from. "Nothing I don't already have under control, Shireche."

"I'm glad to hear that. I assume that means you've managed to capture and execute the outsider?"

He didn't bother answering the question. It was pointless. Shireche already knew the answer and was mocking his failure.

"You are aware that this outsider will ruin everything you have built over the past century? All the careful work and planning you've put into making a strong, unified society will be undone if the outsider isn't caught quickly."

He balled his hands into fists. "You think I don't know that!? Why do you think I've mobilized the entire guard to find him?"

"Temper, temper. I am merely an advisor, here to offer you advice whether asked for or not. I want only what you want. If you no longer wish my help, you have only to say."

Lahire pushed away his anger. Damn that outsider—he was even making him lose his temper with his most trusted confidant! Shireche was too important to risk upsetting.

"You are a valuable adviser, Shireche, and I appreciate all the suggestions and information you have given me since we began rebuilding Wonderland. I apologize for my earlier tone."

Lahire waited for an answer, hoping his apology would be accepted. As the seconds passed, he began to worry Shireche had left, but finally the deep voice spoke again.

"Your apology is accepted."

He felt his annoyance ebb away. He should know better than to raise his voice to Shireche. The kingdom had been built on the advice Shireche had provided, and Shireche had saved his life on many occasions. More than once, Shireche had pointed out threats to Lahire or the kingdom before his own people had begun to suspect anything. Many who he had thought of as friends had turned out to be nothing more than traitors.

Without Shireche's help, he would have been killed a long time ago by the terrorists who plotted against him and his kingdom.

He cleared his throat. "Do you have any advice for me now?"

"I am sure the outsider won't want to stay in the city for long. If nothing else, the terrorists will want to make contact with their cells in other kingdoms. No doubt starting with the Club Kingdom."

He nodded. "Of course. I will increase the guards on all walls, gates, and ports, and keep a close eye on the Club Kingdom for any sign of subterfuge."

"I wish you all the best," replied Shireche, before falling silent. From the tone of the voice, he wondered if Shireche somehow found humor in the situation.

Dismissing any further thoughts about Shireche, Lahire made his way back to the throne room to alter the search.

CHAPTER 6

James was several yards down the ladder when Kara closed the door to the room above, plunging them into darkness. He stopped climbing.

"Keep going, you idiot." Kara's disembodied voice floated down from the top of the ladder. "I'll light a lantern when we get to the bottom." Seeing he had little choice in the matter, he continued. Kara closed the hatch and began climbing down after him.

After another ten yards or so, he found himself stepping onto solid ground. Reaching out, he realized he was in another tunnel. He was relieved it wasn't a sewer.

He stepped back blindly as Kara neared the bottom of the ladder. She struck a match. The light flared, revealing their surroundings as Kara lit a lantern she carried. Not that it had much to illuminate. The featureless tunnel, about three yards in diameter, stretched out beyond the lamplight in either direction. The round shape could have been creature- or machine-made–he wasn't sure which–but it definitely wasn't natural. Nor had the tunnel been created by hand.

Kara resumed walking, and he trailed along behind.

"So, what made the tunnels?"

"No one knows." Kara didn't bother turning as she turned down a left branch in the tunnel. "Only a few people know about them, which is good for us. It lets us move around the city out of sight."

James nodded, following in silence.

Kara glanced back. "What happened back there, after you fell?"

"The people inside the house were criminals of some sort. They heard me fall off the roof and grabbed me after you left. They were going to turn me in for a reward, but White Rabbit turned up."

Kara stopped. "White Rabbit? You met him again?"

He grimaced. "Yeah. He killed the people in the house and wrapped my ankle while I was unconscious. He left after I woke up. He said he had been following us, and that he wanted me to see Gryphon."

Kara continued walking without saying anything.

He cleared his throat. "So, why is White Rabbit so special?"

"He's a mercenary. He has no morals at all and is willing to work for almost anyone if they'll pay. He'll happily let innocent people die if it means he can complete his job. He has no love for the Heart King, which is a point in his favor. Gryphon has tried to get him to join the resistance, but he refuses. There are rumors that he was the last person to leave the White Kingdom before it disappeared, but he refuses to talk about it. He can't be trusted."

"So why is he interested in me? Both times I've met him, he's said he's sorry about bringing me here. He even said he brought me here because of a promise to someone. Who did he make the promise to?"

"How the hell would I know? Maybe Gryphon knows more. All I know is that, if White Rabbit is involved, it's bad news."

A question occurred to James, one he'd planned to ask in the shop. "You call him White Rabbit. Is it the same White Rabbit who met Alice, like your father did? He seems young."

Kara shook her head. "His father would have been the person who met Alice. He was an ambassador who worked for the Heart Queen, visiting the other kingdoms on her behalf. His son, the current White Rabbit, trained with his father. The father was executed by Lahire soon after he took over, and the son took on the name to honor him."

"Oh." He frowned. The more he learned about the current Wonderland, the less he liked it.

The tunnels proved to be something of a maze, rising and falling with many branches. James quickly lost track of the path they had taken. As they turned a corner that looked no different than every other corner, they arrived at a large wall with a metal door in the middle. Kara stepped up to the door and knocked.

"That's it? That's the security system? You knock?"

"As I said, only a few people know about these tunnels. Even less know how to navigate them. And this place holds a few surprises for uninvited guests." She pointed to areas in the sides of the tunnels.

Looking closely, he could see that some areas of the stone were a slightly different color to the surrounding rock. "I'm rather proud of them, even if I do say so myself."

A narrow slot opened in the door. It closed almost immediately, but the sound of bolts being slid back on the door indicated they had been accepted. With a loud clang, the door opened.

A huge man stood in the doorway. He was easily six and a half feet tall, and built like a pro wrestler. A scar running from his cheek to the top of his bald head suggested he had seen his fair share of fighting. The man fixed Kara with a steely gaze. "I should have known you were the cause of all the racket in the city." His voice was deep, with the tone of someone used to giving orders and having them obeyed.

"Not me. Him." Kara indicated James.

The man looked him up and down, then looked back to Kara. "Get in." He jerked his head to indicate the two could enter.

James wasn't expecting the huge area beyond the door. It was only dimly lit by lanterns scattered around the area, but it was at least a hundred yards across. Two other doors like the one he had come through, and many more alcoves that could have contained additional doors, were visible in the shadows. Several people moved about in the room, but no one approached them.

The man closed the door. The sound of heavy locks echoed throughout the chamber, then he turned to James. "So, I assume you're the outsider I was told to expect?"

Kara scowled. "You knew he was coming? Why didn't you say something? What has White Rabbit told you?"

Gryphon ignored her questions. "We should go to my office." He turned back to James. "I saw you limping. You're injured?"

James nodded. "My ankle. It's been wrapped, but it really needs some ice and rest."

"I'm afraid that isn't feasible at the moment."

"What do you mean?"

Gryphon said nothing as he turned and started walking. Kara followed and, with no other option, James joined her.

They passed three metal doors in the wall as they followed the gentle arc it made around the room. The fourth door was a plain wooden affair, and it opened into a section of tunnel that had been closed off to make a study. The walls had been carved out to make the room more square, and several bookshelves and other items of furniture filled the area.

Gryphon motioned for James and Kara to sit, then sat in a large worn chair facing them. "I was told to expect you, but not why. Given the racket up in the city, I assume the king knows you're here, too. What's your story?"

"What do you mean?"

"Why did White Rabbit need my help to bring you to Wonderland?"

Kara looked indignant. "You helped White Rabbit? Are you mad? Why would you do that? How did you do that?"

"He needed to know when Taxard was next going to the Otherworld because he wanted to bring back an outsider. He seemed to feel it was important. I told him what we knew about Taxard's schedule."

"You handed over valuable information just like that? "

"There was a trade. The details aren't important." Gryphon turned back to James. "This is where you talk."

"I don't know. White Rabbit said something about a promise, but he didn't give me any details. He just told me I had to get to you, and that you'd fill me in, whatever that means. He seemed to think you'd know what to do."

"It could have something to do with his mark," said Kara.

Gryphon frowned. "He's an outsider. He shouldn't have a mark."

"See for yourself."

Gryphon motioned for James to bare his arm. He reluctantly lifted it from under the cloak to display his tattoo. Gryphon drew a sharp intake of breath at the sight of the two knights.

Kara told him, "He had a run-in with Taxard, then got brought here by White Rabbit as he was escaping. White Rabbit even saved him from some thugs when we were on the surface. What's going on? And why is White Rabbit involved?"

"Interesting." Gryphon sat back and rubbed his chin as he stared thoughtfully at James.

James realized he had been bouncing his good leg up and down and forced himself to stop. "None of this makes any sense. It has to be a dream."

"No, I imagine it doesn't. But it's not a dream." After a few moments, Gryphon asked, "Do you know why the mark you have on your arm is unusual?"

James shook his head.

"Everyone in Wonderland is born with a mark to show their kingdom and social status." As he spoke he rolled up his sleeve to

41

show a tattoo of a playing card with the Eight of Hearts on it. "This mark can be changed if the owner increases or decreases their position in society, by job or marriage. There are ways to temporarily change the appearance, but they are rare and extremely illegal. It's always been this way, for as long as recorded history has existed in Wonderland."

"So?"

Gryphon stood and moved to a bookcase at one side. He took down a large leather-bound book and brought it back to his chair. He quickly flicked through the book until he found the page he wanted, then handed the open book over to James.

He looked at the open page. The beautifully illuminated picture showed two hierarchy trees, mirror images of each other. On one side, the items were all painted in red, while on the other, they were painted in a silvery-white. He recognized the symbols in the hierarchy in an instant. They were all chess pieces, from pawn to king, arranged in the usual points order from a chess set with the king at the top and the pawn at the bottom. But what surprised him most were the symbols used for the knights. They were the exact same as the ones used on his tattoo, right down to the direction each color faced.

James stared at the page. "I still don't understand. You're saying someone from Wonderland did my tattoo? Or that a copy of this picture ended up in my world, and a tattoo artist found it?"

Gryphon shook his head. "Even if that were the case, when you came here, your *tattoo,* as you call it, would change or disappear. As a mark, what you have on your arm can't exist in Wonderland, no matter how much someone tried to create it. The fact that it does exist means something important."

James started to tremble. As he stared at the pages of the book, the feeling that it was all real, and that he really was in Wonderland, began to overwhelm him. It wasn't a thought or a suspicion. Every part of his heart and soul told him it was real. That Wonderland was real.

"This doesn't make sense. It doesn't make sense. None of it makes sense." He dropped the book to the floor and staggered to his feet. The dull headache that had been in the background the last hour flared up, and his vision began to swim again.

"A dream. It's all a dream. It can't be real. None of it's real. I've got to wake up. Got to go home." He stood and took a step away from his chair, then stumbled as his injured ankle gave way. Gryphon caught him before he could hit the ground and gently helped him back into the chair, then a glass was forced into his hand by Kara. It had some sort of juice in it. She guided his hand up so he could take a sip. The flavor was unfamiliar, but the sweetness of the juice and the coolness of the liquid helped his mind focus. His vision cleared, and his panic receded.

Kara and Gryphon moved back to where they had been sitting, and continued staring intently at James. After a few more sips, he managed a weak smile.

"Sorry," he mumbled.

Gryphon's voice had an understanding tone. "This is all a shock to you. I'm not surprised you feel scared."

James nodded in thanks. "What does it mean? My tattoo, I mean."

"I don't know." Gryphon smiled apologetically. "In an ideal world, we'd ask the Red or White Kingdoms for help to figure it out, but that's no longer possible."

"Why not? Kara said something about the White Kingdom disappearing, but I didn't understand that."

"How much did Hatter tell you about Wonderland?"

"Not much. He mentioned that there were six kingdoms, but he didn't say anything about them. He didn't get a chance to. The alarm sounded, and we started running."

"Wonderland had been broken up into six kingdoms for as long as history has been recorded. That all began to change when the Queen of Hearts was assassinated, a little over a century ago. After the death of the queen, the King of Hearts went to pieces. Despite her occasional temper tantrums, and she certainly had her temper tantrums when she would threaten to chop off everyone's heads, he loved her dearly.

"To give him time to grieve, their son, the Knave of Hearts, was given the power to run the kingdom. It was intended to be only a temporary arrangement, but then the king fell ill. With the king on his deathbed, the nobles of the kingdom agreed that the right of rule should formally pass over to the knave."

"That sounds too convenient. Was the knave the one who killed the queen?"

"No one knows for certain. And anyone who speculates too loudly is likely to end up beheaded. But that is certainly what we believe. Anyway, immediately after coming to power, King Lahire began to change the kingdom. He restructured society, building huge factories and forcing people to work there for minimal wages. Any hint of grumbling or disobedience was considered treason, punishable by death or being sent to the mines. The mines began supplying ore to the factories, and the factories began spewing out all manner of machines and devices of war.

"Then the conquests began. Lahire decided that the Heart Kingdom wasn't enough for him. Perhaps that had always been his plan. He wanted to rule a vast empire that covered all of Wonderland. The Spade Kingdom made a formal alliance with the Heart Kingdom almost immediately, and it has always received preferential treatment as a result. The Diamond Kingdom fell without a fight; the Heart armies marched across their borders and straight to the central castle. The Club Kingdom tried to fight, but were forced to surrender after several months when they realized how outnumbered they were."

"What about the other two kingdoms? The Red and White ones?"

Gryphon's expression turned somber. "As soon as the first signs of Lahire's plans became obvious, the Red and White Kingdoms, or the Island Kingdoms as they were also known, ceased their fighting. Everyone assumed they were going to join forces. Both kingdoms had been at war for centuries, so their armies were seasoned and well-equipped. It's likely that by working together they could have stopped Lahire, but we'll never know. When the Heart armies reached the Island Kingdoms, the White Kingdom had disappeared."

"Disappeared? What do you mean disappeared? How can a kingdom disappear?"

"It was gone. Vanished. The land was still there, but there was no sign of any of the people or their buildings. The Red Kingdom fought on alone, long past the point of surrender. They were a proud kingdom. To them, surrendering to an enemy was unthinkable."

Gryphon sighed. "Lahire totally destroyed them. Every member of their army was slaughtered when they refused to surrender or retreat. Every building was reduced to rubble. A few civilians managed to escape before the fighting, but the rest, those still alive, were rounded up and taken to the mines. There are still a few people from the Red and White Kingdom living in hiding, but neither kingdom now exists."

"And now I have a tattoo with the mark of the two kingdoms."

"Exactly."

"And you have no idea what it means?"

Gryphon shook his head. "I don't for certain, but there is someone who might." He turned to Kara. "You have to take him to see Caterpillar."

Kara looked shocked. "What? You can't be serious. No one has been able to find Caterpillar in years. Not since Lahire forced him into hiding."

"Nevertheless, he is the only one who will be able to say what this all means, and what we need to do." Gryphon's face took on an unreadable expression. "I heard a rumor that Caterpillar was last seen in the Tulgey Wood."

Kara put her hands up as if to push the suggestion away. "No, no, no. Finding Caterpillar is one thing. Going to Tulgey Wood is suicide."

"What's Tulgey Wood?" asked James.

"A dangerous place. Even the plants there will try to attack you, not to mention all the deadly creatures that roam throughout. It's crazy." She turned back to Gryphon. "I won't do it."

Gryphon sat back in his chair. "Then we might as well all walk up to the castle and turn ourselves in to Lahire. In case you haven't noticed, our numbers are dropping. The citizens are getting more and more scared by Lahire and his thugs each year. The resistance in the Diamond Kingdom has been totally wiped out, and even the resistance in the Club Kingdom has been limited since Lahire's raid three years ago. It won't be long until our own people begin to turn each other over in some misguided attempt to save themselves. And when Lahire manages to find this place, and one day he will, it will be all over."

He looked intensely at Kara. "We need something to shake things up. James could be it. We won't know until we find out more from Caterpillar, and you have to take him there."

Kara sighed resignedly. "Fine. But you're going to owe me, big time."

The words slipped out before James realized he was about to speak them. "What if I say no?"

Gryphon and Kara stared at him. He stumbled on, not sure what he was saying. "I mean, this isn't my world. I don't belong here. I can't do anything to help. I don't know how to fight, and I'm not a leader. I'm just an IT consultant who's supposed to be on holiday…"

"You selfish bastard!" Kara's words surprised him. The slap she gave him surprised him even more. "Do have any idea how many people have died under Lahire's reign? How much we all risk every day being a member of the resistance, not to mention every time we try to disrupt Lahire's plans? We're all living under a death sentence here, and all you care about is some holiday?"

"I… I didn't mean it like that—"

"You're right. Go home. We don't need you. The last thing we need is an immature crybaby who will get us all killed." Before he could respond, Kara turned and fled the room, slamming the door behind her.

"Don't worry about her. She'll calm down in a few minutes. She has a bit of a temper, and she's been under a lot of pressure lately. She didn't take Mock's death well."

"So I gathered," said James quietly, remembering her outburst from before. "Was it recent?"

"Just over a month ago. We got a tip-off that Lahire was sending a shipment of new weapons to a garrison in a nearby town, so we made a plan to intercept them. Kara's designs are better, but harder to make with our limited resources. Unfortunately, it was a trap. Mock acted as rear guard and slowed them down long enough for the rest of us to get away cleanly. He saved us, but at the cost of his own life. Kara wanted to stay behind to help him, but he wouldn't let her."

James sat quietly, wringing his hands and cursing himself for his own doubts. He shouldn't have said anything.

Gryphon spoke after a few moments. "If you want to go home, you'll need to see Caterpillar, anyway. Lahire has blocked most of the ways to get to the Otherworld. Caterpillar's probably the only one in Wonderland who could tell you how to get to your own world."

"I guess I don't have any choice then, do I?"

"Not really."

He sighed. "What do I need to do?"

CHAPTER 7

James took the pile of clothes Gryphon gave him and changed once he was alone. His ankle ached, his head throbbed, and all he wanted to do was lie down and go to sleep. But according to Gryphon, he had to get to the port and find a skyship. Or, more accurately, Kara had to find them a ship. He just hoped Kara had calmed down enough to talk to him again.

Gryphon had chosen the clothes well. The white shirt, trousers, waistcoat, and jacket all fit him perfectly. He looked like an extra from *A Christmas Carol*, but at least he wouldn't stand out in a crowd anymore.

He stepped out of the room and began searching for Gryphon or Kara. He finally spotted them on the opposite side of the cavern. The area had been set up as some sort of lab, with all manner of crazy equipment around. Kara was busily packing some of the strange equipment into a backpack, with Gryphon speaking to her as she did so. The way she was throwing the items into the backpack didn't fill him with hope that she had calmed down.

She looked up as James neared. "Here, make yourself useful." She picked up a second backpack and threw it at him. He managed to catch it, surprised at how heavy it was. Kara closed the backpack she had been packing, then slung it over her shoulder.

"Let's go," she said, not looking at him.

"Kara, I—"

"Save it." The note in Kara's voice stopped him from trying to say anything further. Without another word, she walked past him, toward another section of the cavern.

"She'll calm down soon enough," said Gryphon quietly.

"That's what you said before."

"I may have underestimated how long she would be upset. Give her a bit of space for the moment."

James nodded and followed Gryphon in the direction Kara had gone. She was waiting by a different door than the one through which they had arrived. A man stood next to her, holding yet another strange device in his hand.

Gryphon looked at James. "There's one more thing we need to do before you leave. I need you to roll up your sleeve on your left arm."

James did as he was told, not sure what Gryphon was planning. It became obvious when Gryphon lifted the device to his arm and strapped it on so it covered his tattoo.

"This may feel a little strange," said Gryphon, then he hit a button.

At first, nothing seemed to happen. Then, he noticed that the device was getting warm. Suddenly, it generated an intense flash of heat. He let out a shout of surprise. The flash only lasted a moment, but it stung like a sunburn once the heat had gone.

"Baby," said Kara.

Gryphon unstrapped the device. His tattoo had been replaced by a Four of Hearts playing card.

"It's only temporary and won't pass a detailed inspection, especially in daylight, but it should be enough to get you past any guards you run into on the way to the port."

"Thanks."

Gryphon turned to Kara. "This should be enough." He handed her a small bundle of paper that looked like the old-style banknotes. "I don't have to tell you to be careful. But be careful."

Kara gave him a hug. "You'll tell Father where I've gone?"

"Don't worry about it. We'll take good care of him." Gryphon turned to James and shook his hand. "Good luck."

Moments later, they were back in the tunnels, the heavy metal door behind them clanging as the various locks were put back in place.

Kara set off at a brisk pace. "We need to hurry. They're probably going to shut down the ports soon, so we need to find a captain who's happy to leave on short notice. If we're lucky, we'll be able to hire a ship to take us directly. If we're not, we'll have to get a ship to another kingdom and try again. We'll have to stay clear of the passenger ships, as they'll be checking them closely. Our best bet will be some sort of cargo transport."

James did his best to keep up, not wanting to add fuel to Kara's displeasure. Neither of them spoke for the rest of the trip through the tunnels. He estimated they had covered at least a mile before they reached another ladder. Kara waved him up, and he ascended to another trapdoor. It was heavy, but he managed to open it and climb into another back room of a house. Kara quickly joined him, closing the hatch and covering it with the rug that had been displaced.

Footsteps thudded on the floor above, then someone descended the stairs.

"Wait here." Kara exited out of the room. Someone greeted her by name, and they had a brief discussion, but he couldn't make out the details.

Kara returned. "We're in luck. They haven't locked down the port yet. Come on."

James followed her out, past the intense gaze of an older man on the stairs and back out onto the streets. The part of the city they emerged into seemed much more upscale compared to the previous section he had seen. The houses were a little larger with more ornamentation on their front architecture. Unlike the other area they had travelled through, people were out on the streets here. Some moved quickly, as if they had a purpose, while others—usually in groups of three or more—were suffering the effects of too much drinking.

The structure ahead drew his eye. The port had looked impressive when he had seen it from far away, but up close, it was awe-inspiring. The framework of the structure rose like a skyscraper into the night sky. Lights mounted on and around the base of the port illuminated it clearly, making it stand out in the darkness. Large ships that looked like a weird cross between an airship, a train, and a ship hung at various points on the structure, obviously docked. Large bundles of cargo were being raised and lowered at points all over the structure. He could make out people moving on several of the larger metal beams, further indicating how huge it was.

"Impressive, isn't it?" Kara finally spoke to him as they walked.

"I've never seen anything like it at all," said James with amazement.

"They're constantly expanding it, since skyship traffic is on the rise. There are similar ports in the other kingdoms, but none as large as this one. We have the biggest and best."

James spent a bit of time looking at the ships. Something about them didn't seem right. Finally, he realized what it was. "How do the ships stay in the air?"

"What do you mean?"

"The bags on the ships aren't large enough to keep them up in the air. They couldn't store enough helium to lift that much weight. So what makes them float?"

Kara laughed. He was glad to see her in a good mood again, even if it was because of his ignorance. "Our skyships haven't used helium since the first prototype. Their frames are made of an alloy of aethium. It allows the ships to be neutrally buoyant in the air, up to a certain weight at least. The ship then pushes on the aether to travel through the air."

"Aether?"

Kara sighed, shaking her head as if she were talking to a simpleton. "Aether is all around us, like air. It's what allows light to travel. The skyships use the aether like a boat uses water. The engine turns a propeller to move the ship forward, and rudders provide steering."

James frowned. "I remember aether now. It was a theory in Victorian times. But they proved it false almost a century ago."

Kara shrugged. "What is true in your world isn't true here, and vice versa. They only share some similarities."

"Like the fashion." He watched the people they passed. The way the clothes were vaguely Victorian, but not exactly, continued to bother him.

Kara shrugged again. "Lahire was the one who brought in the current forms of dress. In fact, he was behind most of the changes in Wonderland. The skyships, building the Kingdom capitals up as they are, everything. He totally turned Wonderland upside down and wouldn't listen to anything said against his plans."

"You two! Stop!" a voice called out to them from behind.

"Ignore it," hissed Kara, not slowing down. "They may let us go."

"Hey! You two. Stop in the name of the king!"

"Damn." Kara stopped and turned around. Her voice took on a sweet, innocent tone. "I'm sorry, were you talking to us?"

"That's right," said the voice. Turning, James's heart skipped a beat. Three Heart Guard were heading their way. "There's a dangerous criminal on the loose. We need to check every citizen's mark. Bare your arms."

"A dangerous criminal? Oh, my!" Kara began to lift up her shirt arm, and James hurried to copy her. The guard glanced at their arms. James noticed that Kara's mark was the Four of Hearts, just like his fake one.

"Where are you going?"

"To the port." Kara grabbed his arm and leaned on it. It took him by surprise, although he found the experience pleasant. "My sister is getting married, and we need to book passage on a ship."

"And where is this wedding?"

"The Diamond Kingdom," replied Kara excitedly. "I've always wanted to see the crystal-clad buildings there at sunset. It will be a lot of fun. Right, honey?"

James nodded awkwardly, trying to smile as the guards stared at them. He suppressed the sudden urge to run and tried not to appear as nervous as he felt. The guard who had spoken motioned for them to continue. "Carry on."

Kara didn't ask twice and almost pulled him away as they resumed walking. She let go of his arm once the guards were out of sight and returned to her regular manner.

"That was almost too easy," commented James.

Kara shrugged. "They're not expecting an outsider to have a mark, or to be walking around in the open. But the next group of guards we find might not be so careless. We need to hurry."

Kara picked up her pace, and James did his best to keep up.

CHAPTER 8

The sound of music, laughter, and loud carousing became audible in the distance, and before too long, numerous pubs and bars filled with revelers were visible. Kara obviously had a particular destination in mind, and she led them to a pub that had less people around it than the others. On the outside, it looked like one of the nicer places, but it had a strange air of unwelcoming about it.

"A lot of the ship captains come here," she replied to James's questioning look. "Hopefully, we'll find one that will take us."

Kara's words proved to be optimistic. The first five people she spoke to all shook their heads as soon as she explained that they wanted to leave that night, apparently more interested in the drink and ladies in the pub than taking Kara's money.

Kara was searching for a new captain after the fifth knock-back, when she stopped dead. "I don't bloody believe it." She stared toward a table near the back.

"Believe what?" But Kara was already moving forward. James moved to keep up.

At the table, a tall, thin man in his early thirties sat flanked on both sides by women wearing too much dark eye shadow. His short-cropped hair and Errol Flynn mustache matched his worn black leather jacket, and he smiled widely as he spotted Kara approaching. He kissed each woman on the cheek, then shooed them away.

"Kara, dear, how lovely to see you!"

"Don't *Kara, dear* me, you jackass."

"Temper, temper. That's hardly a polite way to greet someone you haven't seen in ages."

"No thanks to you! You left me in the Spade Kingdom without so much as a goodbye, let alone any way of getting back home."

The man shrugged with an apologetic grin. "What can I say? Business negotiations had gone bad, and it was necessary to leave at short notice. Besides, I knew you'd be fine. And obviously I was right. Here you are, all safe and sound."

The man looked at James, who stood silently next to Kara. "My, my, what have we here? He doesn't seem like your usual type of boyfriend."

"He's not my boyfriend," said Kara with annoyance. "He's a... friend."

"Indeed." The man stared intently at James for a second, as if trying to read his mind. After a moment, he turned back to Kara. "I hear you're looking for a ship, and with short notice at that."

"What if I am? It's no business of yours."

"Now, that's where you're wrong." The man leaned forward conspiratorially. "The port is about to be shut down. I got the word a few minutes ago. No captain will be willing to leave now. You'll be stuck here for at least a day, if not more. And I suspect you want to leave well before then."

When Kara didn't respond, the man leaned back with a playful smile. "Of course, I might be persuaded to leave immediately. For the right price."

"I'd rather eat glass."

"I hear the Heart Guard have all sorts of special presents for their guests, so I'm sure that could be arranged." The man shrugged. "It's no skin off my nose if you take me up on the offer. I'm in no hurry. But there it is, take it or leave it."

Kara stared at the captain, then sighed. "Fine. How much?"

"That depends on where you want to go."

"South."

"South is a direction. I need a distance as well."

"Just south for the time being. I'll give more precise directions later."

The man gave Kara a knowing smile. "Fine, south for a bit to visit warmer climes. Five hundred."

"You're kidding. Two hundred."

"It's a sellers' market, honey, but fine, I'll play. Four hundred."

Kara rolled her eyes. "Please, that's highway robbery, and you know it. Three hundred."

The man laughed. "Three hundred? I've a wife and sick kids to take care of. How can you expect me to look after them with such a small amount?"

"You've never been married a day in your life. The only way to get you married would be to knock you out first."

"Fine, there's no wife. But I'm sure I have kids all over the place, and at least one of them is probably sick at the moment."

"Three hundred. You owe me for last time."

The man sighed. "Fine, three hundred it is. Think of it as a family discount. We leave immediately." He stood. "I was getting bored with this place anyway. Try to keep up."

"Family?" asked James, as they followed the man out of the bar.

"He's my uncle," said Kara. "My mother's brother."

"And he left you behind on a trip?"

"I didn't say he was a particularly loving uncle. He's in it for his own gain, and no one else's."

"Can we trust him?"

"Not at all. He may be family, but that doesn't mean he won't turn us over to the Heart Guard if it's more profitable for him to do so. We tell him nothing."

"Does your uncle have a name?"

"You mean apart from lying, unreliable, two-faced scum?" She sighed. "He calls himself Coulter Tyrrel, although his last name was originally Seppings."

"Why did he change it?"

"He thinks Tyrrel sounds cooler and makes him a bigger hit with the ladies."

"Does it?"

Kara wore a look of distaste. "Unfortunately, yes."

James nodded and continued to follow. The large metal structure of the port was only a couple of hundred yards away, looming over them like an enormous web created by an insane spider. Three skyships hovered near them, attached by nothing more than a couple of ropes and thin metal walkways that jutted out from the iron structure.

They had reached one of the main support structures on the side of the port—James could see it had some sort of lifting platform in between the thick beams—when a loud bell started ringing.

"That's the start of the lock down," said Coulter with distaste.

"We have to go now," said Kara.

"I know, I know! Keep your shirt on, girl." They boarded the lifting platform. As another couple were about to board, Coulter held up his hand. "We're grabbing crates of Siffle next level up. It's an especially ripe batch, and I think one of the crates has a crack in it. You might want to grab another elevator."

The couple wrinkled their noses in distaste and stepped back. Coulter gave them an apologetic smile and hit the button to ascend.

They traveled on the elevator in silence, although the loud bell made deep thought almost impossible. It finally stopped halfway up the structure. Coulter was off before it had fully stopped, moving at almost a jog. James followed as best he could, limping as his ankle began complaining at all the movement he had forced it to do.

After traveling along a ten-yard-wide metal platform, they turned onto a narrower walkway that stuck out into the open air. At the end of it sat what James assumed was Coulter's ship.

It wasn't the largest ship docked at the port, but it had the look of being built for speed. The main body of the craft was the balloon-like structure that James expected from a normal airship, but there the similarities ended. A framework had been built around the central body to support a deck, while a strange corkscrew propeller jutted out slightly from underneath, and all sorts of rods and a smoke stack poked out the top.

Coulter turned as they reached the narrow gangplank. "Welcome to the *Nighthawk*. The fastest ship in Wonderland."

"It's smaller than your last ship," said Kara. "I thought you said bigger was better."

"What can I say? This one was a better deal."

"You lost the last one, didn't you?"

Ignoring Kara's question, Coulter turned back toward the ship. "Ahoy, Marco! Prepare for departure."

"Captain?" A tall man stepped out of a door in the balloon hull. He was thin, but carried himself like someone ready for trouble. "Are you sure about that? What about the lockdown?"

Coulter sprung from the gangplank onto the ship's deck. "What lockdown? I don't hear any lockdown bell, do you?"

"No, Captain. Must have been mistaken." The man spied Kara and James stepping on board. "Well I'll be. Little Hat! I never thought I'd see you again on board one of your uncle's ships. Not after last time."

"Hello, Marco." Kara smiled and gave the man a quick hug. "He wasn't my first choice for ship captain."

Coulter cleared his throat noisily. "I believe I mentioned something about a quick departure? I could have been wrong. Perhaps I was talking to myself?"

"Sorry, Captain. Right away, Captain." Marco gave Kara a wink, then began shouting orders to the crew. Men moved around quickly, getting everything ready.

"Try not to get in the way or fall overboard," said Coulter, before departing to organize the rest of the ship.

Kara led him toward the back of the ship. "I'll go and help the crew get ready to sail. You wait here until we're under way."

"Sure, I guess." James sat down on a crate as Kara headed over to a group of sailors. They greeted her with obvious recognition, and she set about helping them work. He tried to push away the feelings of being lost and useless and took a moment to take in more of the sights.

The rail he was leaning against was on the same side as the port structure, so he had a good view of what was happening. Unsurprisingly, a few people had already noticed the activity on the *Nighthawk* and were pointing in their general direction.

Two Heart Guard strolling along the main walkway also noticed the activity and began running in their direction. He was about to call out and let someone on the ship know about it when the ship suddenly jerked and started to move away from the docking spar. In only a few seconds, the gap was over ten yards, and by the time the guards arrived, they had pulled away to over a hundred yards and were beginning to gain speed.

"Better luck next time, guys," muttered James under his breath, as he watched them getting smaller and smaller in the distance.

"My, my. Only a few hours in this land, and already you're a wanted criminal," said an unknown voice beside him. He jumped, standing and turning to look in the direction the voice had come from. He could see no one.

"Careful there. Wouldn't want you to fall overboard, now, would we?" The voice had moved behind him. He whirled about, but again saw no one.

"Really now, anyone would think you didn't know if you were coming or going, the way you keep turning around like that."

James feinted, turning in the direction of the voice, then immediately turned back. To his surprise, he found a cat's head with a large grin on its face floating in the air above the railing. It didn't look quite like a normal cat's head. The eyes were too wide, and the head was slightly misshapen. But a cat it was.

"You're the Cheshire Cat!" said James in surprise.

"Well, well, my name and fame precede me, I see. It's always nice to be recognized in the streets, don't you think? Oh, my. I guess you don't want to be recognized. How inconsiderate of me."

"What are you doing here? How did you get here?"

"One could ask you the same question, you know."

"You could, but I asked first."

"Ah, a bit of a debater I see. Very well. In answer to your question, I'm here because I heard there was a fuss, and I wanted to see what all the commotion was about. And what do I find? An outsider! It's been so long since we had one in Wonderland. I'm sure everyone will be most excited when they find out."

"I don't think you want to go telling anyone about me. From what I've heard, outsiders aren't too welcome here. You'd probably get in trouble with the king if he found out you'd been talking to one."

"Oh, yes, I'd forgotten. The King of Hearts isn't too fond of outsiders visiting. I expect he doesn't want any outsiders around because they always cause an upheaval whenever they make their way here."

"Well it's not like I came here by choice. If I could go home, I'd do so in a heartbeat."

"Really? I don't blame you. Wonderland is a strange place."

"You can say that again." James looked at the retreating port structure. "It's certainly nothing like the books."

"What's not like the books?" asked Kara, as she moved up beside him.

"This place. Wonderland. I was just telling..." James stopped as he turned to where the Cheshire Cat, or its head at least, had been hovering. It was nowhere to be seen. "Where'd he go?" He looked around, to no avail.

"Where did who go?"

"The Cheshire Cat. He was here a minute ago."

Kara looked at him quizzically. "No one was here. You've been standing here by yourself the entire time."

"But I..." James shook his head. "Never mind. I'm probably going nuts."

"Why don't you get some rest? Coulter has given us a cabin, and you look like you could do with a rest."

"Only the one cabin?"

"Yes. I expect he did it to get a rise out of me, but he'll be sorely disappointed."

"Thanks," said James, surprised at Kara's generosity. "Sleep sounds good."

* * *

Lahire stood in front of his throne and stared at the two men and the woman kneeling in front of him. They all wore Heart Guard uniforms with regalia to indicate their high rank within the guard.

"You mean to tell me that your men sighted the outsider, yet failed to apprehend him?" Lahire kept his voice perfectly calm, with no hint of any emotion.

"Th-that's not quite how it happened, Your Majesty," replied the man kneeling slightly forward of the other two. The tremor in his voice was audible. "The alarm was sounded as soon as the ship tried to leave port. Unfortunately, it was too far away by the time other guards arrived on the scene. We signaled the nearby patrolling ships, but the vessel was too quick. Our ships lost sight of it an hour out from port."

"I see. And what about the fliers? Why weren't they used to chase down and disable the fleeing vessel?"

The man coughed uncomfortably. "Unfortunately, they were unavailable, Your Majesty. We received your orders to upgrade the fliers, and they were all either in transit to the workshop, or in the process of having the upgrade applied. We were unable to get any ready in time to chase the escaping ship."

Lahire stared impassively at the man, who continued hurriedly, "However, it wasn't a total loss. We managed to determine the name of the ship that the outsider is on. The *Nighthawk*. I've sent out a general alert to the other kingdoms and patrols ships in the area, so—"

"That's enough. I gave you a simple task. Track down and capture one outsider. You had the resources of the entire Heart Guard at your disposal. You couldn't even manage to do that. On top of that, it would seem the outsider has managed to acquire help, most likely from the terrorist cell in the city. A terrorist cell, I might add, that you have constantly failed to eliminate. I think you've lost the right to suggest any next steps, don't you?"

The man groveled at his feet. "Sire, I've been a loyal servant for many years, and my loyalty is only to you and the Heart—"

"ENOUGH!" He glared at the man. "I will no longer listen to your excuses. Guards, take this man to the dungeons. I want his head on a pole by midday tomorrow."

"Please! Your Majesty!" The man leapt to his feet, but was immediately grabbed by two guards.

Ignoring his pleas for leniency, Lahire watched as the man was dragged out of the throne room. "Mercy leads to lack of respect," he muttered under his breath. "Something Mother never learned." He turned back to the remaining man and woman, both of whom looked slightly pale. He focused on the woman.

"Congratulations on your appointment as commander of the Heart Guard. I expect better results from you than your predecessor."

"Sire!" The commander bowed low, a faint tremble visible on her slight frame.

He sat on his throne. "Notify all patrol ships and guard outposts with the description of the outsider, everyone he had been seen associating with, and the details of the ship he was on. And find out who his contacts in the city were. I want to know where they are going, what they are planning to do and, most importantly, I want them tracked down and caught. Do I make myself clear?"

"Yes, Your Majesty." The woman bowed again. He dismissed them with a flick of the hand. The woman and man quickly stood and left the throne room.

Lahire motioned at a heavily curtained section of the wall.

Taxard was kneeling before him in an instant. "Your Majesty?"

"The outsider escaped the city. I gave you explicit instructions that he was to be hunted down and captured. You failed me."

Taxard bowed lower. "Yes, Your Majesty."

"Do you have anything to say for yourself?"

Taxard paused. "I believe I know the identity of the one who brought the outsider to Wonderland."

Lahire narrowed his eyes. "Go on."

"I found a house where the occupants had been killed, in an area where the outsider had been sighted. They had all been killed by thrown knives."

He slammed his hand down on the arm of the throne. "White Rabbit!"

59

"I believe so, Your Majesty. He is familiar with accessing the Otherworld and has been known to associate with terrorists."

Lahire growled. "I knew I should have had him removed when I took care of his father. The treachery of his family knows no bounds. Find him and the outsider. Find them both and eliminate them."

"As you command." Taxard bowed again, then quickly left the throne room.

Lahire sat back heavily in the throne. The outsider had managed to escape the city. And White Rabbit was involved! It was the outcome he had feared. Dark days were in Wonderland's future if he didn't get the situation under control again.

CHAPTER 9

Despite being exhausted, James slept fitfully. The bed looked older than he was, and no matter how much he tried, he was only able to sleep for short bursts at a time. The mix of a sore head, keeping his aching ankle elevated, and the strange sounds of the ship, not to mention the unbelievable situation he found himself in, all combined to make sleep elusive.

Wonderland! Could it be real? Was he actually here, or was it all a dream? His mind kept telling him it was impossible, and each time he closed his eyes and managed to doze for a few minutes, he half-expected to wake up again in his own bed, the whole ordeal merely a bad dream.

But in his heart, he somehow knew it was real. He really was in Wonderland.

By the time light began to filter into the cabin, James had finally admitted to himself that getting any more sleep would be impossible. A glance at his phone said it was just after five o'clock, although he had no idea if time was even the same in Wonderland. After attempting to get his hair into some sort of order, he opened the cabin door and stepped out onto the deck.

The ship was deserted. It was light enough to dimly illuminate everything, but there certainly wasn't enough light to do much by. His ankle hurt when he walked, but the rest had done it some good, and the pain was reduced. He made his way to the bow of the ship to look out at where they were going.

The view was breathtaking. The land spread out below him, a seemingly untouched landscape of trees, grass, hills, and valleys. The first rays of sun were beginning to poke above the horizon ahead, and with it, the land was beginning to lighten. They passed over an area of low mountains, although to the right, he could see a much taller range that looked ominous and impassable. Occasionally, he thought he could see some sign of movement below, but they were too far up, and the light was too poor, to make out what it could be.

As he looked at the horizon ahead, something gnawed at the back of his mind. He was missing something, something obvious, but he couldn't put his finger on what.

The sound of loud hammering, followed by a stream of cursing, brought him out of his thoughts. Looking back down the deck, he noticed someone hanging by their legs off the side of the ship. At first, he thought they had fallen overboard, but then the hammering and cursing resumed from where the person hung.

As James moved over to the rail, a round man in rough navy-blue trousers and a grubby white vest became visible, hanging over the side and hammering on something on the outside of the hull. The man continued to curse as he hammered, but stopped when he noticed James at the railing.

"You must be the stranger I heard about." The man spoke with a gravelly voice. "Make yourself useful and pass me that wrench, would you?"

"Sure." James looked in the toolbox beside the rail. He found the wrench and knelt to pass it down. The round fellow took it and adjusted the object he had been hammering.

"Mind if I ask what you're doing?"

"One of the aether vanes is playing up. It's messing with the steering a bit. Nothing serious, but the captain wanted me to fix it as soon as possible, so here I am. Besides, I prefer working in the morning. Less people bothering me."

"Sorry, didn't mean to get in the way."

"Nah, it's fine. Pass me the wire."

James rummaged in the toolbox, then handed down the wire. "Worked on this ship long?"

"This ship? Nah. Captain's only had it a couple of months. Been with the captain for over ten years, though. He's had six ships in that time, and I've been the poor sod who's had to keep them all running.

There we are, all done. That should keep him happy." The man pulled himself back up through the railing.

"Six ships? What happened to all of them?"

The man laughed as he wiped his hands on a rag. "Various things. Two got shot up beyond repair. He lost one in a poker game, although I still say the other guy was cheating. One was impounded by the Heart Guard when we dallied too long in the Spade Kingdom—barely managed to escape getting caught ourselves. One he sold, and one was taken by other pirates. I'll say one thing about the captain, he's always one for new adventures."

"From the little I've seen of him, he certainly seems to be a unique individual."

"That he is, that he is." The man held out his hand. "The name's Sasha."

He took the hand. "James."

"So I've heard. You're the man who's stolen Little Hatter's heart."

"No, no, it's nothing like that," replied James hastily. "She's just helping me. I don't know that we're even friends."

Sasha laughed, slapping him on the shoulder. "Don't be so serious. I'm pulling your leg. Had a bit of trouble with the Heart Guard from what I hear." He laughed again. "Don't worry. We're all wanted by the Heart Guard for one thing or another. You don't get to go around being a pirate without getting your name on various wanted posters around the place. We're just lucky the Heart Guard aren't too great at finding us."

James let the pirate thing go. That much had been obvious from when they had arrived. But he did remember a comment Kara made the night before.

"Kara mentioned that the captain is her uncle?"

"Yep, that he is." Sasha collected his tools and walked toward the back of the ship. He followed. "On her mother's side, of course."

"I didn't get to meet her mother."

"I doubt you will. She's not exactly the stay-at-home type, if you know what I mean. She's probably out raiding a cargo ship or some such thing right now. Either that or living it up in a tavern somewhere, celebrating her latest spoils."

"She's a pirate, too?"

"Of course she is! Don't tell me Little Hatter didn't tell you?"

"We haven't had a chance to talk much. Things were a little hectic."

Sasha nodded in understanding. "Yeah, Little Hatter's mother is a pirate. Lydea Hawthorne, the terror of the skies! Beautiful and ruthless, always a dangerous combination. Don't really know how Lydea met Little Hatter's father, but soon after Little Hatter was born, Lydea gave her to her father and returned to her pirating ways. Little Hatter traveled with us for a few months about a year ago, hoping to meet her mother. No idea if she managed to track her down after she left the ship."

"I didn't know any of that. It sounds awful, having her mother abandon her like that."

"Yeah, well, life's a bitch. Smoke?" Sasha offered him a hand-rolled cigarette.

"No thanks."

Sasha shrugged and lit one himself. They arrived at a large metal door at the back of the ship, the sound of heavy machinery coming from within. Following Sasha inside, James found himself in what was obviously the engine room.

It was hot. A huge furnace burned, while several large machines he didn't recognize took up most of the space. Smoke and steam filled the room, making his eyes water.

"Did you fix the vane?" asked Kara, walking out from behind one of the large machines. She had exchanged her earlier dress for trousers, a vest, and a jacket not unlike the one Sasha wore. She stopped when she saw James, suddenly seeming a little awkward. "Oh, hello. I figured you were going to be asleep for a few hours yet."

"I couldn't sleep too well. What about you?"

"I don't need much sleep. I got a few hours earlier, and now I'm down here helping Sasha with the engines. The ship may look nice on the outside, but someone's tweaked the engine so much for speed that the damn thing is temperamental. It needs almost constant babysitting if we're moving at any sort of speed, and we needed the speed last night to get out of the Heart Capital."

As if to illustrate her point, a loud explosion of steam burst from one of the machines. A loud whistle blew.

"Don't just stand there. Give me a hand," yelled Sasha. Kara was already moving over to the machine where Sasha was frantically trying to adjust something with his wrench. James stood still, not sure what to do.

Kara began to turn a small wheel. "James! Turn that wheel over there when I say." She pointed to a wheel similar to the one she was turning. She watched a gauge intently. He moved over to where she had indicated. "Now! Turn it clockwise as fast as you can!"

He complied. The wheel was stiff and hard to turn at first, but loosened quickly. By the time he had turned it as far as it would go, the whistle sound stopped, and the steam dissipated to earlier levels.

"Damn stupid engine," said Sasha, grumbling at the large machine as he wiped his brow with the back of his wrist. "Hunk of junk. Told the captain it would be no good, but he wouldn't listen." He muttered some more to himself as he moved around, checking the other gauges on the machines.

"Probably best if we don't talk to him for a little while," said Kara. "He gets into a bit of a mood if the engine starts playing up."

James nodded. Then, he finally realized what had been bugging him since he'd watched the approaching dawn over the side of the ship.

"You told Coulter we wanted to go south, right?"

"Yeah, I did. We won't get to Tulgey Wood going south—we need to veer to the west a bit—but it's a good enough start. Why?"

"Because we're going more east than south."

Kara stared at him for a moment, then cursed and headed for the door. He followed.

* * *

"Why the hell are we heading toward the Diamond Kingdom?" demanded Kara, as she stormed onto the bridge.

"And good morning to you, too," replied Coulter casually from the map he had laid out on a table to the side of the room. "You're looking bright and cheerful today. Obviously, you had a good rest. Have you done something with your hair?"

Kara advanced on Coulter. "Don't try to change the subject. You heard me. Why are we going toward the Diamond Kingdom?"

"You said you wanted to go south. We're heading south. It's just... an easterly version of south."

Kara glanced at Coulter's map. Her eyes widened. "How did you get hold of a route map for the Soundy Trading Company?"

Coulter shrugged casually. "You know how it is. When you're having a few drinks with some new friends, and you decide to play a few friendly hands of poker to pass the time, sometimes people might bet more than they can afford. And in their inebriated state, they might not think about what it is they're offering in exchange for their life.

Who am I to turn down a trade offer from a friend in return for canceling their debt?"

Kara glared at Coulter. "That's why you wanted to leave the Heart Capital so quickly. When they figure out the map is gone, they're going to change their routes, so you only have a short window of time to get to your ambush point. The lockdown would have ruined your chances."

Coulter smiled. "Business is business. You should know that by now."

"Yes, I should," said Kara bitterly, seemingly more to herself than Coulter.

"Cheer up. In a few hours, you'll be able to take part in a successful raid on a Soundy cargo ship, one of the few ever carried out. Think of how much your share will be. You'll be able to buy all the dresses, jewels, and gadgets your heart could desire. You could even put your father into a much nicer place, like he used to have."

"Don't you dare bring my father into this!"

"How do you know it's real?" asked James, who had been examining the map as the other two argued.

"What do you mean, how do I know it's real?" Coulter turned to look at him. "Of course, it's real. Look at it."

"I mean, I don't know anything about this Soundy company, but it sounds like this map is rare and valuable. And it does sound like it fell into your hands awfully easy. Don't you think that might be a little suspicious? If this map is as important as you two say it is, would someone just hand it over when they're a little drunk and owe some money?"

Coulter grabbed the map and rolled it up. "Don't be ridiculous. I spent a lot of time, not to mention money, setting up this plan, and I'm not going to listen to anything negative about it. Get off my bridge! If you're not going to take part in the raid, then stay out of my way."

"What about us?" asked Kara. "We need to go south, not to the Diamond Kingdom."

"Fine, fine. Once we've raided the cargo ship, we'll drop you two off wherever you want to go, and you can go do... whatever. Happy?"

"Not at all, but I guess it's the best I can expect from you."

Coulter stepped past Kara to the wheel, ignoring her as he looked out the large glass panels in front of him. Kara let out an exasperated sigh and stormed off the bridge.

Once outside, Kara leaned against the rail and looked out over the side. "You raised a good point, you know," she said, as he moved to stand beside her. "The Soundy's never let their trade maps go. They're too valuable. Coulter's story, assuming he was telling the truth, sounds like it was too easy. And given how pleased he was about it all, I believe that is how he got the map."

"So what are we going to do? If it's a trap, we don't want to be in it."

"I don't know. I'm still trying to work that out. There's a chance Coulter might see reason, now that we've planted the seeds of doubt in his mind, but that's a long shot. We'll need to think of something else."

"Well, it seems like the only three options we have are mutiny, sabotage, or jumping overboard. None of those ideas seem particularly palatable."

Kara snapped her fingers. "That's it! We jump overboard. In a manner of speaking."

James looked at her warily. "Am I going to like where this is going?"

Kara gave him a smile that he didn't buy. "Absolutely. It'll be fun! Come on."

CHAPTER 10

Several minutes later, James asked, "And what exactly am I looking at?" Kara had led him inside the ship, detouring to collect their belongings, and down to the bottom of the hull. They stared through an open hatch at a strange framework of metal that looked suspiciously like some sort of ultra-light aircraft.

"My pride and joy. It's a two-person flier I designed and built when I was on Coulter's last ship. It's like a powered glider." Kara nimbly climbed down into it. "I noticed it when we were boarding. Coulter must have managed to keep it somehow. We can use it to leave the ship and shadow them at a distance. If it's a trap, like we suspect, we can get away and continue on by ourselves. If everything works out for them, we can come back."

He looked past the framework of metal to the ground far below and gripped the bar he held tighter. "Why don't we sabotage those aether vanes Sasha was working on? Seems like it would be easier. And safer."

Kara shook her head. "Coulter would know it was us, and I honestly don't know what he'd do if he found out we sabotaged his ship. He's too convinced that he's about to become rich, so he isn't thinking clearly."

He looked dubiously at the craft again. "It doesn't look that safe."

Kara finished storing the second pack. "It's not going to break up, if that's what you're worried about. It's stronger than it looks. And besides, it's made of aethium. It's not like it's going to fall out of the sky. Trust me."

He sighed. "If you say so."

"Come on. We need to get going before anyone realizes what we're up to."

"Too late," said Marco from behind them. James jumped slightly, and Kara whirled.

"Marco—"

"Save it." Marco held up his hand. "I heard your conversation. I'm not going to stop you. I'm glad you're leaving the ship before this raid."

"You have doubts, too?" asked James.

"Of course. But I won't say a word against the captain. It's his plan, and he's put a lot of work into it. I'm going to see it through to the end, no matter what the result. But if the ambush does go wrong, it would be better if the two of you aren't on the ship." He looked directly at James. "Especially if what they say is true."

"What do they say?" asked James.

"That an outsider arrived in Wonderland, and that Lahire's in a panic about it. I don't know why Lahire would be afraid of a single outsider, but I figure if he's afraid, then that's all the more reason to keep him alive. Don't you agree?"

James shuffled his feet awkwardly, but didn't reply.

Kara climbed out of the flier. "Thank you," she said, crossing over to Marco and giving him a hug. "Be careful."

"I always am." Marco returned her hug. "Now, get going while you can. Stay low and well behind the ship. If anything does go wrong, they're less likely to see you if you're close to the ground. Just get away and do whatever it is you have to do."

Kara motioned for James to climb into the glider. He did so gingerly, feeling exposed and uncomfortable in the relatively open frame. Kara paused to put on the goggles he'd seen her wear the night before, then climbed in to sit in the pilot's seat in front of him.

She looked up and nodded. Marco, standing at the hatch, hit the release for the glider. James felt it lurch as the clamps holding the flier in place released, then they fell away from the ship.

* * *

Lahire sat on his private balcony overlooking the city. His breakfast and cup of tea had long since gone cold, and despite it being a glorious day, the sight of the city did nothing to improve his mood.

The outsider was out there. Somewhere.

His dreams, when he had managed to sleep, had been visions of disaster. The kingdoms falling. Wonderland burning. His people dying. The entire time, the giant shadowy form of the outsider had loomed over the images, laughing evilly at the misfortune being inflicted on Lahire's creation.

Damn Taxard! He was the one who had allowed the outsider to sneak into Wonderland, and had failed to track him down within the city. It was a definite sign that the current model was starting to break down.

He berated himself. He had allowed himself to get too attached to that one. It should have been replaced years ago, but he had felt a sense of empathy with it. The model had reminded him a lot of the first automaton Dr. Keron had created for him, all those years ago, the model that had assured his ascension to the throne.

He shook his head. It was no time for sentimentalities. He had to be strong and lead his kingdom through the current crisis. Shireche had convinced him long ago that only by his hand would Wonderland be safe, and so far he had been right. The outsider would be a minor footnote in the history of his reign, nothing more.

Behind him, someone coughed politely. One of the court officials had entered.

Lahire turned. "What is it?"

The official bowed. "I'm sorry to disturb you, Your Majesty, but you have an appointment with the King and Queen of Clubs in ten minutes."

He waved his hand. "I will be there in due course." The official bowed again and scurried off. He stood, taking in the view of the city one last time, then turned and made his way to the throne room. By the time the King and Queen of Clubs were shown in, he projected the air of being in control.

"Your Majesty," said the king and queen in unison, bowing deeply when they reached the area in front of the throne.

Lahire bowed slightly in acknowledgment. "I understand you wished to speak with me on personal matters."

The queen cleared her throat. "Your Majesty, we wanted to speak with you about our children."

"Of course. I can assure you they are all happy here and enjoying their stay in the castle. Their education is progressing well, and I'm told they are well behaved with their nanny and the tutors."

The queen stepped forward. "Please, Your Majesty. We miss them terribly, and we get to see them so rarely. If we could spend some more time with them, visit them every day or two—"

Lahire shook his head. "Out of the question. You know the rules. All children of the kingdom rulers will live in Heart Castle between one and twenty years of age, with their parents allowed to visit for one hour, once a month. I can't make exceptions; otherwise, the other families would want the same thing. Besides, think of the children. It would be a huge distraction to their studies to have so many visits. Their learning and development would suffer."

"But they hardly recognize us anymore!" Realizing she had raised her voice, the queen continued in a more gentle tone. "We beg you to allow us to be more involved with our children as they grow up, so they know who we are and learn about the history of the Club kingdom."

"Your children know who you are. They're getting the best education and upbringing possible, and I have seen to it myself that they have private tutors with detailed lesson plans. They will grow up to be men and women you can be proud of."

The Club King took a step forward to join his wife. "Please, Your Majesty. Our children are our life. We can't bear to be without them. Can't you see it within your heart to let us at least spend more time with them, if not remove the rule entirely so we can take them home with us?"

Lahire drummed his fingers on the arm of the throne. "You know full well that the children are here to *protect* them from incidents like the one three years ago. A huge terrorist cell in your own kingdom, and you knew nothing about it? A terrorist cell that had Club army weapons and was extremely well resourced?

"Your children were in terrible danger. Imagine what those terrorists might have done if they had decided to target the children? No, it's much better if they are here, safe and sound, until we can be sure that every terrorist has been eliminated in your kingdom."

The Club King cleared his throat. "As we have already explained, Your Majesty, the terrorists had obviously secured a cache of weapons from before the wa... er, unification. Our people were working tirelessly to hunt down members of the cell, when your Heart Guard came in and provided the assistance that made the breakthrough."

Lahire leaned back in the throne. "Obviously, I'm in *no way* suggesting you were involved in any such group. That would be treason, after all, and punishable by death. I merely want to ensure that even if something like that were to happen again in your kingdom, and the terrorists decided to cause trouble for the rightful rulers, that your children would be safe. I'm sure you want your children to remain safe, don't you?"

"Of course, Your Majesty," replied the king resignedly.

"Well then, I'm glad we've had this chat. Now, if you'll excuse me, I have matters to attend to."

The king and queen looked at each other sadly, then bowed and departed.

Lahire watched them leave, then stood quickly. The Club Kingdom had always been a thorn in his side, and he was beginning to suspect that he would soon have to take decisive action to deal with them once and for all. To do that, he needed a Taxard he could rely on, one that wasn't a liability.

It was time to talk to Dr. Keron.

CHAPTER 11

James had to admit that, after the first few minutes of sheer terror, traveling in the flier was kind of fun. Because it was made out of the same strange material as the skyships, unlike a normal glider, the flier could hover. That had been useful once or twice when the *Nighthawk* had slowed down, and they'd needed to lose speed quickly.

Propulsion was provided by a small engine of some kind that turned two corkscrews beneath the flier. He didn't know how the engine was powered, but since Kara had proven to be a mechanical genius so far, he was willing to simply accept that it worked.

After banking in a large circle to come up behind the *Nighthawk*, they had slowly dropped back to keep their distance. They were lucky in one respect. It was a clear day, so they had no trouble keeping the ship in sight. But they had been following the ship for the past four hours without incident, and he was beginning to get bored.

To make matters worse, the open structure of the flier made it difficult to talk. The front canopy protected them from the worst of the wind, but did nothing to reduce the wind noise. So he couldn't ask more about where they were.

Not that he had many questions he wanted to ask about the landscape. The sun had risen high in the sky, and he could clearly see the forest below. Occasionally, they would pass over large plains areas with animals that looked like cattle, but he was too high up to tell clearly. So far, he had seen no signs of civilization—no buildings or roads—but it was possible some could be hiding beneath the trees.

He noticed it at the same time Kara pointed. A dot to the left of the *Nighthawk* had become visible and was moving through the sky at a slow pace. Kara reached into the satchel she kept over her shoulder and pulled out a spyglass. After looking through it for a few moments, she passed it back to James. The dot grew larger when he placed the spyglass to his eye and proved to be a large cargo ship of some kind.

As he watched, the *Nighthawk* changed direction to move toward the cargo ship. It became apparent that the cargo ship was trying to change course to escape, but it was a much slower and less maneuverable ship. He lowered the spyglass for a moment and looked around for signs of any other ships.

"There!" yelled James, tapping Kara on the shoulder. He had spied something moving on the ground below, but after staring at it for several seconds, he realized it was a shadow from something above. Looking up, he could make out another ship high in the sky.

"Give me the glass." Kara killed the forward thrust of the flier and took a quick view through the glass. The wind noise died down as they glided to a stop. She lowered the glass again, her expression worried as she turned back to him. "That's a Heart patrol ship. You were right. It's a trap."

He nodded grimly. They could do nothing as they sat in the flier and watched the events unfold.

The *Nighthawk* drew closer to the cargo vessel. Several warning shots from the *Nighthawk* encouraged the cargo ship to stop, allowing the pirate ship to move alongside. Through the spyglass, he was able to make out the *Nighthawk* crew, led by Coulter, boarding the cargo ship. The pirates met little resistance as they surged on board.

After they had been on board the ship for several minutes, Coulter, Marco, and four pirates suddenly appeared, running toward the *Nighthawk* as if trying to escape. A group of Heart Guard chased after them. A red flare shot up from the deck of the cargo ship.

Kara pointed to the ship high above them. "It's closing in." The Heart ship descended quickly from its overhead position toward the two ships. The *Nighthawk* began to separate from the cargo ship, but before it had opened much of a gap, the patrol ship fired several cannons. The pirate ship appeared to get the message as it cut forward momentum, and the cargo ship again docked alongside the *Nighthawk*.

James looked at Kara. He could see that she was fighting back tears. "What will happen to them?"

"They'll be taken to one of the kingdom capitals. Some of them might be lucky and get a life sentence of working in one of the mines, but most of them will be executed for piracy. Coulter and Marco will be the first to lose their heads." Kara wiped away the few tears that had escaped. "But there's nothing we can do for them. They knew the risks."

He stared at the three ships, the Heart ship in the perfect position to fire on the *Nighthawk* if they tried anything. He raised the spyglass again and observed the movements of the Heart troops on board. He forced himself to relax and let his mind take in everything. He felt the familiar sensation of his mind processing possibilities and probable outcomes, as Melvin had taught him when he had shown James how to play chess.

"We should get going," said Kara finally. "It was my uncle's own stupid greed that got them into it."

"True," replied James distractedly. "But what if we rescued them?"

"How? It's not like we can storm the ships. There's only the two of us. And no offense, but you're pretty useless."

He ignored the insult. A number of Heart Guard moved around on the deck of the *Nighthawk*. Two of them dragged Sasha out of the engine room area, then hauled him and three other crew over to the cargo ship where they were taken inside. Other Heart Guard did a quick sweep of the *Nighthawk*, then attached thick lines from the cargo ship to the bow of the pirate ship.

"They're keeping the *Nighthawk* crew on the cargo ship. It doesn't look like the patrol ship is getting near."

"There's probably a full contingent of Heart Guard on the cargo ship," said Kara sourly. "I bet it doesn't even have any cargo on board."

"It looks like they're planning to tow the *Nighthawk* behind the cargo ship."

"It makes sense. The cargo ship can pull the *Nighthawk* with ease. They're probably going to take it back with them to the Diamond capital. Lahire likes to have his war trophies to parade around."

"Do you think the patrol ship will stick around?"

Kara shrugged. "I don't know. Probably not, if they're towing the *Nighthawk* and keeping the crew prisoner on the cargo ship. Why?"

James lowered the spyglass as his mind began working out several strategies to consider. He gave Kara a smile. "I think I might know how we can save your uncle and his crew."

* * *

"And then the loyal Wonderland boy reported what his parents had tried to make him do to the authorities. They thanked the boy for warning them about the evil terrorists, and he was rewarded with lots of candy. They also gave the boy new parents who loved him very much and didn't try to make him do bad things. They all lived happily ever after. The end."

The eight boys and girls of various ages between three and nine sat in their beds listening with rapt attention as Lahire finished his story. He closed the book to groans and complaints from several of the kids.

"Read us another story, Uncle Lahire," begged one young girl. "Read us the one about the brother and sister and their evil stepmother who hid a terrorist in her house."

He moved over to the girl, the Ten of Clubs symbol visible on her arm, and ruffled her hair as he gave her a smile. "Come now, Lucy, I've already read three stories tonight. It's time you all went to sleep."

A second chorus of "Awwww" filled the room.

"There's no use complaining," he replied with fake severity. "It's time to sleep now. Remember, tomorrow's the big day you all go to the zoo. And I think whoever manages to fall asleep the fastest might get extra time holding the baby hedgehogs."

The children quickly snuggled down into their beds. He moved around, making sure each child was tucked in and giving them kisses on their foreheads.

He stopped at the door. "Nighty night," he said, before extinguishing the light and partially closing the door. He paused for a minute, listening to hear if any of the children spoke or got up. But they were all quiet. With a smile on his lips, he turned and crept away.

"They're so cute and impressionable when they're young, aren't they, Your Majesty?" Shireche's voice came from behind him.

Lahire forced himself not to jump, his jovial mood evaporating. He turned to where the voice had come from. As usual, he could see no form in the shadows.

"They are Wonderland's future," replied Lahire. "I will do everything in my power to protect them from any who would harm them."

"And quite right, Your Majesty. Alas, there are many in this world who would see harm done to the people, even ones as young and innocent as children."

After several moments of silence, Lahire asked, "Was there anything you wanted in particular?"

"I came to offer my condolences. I heard that the ship the outsider was seen leaving on had been caught as part of the pirate trapping program you had begun, but the outsider and his female accomplice were gone."

"What?" He let his surprise show. It wasn't the first time Shireche had known important details before him, but it frustrated him to no end. "I've heard no such news."

"Really? I'm sure there's a reasonable explanation for such a long delay in informing you. Perhaps they've been having communications difficulties. Or maybe the message was simply lost. I'm sure there wouldn't be any attempt to deliberately withhold information from Your Majesty. After all, that would be treason."

"Indeed, it would. And treason of any sort is punishable by death. I will look into the matter at once. Thank you, Shireche. Once again, you have given me valuable information that has been hidden from me."

"I am here to help, Your Majesty. I have only the best interests of Wonderland at heart."

Lahire set off toward the Heart Guard central offices. He expected to find the new commander of the Heart Guard present, and he wasn't disappointed.

When she saw him, the commander quickly stood and bowed low. "Your Majesty." The folder of papers she had been reading spilled to the floor.

"Why wasn't I informed about the captured ship?" Lahire made sure his tone hinted at dire consequences for the wrong answer.

"I'm sorry, Your Majesty, but I'm not sure I know what you're talking about—"

"Don't play games with me. The ship that was captured as part of the Soundy sting. Why wasn't I informed that it was the same ship the outsider was seen leaving on?"

The commander's eyes went wide in surprise and alarm. "I hadn't been made aware of that information myself. There have been some communication problems with the ships involved in that operation all day. We got a confirmation message that the operation had been a success, but no further details."

Lahire narrowed his eyes, examining the commander's expression closely. She seemed to be telling the truth, but it could be hard to tell at times. For the moment, he would give her the benefit of the doubt. "Go on."

The commander hurriedly continued. "I'll dispatch another ship at once to rendezvous with the bait ship and have the captured crew brought directly here. We'll interrogate the prisoners and find out what they know before sunrise."

"See that you do. It would be unfortunate if you were to have a major failure so early in your new position. I would be forced to reconsider your appointment."

CHAPTER 12

The flier moved quietly through the night sky toward the slow-moving cargo ship which towed the *Nighthawk*. No lights were lit on the pirate vessel, and only a thin wisp of smoke wafted from the engine's chimney. The ship was a dead weight behind the cargo ship.

Kara killed the flier's engine when they were a few hundred yards from the two ships and glided it silently forward. She directed the flier to below the pirate ship, shedding speed as she headed toward the mounting structure underneath. By the time they drew near the launch point, they had almost matched the speed of the *Nighthawk*.

James stood, and with the hook and pole Kara had showed him earlier, reached out and managed to snare one of the metal struts underneath the ship. He slowly pulled them into the docking bay, Kara helping him guide the flier in the final yard and making sure the clamps locked on so the flier wouldn't drift.

"I hope the ship is as deserted as it seems," whispered James, as they climbed up to the hatch.

"We'll find out in a moment." Kara pulled the release lever to open the hatch. The sound of the hatch opening echoed loudly through the ship. James held his breath for the shout of alarm he expected at any second, but only silence greeted them. They climbed quickly into the ship and closed the hatch behind them.

He looked around, imagining guards in every shadow. "Maybe this was a bad idea."

"It was your idea, remember?" Kara removed her gun from the satchel she carried.

"Just because I came up with the idea doesn't mean I want to do it."

Kara didn't reply, and he followed her through the ship without further complaint. To his relief, no guards were on board. Several minutes later, they had reached their destination.

Unlike his first visit, the engine room was almost clear of steam and smoke. The furnace gave off a faint glow, but it had obviously been left to go out on its own. Kara handed him a shovel, then grabbed one herself.

The two began shoveling, putting fuel—not coal, as he first thought it was, but something that looked similar—into the furnace. The flames immediately grew brighter and hotter. After several minutes of shoveling, Kara stepped over to the side and read the dials hanging from various pipes, tapping a few of them to make sure they hadn't stuck.

"Okay. By the time we get everyone off the cargo ship, the engines should have built up enough steam to get us out of here. Now, wait here while I go get the climbing gear."

He nodded silently, and Kara departed. Putting down the shovel, but not sure what to do until Kara returned, he slowly wandered around the engine room examining the various gauges and strange attachments.

"So, a daring nighttime rescue," said the Cheshire Cat, from above and to his left. He looked in the direction of the voice. The cat sat on top of one of the large machines, its tail flicking around. "How exciting. A bit risky, though, don't you think?"

"We can't sit back and do nothing," said James defensively.

"Indeed." The Cheshire Cat's tail twitched. "Hunted throughout the kingdom, wanted dead by the king himself simply because you exist, and yet you return to a nest of Heart Guard to rescue cutthroat pirates. Some would say you're mad to even consider it."

"Yeah, well, being called mad is nothing new. Besides, isn't Wonderland supposed to be full of mad people?"

The cat grinned. "There are many who say that."

"So are you here to help, or are you just going to heckle?"

"Oh, I couldn't possibly get involved. I'm much more of an observer of life. One day I should write a book about it." The Cheshire Cat held up his paw in front of his face and flexed his claws as if reminding James about the absurdity of the suggestion.

"I'm sure stranger things have happened here."

"You have no idea." The cat turned his head to one side. "Most of them are drinking tonight, you know."

"Who are?"

"The guards. They don't normally get to celebrate or drink much. The king doesn't allow it. But it seems that after some thought on the matter, and one or two suggestions from an outside source, their officers decided it would be a good idea to hold a party for the men. After all, the alcohol on this ship would have been thrown away otherwise. Only a few of the guards are actually keeping watch." The cat stood and stretched. "Avoid the front of the ship, and you should be fine."

"Thank you. But why are you telling me this?"

"It makes things interesting," replied the cat with another large grin.

The door to the engine room opened again, and Kara returned carrying several items. James glanced back to where the Cheshire Cat had been sitting, but he was nowhere to be seen.

"Found the harnesses and the other items we'll need," she said, handing one of the harnesses to him then putting on one herself.

He looked dubiously at the poorly made item. "You're sure this will hold me if I fall?"

"Of course, it will. It's stronger than it looks."

He shrugged and put it on as Kara showed him. He debated telling her what he had learned from the Cheshire Cat, but decided to say nothing. He didn't know if the cat's information was true, and if it wasn't, they could get themselves into a lot of trouble very quickly.

Once he'd finished putting on the harness, he followed Kara back onto the deck of the *Nighthawk*, and they walked toward the bow of the ship.

A huge rope ran from the ship to the cargo ship twenty yards ahead. Although as he looked closer at it, he realized *rope* wasn't the right word. It looked like rope, but from how the two ships were moving, it had to be much stiffer than rope. It looked as though it acted more as a shock absorber between the two ships.

He connected his harness to the not-quite-rope as demonstrated by Kara, then the two of them made their way across as quietly as possible.

They were halfway when the sound of footsteps on the deck of the cargo ship became audible. He froze. He was too far from either ship to find a hiding place in time. In front of him, Kara had stopped as well. She dropped to lie on the rope, and seeing little other option, he did the same—just in time, as a Heart Guard stepped into the light.

James held his breath, not moving. They had the advantage of the guard standing near a lit lantern, so his night vision would be poor, but James had no doubt that any sound or movement would alert the guard to their presence.

Without warning, the rope bucked. James did his best to hold on and suppress the cry of surprise on his lips, but as the rope stabilized, he realized his grip was slipping. He tried to tighten his hold, but felt himself slowly sliding around the rope. He risked a glance toward the guard, but he stood at the stern of the cargo ship.

As he was about to fall and give away his location, the guard resumed his patrol. James managed to hold on the few extra seconds it took for the guard to move out of sight around the deck of the stern, before his grip finally failed. He fell.

Luckily, Kara hadn't been lying. He was almost winded by the harness as he jerked to a stop after falling a yard, but at least he was safe.

Kara inched her way back to where he dangled. "Grab your tether and climb up. I'll help you."

He struggled, but with Kara's help, was finally able to get back up onto the rope.

Kara turned back toward the cargo ship. "We'd better hurry. We don't want to be stuck out here again if another guard comes."

He nodded, shaken from the fall, but he obediently crawled forward. Safely on the stable deck of the cargo ship, he took a moment to breathe deeply and let his pulse rate return to normal while Kara again took her gun out of her satchel. The sound of men laughing loudly was faintly audible in the distance.

Kara obviously heard it, too. "They sound like they're having a party of some sort."

"Maybe they've taken the alcohol off the *Nighthawk*," suggested James, echoing the information the Cheshire Cat had given him. "They could take advantage of being in a remote location, where they won't get into trouble for drinking."

Kara shook her head in amazement. "I've never heard of that happening before. Hopefully, that means there will be less of them keeping watch."

The two of them crept along the deck of the cargo ship. Reaching a door, Kara carefully opened it. She glanced inside, then motioned for him to follow.

They entered a huge open section of the ship, where they stood on a metal gangway ten yards above the floor. As far as he could tell, the expanse was one third of the ship's hull area. In the dim lighting, he could see a similar door and gangway on the other side of the space, with the area being partitioned from the forward sections of the ship by a wall. The gangway was also partitioned, with doors separating that area from the rest.

Below, a large metal cage had been placed in the cargo area. The crew of the *Nighthawk* were inside, lying down on the floor or leaning against the bars. Two guards sat near the cage. They were drinking and playing some sort of game. They weren't paying attention to anything going on in the cage, but it was obvious they would see James or Kara if they tried to cross over to the pirates.

Kara moved forward silently along the gangway to the top of the stairs located at the end. He followed, moving slower in an effort to not make a sound. Luckily, he didn't, and he reached where she was crouching.

Kara waved at the pirates in the cages, trying to get their attention. Marco finally noticed Kara, although other than a nod, he made little motion of seeing her. Instead, he casually stood and walked over to Coulter, where they had a brief whispered conference.

"That's right," said Marco loudly, pushing Coulter. "I said this was all your fault."

"I didn't hear you complaining about the idea." Coulter pushed him back. "In fact, you were the one carrying on the most about how rich you were going to be, and how many women you'd be buying when we got back to port."

"A man can dream, can't he?" Marco pushed Coulter again, harder than before. "Besides, at the first hint of someone disagreeing with you, you throw a hissy fit. None of us wanted to deal with another one of your sulks."

"And I suppose you think you'd do a better job of captain than me." Coulter shoved Marco into a group of pirates standing at the side.

"Maybe I would." Marco almost launched Coulter into the cage wall.

"If you want it, come and get it." Coulter motioned for Marco to come at him.

Marco threw himself at Coulter. The two guards, who had stopped their game to watch the argument, made their way over to the cage.

"Hey! Knock it off, you two," yelled one of the guards, raising his weapon. Marco and Coulter continued to wrestle. The other pirates had all jumped to their feet. A few egged the fight on, shouting in support of one side or the other, while others tried to break it up, throwing in the odd punch into others at the same time.

The fight was enough of a distraction to ensure the guards didn't hear the sound of Kara's gun charging as she carefully lined up her shot. James remembered to cover his eyes as the electricity crackled from the gun to the guards. Kara's whispered "Yes" told him her shot had been successful.

Coulter and Marco immediately stopped fighting and restored order to the pirates as Kara moved over to the door on the cage.

"Nice shooting," commented Marco. Kara grinned. The bolt cutters from her satchel made short work of the padlock.

"The other guards are having some sort of party," Kara told Marco and Coulter, as they stepped out. "If we're quiet, we should be able to get back to the *Nighthawk* before they realize anything is wrong."

"Using my alcohol!" steamed Coulter.

"Why don't you go and have a word with them, then?" snapped Kara. "I'm sure they'll happily give it back to you."

Coulter stared at Kara for a moment, then shook his head. "Let's get out of here."

"It's no use," said Sasha. "The engines will be too cold by now. We'd need at least half an hour to build up enough steam, and they're sure to notice we've escaped before then."

Kara gave him a large smile. "We've already taken care of that."

"That's my girl!" said Sasha happily, a little too loud. Several pirates shushed him, and he looked away in embarrassment.

"I'm surprised you came back," said Coulter to Kara.

"I almost didn't." She pointed at James. "He was the one who came up with a plan to get you out."

Coulter looked at him with surprise. "I guess I underestimated you." His voice held a hint of respect.

James had been continuously scanning the cargo bay. "We're still not out of here. We need to get going. We have no idea how soon someone will come by to check on the guards."

Coulter turned to the other pirates. "You heard the man. We're getting out of here. Stay quiet, or you're getting left behind."

One of the pirates grabbed the weapons off the Heart Guard, but a cough from Coulter saw the pirate hand over the pistol to Coulter. Marco took the other pistol, and with a nod, led the pirates onto the gangway and toward the door.

"There was a guard patrolling the deck," whispered James to Marco. Marco nodded, then motioned for everyone to stay still and be quiet.

He listened carefully at the door, then cracked it open and looked out. Motioning the all-clear, he opened the door and stepped out. As they neared the stern, Marco held up his hand in warning. Everyone stopped moving. James could hear the sounds of footsteps ahead, and his heart leapt into his throat.

Marco moved forward silently, crouching low. He glanced around the corner, then leapt around it in one smooth movement. The sound of a sickening snap, then of Marco carrying something heavy for several steps on the deck, told James all he needed to know about the fate of the guard. After a few moments of silence, Marco returned and motioned for everyone to continue.

The pirates began crossing the rope, none of them showing concern at their lack of safety equipment. He stopped to attach his harness to the rope.

"No time for that, lad," said one of the pirates, grabbing his shoulders. "Just move forward and don't look down." James stifled a yell of surprise and did his best to not fall off as the pirate moved him forward. He was unsteady on the rope, but the pirate managed to keep him upright, and he crossed back to the *Nighthawk* without incident.

Marco assigned several pirates to remove the tow rope on his signal, while others moved to their assigned positions on the ship. Kara and James followed Sasha to the engine room, where they quickly set to work.

"Are we ready to go?" Coulter's impatient voice emerged from a metal tube in the middle of the room. Sasha stopped what he was working on and leaned over to a similar tube. "Ready when you are, Captain."

He felt the ship lurch slightly, then list as it was put into a sharp turn. The bridge signaled for full speed, and following Sasha's orders, they pulled levers and turned wheels in a complex pattern that made no sense to James. The noise in the room increased as the large machines began moving.

Several seconds later, the ship shuddered slightly as several cannon shots were fired. At first, he thought the cargo ship was firing at them, but when he heard no sounds of impacts or shouts of alarm, he realized it had been the *Nighthawk* shooting at the cargo ship. James hurried out of the engine room onto the deck. The cargo ship slowly swung into view as the *Nighthawk* completed its one-hundred-eighty-degree turn. The cannon shots from the pirate vessel had struck their targets on the cargo ship. A fire had broken out near the rear, and the ship had taken on a slight list.

Heart Guard appeared on the deck of the cargo ship, but the *Nighthawk* was already well out of range.

He allowed himself a smile. They had done it! They had done the impossible and managed to escape.

CHAPTER 13

The lack of sleep for a second night had left Lahire in a bad mood, and he tapped his fingers on the arm of the throne as the commander of the guard gave her report. She trembled as she delivered the news, obviously expecting her life to be forfeited.

He cut off the commander's report with a wave of his hand. Once again, the outsider had slipped through his fingers, and he had made a mockery of the Heart Guard name.

"When the guards on the cargo ship return to the capital, they are to be publicly executed for dereliction of duty. I want every patrol ship sent in the direction the pirate ship was last seen heading. The vessel is to be destroyed on sight, and everyone on board is to be killed. I will accept no more mistakes in this matter. Do I make myself clear?"

"Y-yes, Your Majesty." The commander bowed nervously and made a hasty exit.

"Guards!"

The senior guard stepped through the door into the throne room. "Your Majesty?"

"Tell the head executioner I want ten prisoners brought out for immediate execution. I will not have the citizens of this kingdom thinking my rule has gone weak, and they can take advantage of me. Understood?"

"Of course, Your Majesty. Right away."

The guard left. Lahire let out a frustrated sigh. It was as though the outsider was mocking him. Twice, the outsider had been within his grasp, and twice, the outsider had managed to slip away. His guards were useless. His assassin was no longer reliable. Everyone in his kingdom was failing him at the very time he needed them to do their duty.

As if summoned by Lahire's thoughts, Taxard stepped out from behind a curtain at the side of the room and made his way to the front of the throne. He kneeled in silence.

He eyed his assassin coolly. "I told you to only return once you had dealt with White Rabbit and the outsider. Since you kneel before me, I can only assume you have carried this out?"

"No, Your Majesty. I return because of more urgent news."

"Go on."

"I was able to track White Rabbit's movements. He left the city and headed toward the Club Kingdom. When I arrived there, I observed that the Club rulers have begun their own search for the outsider in secret, separate from the search your guards are carrying out in their kingdom. I also saw suggestions that the terrorists in the kingdom have re-armed, and they appear to be getting ready to revolt while you are distracted with the outsider situation. I believe White Rabbit is helping them and is now working for Ariston Bachrach."

Lahire scowled at the name. "So, the general is finally going to make his move. And the former rulers will risk their own children to be a part of it. They will live only long enough to see their precious kingdom razed to the ground when the Heart army marches across it again."

He looked at Taxard. "You have not done what I asked, but the information you returned with is valuable. The situation has changed. Stay in the castle, but be ready to leave at short notice. Whether it's the Club Kingdom or the outsider, I will need your services shortly. I want no mistakes this time."

"Of course, Your Majesty." Taxard stood and left the room.

Lahire left the throne room and retreated to his private chambers. He stood at the edge of the large map of Wonderland he had mounted on the central table in his study all those years ago, the day he had taken over as ruler of the Heart Kingdom. The six kingdoms were arrayed in front of him, each displaying a Heart flag stuck into the location of the kingdom capitals.

"So, the Club Kingdom wants war, do they? Your kingdom was conquered once. The Heart army will be ready to conquer it again if you try to revolt."

He sat down at his desk and began writing out the orders for his armies to march to the Club Kingdom's borders.

* * *

Coulter stared at Kara in disbelief. "You want to go where?"

It was late in the day after their escape from the cargo ship the night before, and Kara had finally told Coulter their real destination.

"Tulgey Wood," repeated Kara evenly.

"I knew you were a risk taker, but I hadn't realized you'd turned suicidal. You won't last five minutes in there. You know what that place is like. It's a death trap on roots."

"Nevertheless, that is where we need to go. You don't have to come with us. You can wait for us at the edge of the forest."

"You're damn right I'm not coming with you." He glanced at James, who had been standing quietly as the two argued. "You're taking him to see Caterpillar, aren't you? You want to know if you can use him to overthrow Lahire."

"I don't know what you're talking about."

"Come on, I heard the rumors before we left the capital. An outsider was loose in the capital, and the entire Heart Guard had been turned out to find him. Then, you show up with a stranger, wanting to leave immediately. It doesn't take much effort to piece the two together."

"You can think what you like. We need to get to Tulgey Wood."

"Fine." Coulter threw his hands in the air. "You want to go to Tulgey Wood, I'll take you to Tulgey Wood. But you're going to get yourself killed."

"That's never worried you before."

Coulter said nothing, turning to focus on the maps in front of him and making a large show of plotting a new course. Kara gave an annoyed sigh, then exited the bridge. James quickly followed her.

"Like he actually cares if I live or die," said Kara fiercely, when they were back on the deck.

"Maybe he does, but he doesn't know how to show it."

"Yeah, right." Kara leaned against the railing and looked out over the side of the ship. "And he showed it by leaving me in the Spade Kingdom without so much as a 'See you later.' Then there was putting us in the middle of his 'big payoff' raid on the cargo ship. Look how well that turned out. He's never written, never visited. How dare he try to play the 'It'll be dangerous' card. He's just too chicken to go there himself."

James remained silent, and the two of them stared off at the countryside.

"Did you ever find her?" he asked finally.

"Find who?"

"Your mother. Sasha said that's who you were looking for when you came on their ship the last time. That she was a pirate somewhere."

Kara looked somber. "No, I never did. Oh, I heard rumors, sure. People said they had seen her recently in one place or another. But that's all they were, rumors. She's still alive; I know that much. But I don't know where she is. Or why she abandoned me."

"She might not have had a choice. I don't imagine being a pirate is a healthy environment to raise a kid, and she probably has a lot of enemies."

"She's never even tried to contact me. To write or send word that she's okay." Kara was starting to get worked up. "Not once. I only found out who she was by accident a few years ago, when Father put a little too much brandy into his tea and got tipsy. Every other time I had asked, he was always silent on the matter."

He put a hand on her shoulder. "I'm sorry. I hope you find her one day."

Kara looked as if she wanted to say something else, but then sighed. He took his hand away, and they stared in silence at the scenery below.

Kara broke the silence after several minutes. "Do you miss it? Your world, I mean?"

"Kind of. I mean, yeah, sure. It's only been a few days, and everything has been so hectic, I guess I haven't had a chance to sit down and think about it. With Melvin being killed like he was, I guess I've been trying to put it out of my mind."

"Do you have family back there? A girlfriend or wife?"

"A girlfriend. Well, fiancée, I guess. Her name's Laura. She was the reason I had gone to Melvin's place. We had a fight, and she decided that I needed some time to 'think about what I'd done.'"

He made a face. "Because it's not like she could ever do anything wrong. She was too perfect for that. You know what? I *have* thought about what I've done. I've thought about what I've done over the past eighteen months I've spent with her. She was the one who was wrong, not me. She always wanted me to change, to do only what she liked and stop doing the things that she didn't like. Frankly, she can go to hell for all I care. I'm better off without her." James stood as he delivered his tirade and thumped the rail to drive home his point.

Kara looked at him with a slightly amused expression her face. "What?"

"Nothing," she said, obviously trying to hide her smile. "It's the first time I've seen you get worked up over anything."

He leaned back on the rail and chuckled. "I guess there's a lot of built-up anger there. More than I realized."

"What about family?"

"I don't talk to my family if I can help it. A brief call once a year, at Christmas, that always ends in a shouting match. My family couldn't care less about me. Not after their precious 'Natalie' was born..." His voice trailed off, as he thought bitterly about his sister.

"She was their favorite child?"

He snorted. "The way you hear it from them these days, she's their only child. I was adopted because the doctors said my mother could never get pregnant. When I was seven, the *miracle* happened. I was happy, of course. I thought having a brother or sister would be fun. But once she was born, everything was about her. I couldn't do anything right. I left when I was fifteen and haven't seen them since."

"So you never knew your real parents?"

He shook his head. "I tried to find them after I left home. My mother died in childbirth. I didn't really find out anything about my father."

"I'm sorry."

James shrugged. "Don't be. I've had a lot of time to think about it over the years. I wish I could have met her, my mother, but I know that can never happen. As for my father—well, he abandoned my mother before I was born, so I don't think he was exactly father of the year material."

A thought struck him. It obviously showed on his face, as Kara looked at him quizzically. "What is it?"

"I just realized I've never talked with anyone but Melvin about this before. I tried saying something to Laura once, but she told me to stop moping about the past. It's a nice feeling. Thank you."

The ship began to change direction. "Looks like Coulter has decided to head toward Tulgey Wood."

Kara nodded. "Another two days and we should be there."

"Is it as dangerous as Coulter made it sound?"

"I'm afraid so."

"How are we supposed to survive, then? I'm hardly a great woodsman, and you don't seem to be either. Plus there're only so many shots in your gun."

Kara shrugged. "I don't know. I didn't think that far ahead. I was hoping something would come to me by the time we got there."

He stared at her in disbelief, then started chuckling. His chuckling turned into laughter.

Kara looked at him in bewilderment. "What? What's so funny?"

It took James several tries to stop laughing. "I'm sorry, it struck me that I'm in Wonderland, on the run because the Heart King wants to chop off my head, and now I'm probably going to get eaten by a plant. Then I had the scene from *Through the Looking Glass* playing in my head with the flowers, and I realized how absurd this all is. Being in Wonderland, meeting the Mad Hatter—no offense to your father—and Gryphon. Now, I'm off to see the Caterpillar. When I read the books as a child, I hardly imagined they were real."

"You keep mentioning books. What books do you mean?"

"You're right, I guess no one here would know about the books, since they were published in my world."

He gave a quick synopsis of the two Wonderland books to Kara.

"Interesting," said Kara when he had finished. "Father mentioned this Alice girl once years ago, but I never paid it a lot of attention. I guess the only reason I remember her name at all was because she was an outsider. The few details Father mentioned sound vaguely like the Alice in your story. I wonder what the link is between the visit of Alice and Lahire."

"You think there's a connection?"

"I'm not sure, but everything changed soon after she visited. It seems reasonable to think there's some sort of connection between the two."

"You said Caterpillar is some sort of oracle, right? Perhaps he'll know."

"Maybe. If we survive long enough to find him."

The two of them returned to silence, watching the scenery pass far below them.

CHAPTER 14

"Ship ahead!"

The call rained down loud and clear from the crow's nest of the ship and shook James from his reverie as he stared at the ocean below. It wasn't the first time the call had gone out since they had altered course for the Tulgey Wood two days previous. They'd already passed three small cargo ships and a luxury yacht early that morning, keeping their distance to avoid being recognized. But it was the first ship they'd seen for several hours.

The *Nighthawk* pitched slightly, as their course was adjusted to give the oncoming ship a wide berth.

"Heart patrol ship! Changing course to intercept!"

His heart skipped a beat. Thoughts of *We're all going to die* and *I'll be executed* came unbidden to his mind, but he forced them away. The crew of the *Nighthawk* were good, and the ship was fast. The fastest in Wonderland, Coulter had boasted. He was sure they'd be able to get away with little problem. Even as he formed the thought, the ship lurched forward, picking up speed.

A loud explosion from the engine room shook the ship. He turned to see smoke and steam erupting out the back. Crew ran toward the engine room, with James joining them. As the first crewman reached the door, it was thrown open.

More smoke and steam was released from the room. Kara staggered out, half-carrying and half-dragging the unconscious form of Sasha. The crew helped pull the two of them away from the engine room, and Kara collapsed onto the deck in a coughing fit. He reached her as someone handed her a hip flask. She took a swig, screwing up her face in distaste but obviously happy to have something to help clear the smoke from her throat.

He could see that Sasha was badly burned. One arm and leg looked as if the skin had been removed, leaving bare flesh, and his face was starting to blister.

"What happened?" demanded Coulter, striding to where they stood.

"Don't know exactly." Kara paused to cough. "One minute, we were increasing the engines to full, the next, there's a huge explosion with smoke and steam everywhere. I managed to crawl to Sasha, then get out. I think your dodgy engine finally failed."

"Can you fix it so we can get out of here?"

"Fix it? Are you crazy? It would take hours, days, and that's assuming you even have the parts on board."

Coulter stared at her. When he spoke, he had a softer tone. "You and the outsider get to the flier and get going. We're almost at Tulgey Wood. Hopefully, you'll find out what you need to know there."

"What?" Kara got unsteadily to her feet. "And what exactly are you going to do?"

Coulter smiled grimly. "We're going to show the Heart patrol ship why they don't want to mess with us."

"But that's crazy. You have almost no propulsion. You'll be sitting ducks."

"This isn't up for discussion." He grabbed her arm roughly and threw her toward James, who managed to catch her without the two of them collapsing in a heap.

"Get down to the flier and leave on my signal. I had Marco load it earlier with provisions, so you should be fine for a few days at least."

"But Uncle—" Kara's voice was unsteady.

"No time for goodbyes." Coulter turned to the rest of the crew. "What're you all standing around for? All hands prepare for battle! Ready the cannons. Prepare to repel boarders. Let's show these Heart bastards what we're made of!" A cheer went up among the crew, and they all ran to prepare the ship. Coulter looked at him. "Take care of her, you hear me?"

James nodded mutely. With a last look at Kara, Coulter turned and strode toward the bridge, shouting orders as he moved.

James took Kara's arm gently. "Come on, we'd better go." Kara said nothing as he led her off the deck. Once inside, she seemed to get a hold of herself somewhat.

"Stupid stubborn idiot," she muttered quietly to herself over and over as they made their way down to the flier. He couldn't be sure, but he thought he heard one or two muffled sobs at the same time.

Kara climbed into the flier silently. He followed her, standing as best he could between the bags of supplies that had been stored on board and readying to pull the release lever. Positioned in the open flier below the *Nighthawk*, they could see the Heart patrol ship get closer and closer. It was only a few hundred yards away when a crewman called down to them.

"Coulter says to launch when the cannons fire!"

Kara said nothing, so James yelled out a simple "Got it," to confirm they had received the message.

"They're going to be okay," said James, trying to sound confident.

"Just shut up," said Kara fiercely. He did as he was told.

The time seemed to drag out into hours. Finally, the deafening roar of the cannons filled the air. James pulled the lever to release the flier, and Kara immediately put them into a turn and dive to get away from the two ships.

He looked back to see several of the shots from the *Nighthawk* hit their mark on the Heart ship. He let out a cry of joy, but it was short-lived as the Heart ship swung around and began firing at the *Nighthawk*. At least three shots hit, with huge showers of debris flying from the impact. He also noticed something else that worried him.

"They've released fliers," he yelled to Kara. She glanced back to where he pointed. Three shapes had detached themselves from beneath the Heart ship and were flying their way. Pushing the flier to gain as much speed as possible, Kara dove toward the ocean.

Glancing back again, he saw several of the cannons on the closest side of the *Nighthawk* fire at the Heart fliers as they passed. One of the fliers broke apart in the air when a cannon ball ripped it in half, but the other two survived the onslaught and began to slowly close the gap.

Kara yelled back at him, "It's up to you. Take my gun from my satchel and try to shoot them."

"But I've never shot a gun in my life," protested James.

"Now would be a good time to learn."

He took Kara's gun out of the satchel. It was heavier than he had expected, weighing at least two pounds, and it felt awkward in his hands.

Kara glanced back again. "Turn the dial on the left side to one, and the red dial on the right side to seven. You don't have a lot of range on the gun, so wait until they're within a hundred yards. With those settings, you should have five shots."

He carried out her instructions, holding the gun right in front of his face to see the writing on the red dial. By the time he had the dials set, the pursuing fliers were much closer. When they had closed to within a hundred and fifty yards, the fliers began firing at them. He could make out the puffs of smoke from the large cylindrical devices on the front of the fliers, as if they were some sort of musket Gatling gun. One shot ricocheted off the frame near his head, but the other shots missed their mark.

"Hang on!" Kara began moving the flier around in a random pattern, making it harder for the chasing fliers to hit them. Unfortunately for James, it also made aiming a lot harder. When the lead flier was within range, he carefully lined up and fired off two shots. Both missed their mark.

"Hold it steady for a second," yelled James. Kara nodded, and their flier leveled out.

The lead flier moved to line up its shot, but before it could shoot, James fired. A hit! The flier lost control with part of its wing blown off, and it went into a steep dive toward the ocean. Only one flier remained.

"Tulgey Wood is up ahead. We might be able to lose them there if you can't shoot them."

"I've still got two shots." He tried to target their final pursuer, but its pilot wasn't making the same mistake as the one he had shot. Like them, it constantly changed its position to make it harder to hit. James missed with his first shot. He spent several seconds lining up his remaining shot, praying he would hit so they would be safe.

Just as he pulled the trigger, Kara put the flier into a sharp climb. His shot went wide.

"That's it. I'm out," yelled James. The chasing flier, realizing James and Kara's ship was no longer a danger, leveled out and moved in for the kill. Kara's flying managed to save them from the first two shots, but their luck finally ran out. A shot from the chasing flier struck their left wing, and they began to spin out of control.

"Hold on, we're going down!"

He looked forward. Land was tantalizingly close, only a few hundred yards away, but the ocean was coming toward them at a much faster rate. A loud noise behind him made him glance back. The chasing flier had exploded into a huge fireball in midair. Before he could say anything to Kara, the flier lurched suddenly, then hit the water.

Everything went black.

* * *

"We received confirmation from the patrol that it found the pirate ship in question and was moving to engage the vessel. A brief update several minutes later indicated the pirate ship had suffered some sort of on-board explosion and appeared dead in the sky, but we've received no further messages from the patrol since. I've dispatched three ships to investigate, and I will have their reports by the end of the day." The commander wore a nervous expression as she finished her report.

Lahire had been taking a stroll in the garden, enjoying a moment of respite among the white roses, when she had approached him to interrupt his relaxation. Normally, he would have punished anyone disturbing him, but the outsider matter took precedence over everything.

He nodded. It appeared that his luck was beginning to change. "You have done well. Let me know immediately what the ships find."

"Of course, Your Majesty." With a bow, she backed away and left him alone.

Well, not truly alone.

"Taxard," said Lahire quietly.

His assassin was by his side almost immediately. "Yes, Your Majesty?"

"The ship the outsider was on has been sighted near Tulgey Wood. You know what that means." It was a statement, not a question.

"He was trying to see Caterpillar."

"Exactly. Which means Caterpillar is likely to have come out of hiding in expectation of his visit. This is the perfect opportunity to take care of that problem once and for all."

"I will leave at once, Your Majesty."

"Don't fail me this time, Taxard. I won't tolerate failure, not even from you."

"Of course, Your Majesty." Taxard bowed low and an instant later was gone.

Lahire took a deep breath. For the first time in days, he felt as though the situation was finally under control. With Caterpillar and the outsider gone, Wonderland would be more stable than it had been before. And soon, the Club Kingdom would no longer be a problem. His army would crush the terrorist uprising and remove the meddlesome Club rulers once and for all.

He smiled.

CHAPTER 15

James slowly opened his eyes, blinked, and tried to focus on his surroundings. For the second time since he'd come to Wonderland, his head felt as though someone inside it was trying to escape by using a sledgehammer between his eyes, and his body ached all over as though he'd run a marathon.

The memories flooded back. The escape in the flier, being chased by other fliers, getting shot down, and the crash into the ocean. He tried to get up... and promptly fell back when a wave of dizziness hit him.

An unknown male voice spoke from his right. "You swallowed a lot of water. Take it easy for a few minutes."

He slowly turned his head. He realized he was under some trees at the edge of a beach. A campfire had been built, and the man who had spoken sat by the fire stirring something in a small hanging pot. He looked like a wild man. His clothes were patchwork, and his hair hadn't seen a comb in years. James placed him in his late thirties, although since aging worked differently in Wonderland, he had no idea how old the man actually was.

The man glanced over. "How do you feel?"

"Like someone ran over me."

"You were in a bad crash. If your pilot hadn't managed to pull up at the last second, you'd probably be dead."

James forced his head up to look around. "Kara! Where is she?"

The man motioned toward James's feet. Twisting his head slightly, he could see Kara lying on an old blanket.

He risked sitting up slowly. His head complained, but not too much. "Who are you?"

"I could ask you the same question."

"My name is James Riggs."

"And why were the Heart Guard trying to kill you?"

"Let's just say the King of Hearts has decided he doesn't like us and leave it at that for the moment."

The man nodded, seeming satisfied with the answer.

James remembered that he had seen the second flier chasing them explode. "Was that you? Were you the one who shot the flier?"

"Any chance to take out Heart Guard is worth taking. Besides, it was an easy shot. Watching the two of you firing at each other was embarrassing."

"You never introduced yourself. Who are you?"

"Torre."

"Just Torre?"

"Yes, just Torre. The rest of my name no longer has any meaning."

"Why not?"

"Because he's from the Red Kingdom." Kara's eyes were open, and she was staring at Torre.

Torre slammed his pot stirrer into the ground with great force. James started as he realized it was a large, well-worn knife. "The Red Kingdom doesn't exist anymore. Nor does my family name. Until the King of Hearts is dead and I have avenged my kinsmen, I am simply Torre."

James quickly put up his hands. "Fine by me. Torre it is. Thank you for saving us. We owe you our lives."

Torre stared at him for a moment, then shrugged. He took the knife out of the ground, wiped it on a cloth, and resumed using it to stir the pot.

James crawled over to Kara. "Are you all right?" he asked quietly.

"Fine. Fine. Never been better." Kara sat up and grimaced. "Nothing broken anyway." She seemed to remember something and turned to Torre. "Did you see the two skyships fighting? Did you see what happened?"

"They were too far off to see anything clearly. Both ships were badly damaged and on fire. After several salvos, they separated and moved away. I didn't see what happened after that. They were gone by the time I'd finished saving you."

"Oh." Kara slumped.

"I'm sure they're fine," offered James. "You heard him. The two ships separated and moved away. That means the Heart ship wasn't in any position to finish them off. The *Nighthawk* must have gotten back enough control to escape."

Kara said nothing, simply staring at the ground.

Torre pointed to a tree to one side. "Your stuff's over there. What I was able to fish out, anyway. I wasn't able to grab a lot before it sank."

James looked over to the pile of items under the tree. Kara's satchel was there, along with one of the backpacks and two of the sacks.

"Thanks again for your help," said James. "We'd be dead if it wasn't for your help."

"Well, at least you provided lunch." Torre took the pot off the fire. "Speaking of which, it's ready."

Torre poured a thick stew of some kind into roughly carved wooden bowls. He handed one to each of them, along with some old and misshapen metal spoons.

James ate the food happily. He hadn't realized how hungry he was, and the meal Torre had put together was pretty good. Kara picked at her bowl, eating only a few mouthfuls. Once they'd finished eating—Torre ate the rest of Kara's share—Torre looked at them closely.

"You're looking for Caterpillar?"

"Why do you say that?" asked James, after Kara had remained silent.

"Because that's the only reason anyone would come to this godforsaken forest."

James tried to keep the hope out of his voice. "Do you know where he is?"

Torre shrugged. "I've been looking for him in here for the past five years. I haven't found him in that time. Signs, sure. Evidence that someone has been here. But wherever he is, he's well hidden."

"Three pairs of eyes might be better than one."

"Neither of you look like you're experienced with the outdoors, let alone this place. Having you with me will only slow me down."

Kara finally spoke. "We need to find Caterpillar. We don't have any choice."

"Why?"

Kara and James looked at each other. Kara then looked at Torre, then back at James. "Show him," she said finally.

He lifted his shirtsleeve to reveal the tattoo. Faint traces of the fake Heart tattoo remained, but the two knights were clearly visible again on his arm.

Torre moved like lightening, his knife stopping an inch away from James's throat. He shook with rage. "How dare you! How dare you blaspheme the name of the Red Kingdom! I'll kill you here and now!"

"Stop!" Kara waved her arms as if trying to divert Torre's attention. "He's an outsider! He got the mark in his world. That's why we need to find Caterpillar. To find out what it means!"

Torre stared at Kara, then back at the mark on James's arm. He spat at the ground. "That still doesn't explain why he has the mark of the backstabbing White Kingdom defiling the mark of the Red Kingdom."

"We don't understand it, either. But it might give us the key to finding out what happened to the White Kingdom."

"I know what happened to them. They acted like the cowards they are and ran away, leaving the Red Kingdom to be destroyed. Their betrayal can never be forgiven, and *will* never be forgiven."

"So, we all agree we need to find this Caterpillar," said James, trying to divert Torre's attention from his fixation on the White Kingdom.

Torre sheathed his knife. "You can accompany me. But as I said, I've been looking for him in here for five years. Don't expect to find him any time soon."

Kara smiled slightly. "We'll take our chances."

Torre looked up to the sky. "We're wasting daylight standing here. I have a camp nearby that I use occasionally. We should be able to make it before nightfall if you keep up. We can spend the night there and move deeper into the woods tomorrow."

Torre put out the fire, packed away the blankets and bowls into an old pack, and began putting on strangely constructed body armor. James finally noticed the mark on Torre's arm—a red rook.

Kara's attention was drawn to the armor. Her eyes boggled when she saw what Torre was putting on. "You were a member of the Castle Brigade?" The awe and amazement in her voice was obvious.

Torre ignored her question, and finished tightening the last strap. "Come on. We need to get moving if we want to reach the camp. Don't slow me down." He grabbed a strange-looking rifle that looked nothing like a standard musket and set off at a fast pace.

"Who, or what, was the Castle Brigade?" asked James quietly, as he followed Kara.

Kara whispered, "They were the elite troops of the Red King, sworn to defend him to the death. It's said during the final battle, when the Red armies had been beaten back to their capital city, the remaining members of the Castle Brigade were able to hold off the entire Heart army for five days, no matter what was thrown at them. They were only defeated because their king was killed by an assassin. With the king dead, the remaining brigade members launched a suicide attack on the Heart army. They did a lot of damage, too, before they were all finally killed."

"Obviously, they weren't all killed. If he was actually a member, that is."

"He was. No Red Kingdom citizen would ever pretend to be one. They were the most honored people in the kingdom, after the royal family."

"Can we trust him?"

"We don't have a choice. He's the best bet we have to survive in Tulgey Wood. Besides, he obviously hates the Heart Guard, so that counts for a lot."

"I guess."

James and Kara followed Torre deeper into the woods.

* * *

James awoke to darkness, although he wasn't sure what time it was. The sounds of the woods began to filter into his mind. He'd noticed it when he'd lain down to sleep, but had been tired enough to ignore it. It wasn't just because he'd lived in the city his whole life and wasn't used to camping. Some of the sounds he didn't sound like anything he'd ever heard in nature documentaries.

And he needed to pee. Really needed to pee.

He tried to ignore it, but was finally forced to admit that his bladder was going to win out. He got up as quietly as he could.

The camp Torre had brought them to was small, no more than a fireplace in a clearing, with a basic shelter made from a few branches and leaves, but it had been surprisingly comfortable. It had been made slightly better by the bottle of rum that had somehow survived their flier crash.

Torre had been silent during their journey, and even after several drinks, had spoken very little. Despite his indifference to socializing, James had been impressed with the Red Rook. Several times, Torre had guided them around areas that had looked safe, but proved to contain nasty surprises for the unwary. They had even avoided a confrontation with a huge beast that looked like a strange cross between a rhino and a tiger by hiding next to a particular plant that had masked their scent.

The animal had walked to within five yards of where they stood, but left when it became distracted by another creature.

He had to admit, if they hadn't found Torre, he and Kara would probably have been dead several times over already.

Trying not to disturb the others, James moved as quietly as he could away from the camp. Once far enough away, he took care of business.

As he was about to head back to camp, he heard, "Hello? Is anyone there? I need help." It was a young girl's voice.

"Hello?" Startled, he moved toward the voice. "Where are you? Why are you out here?"

"Over here. Help me, please."

"What's wrong? Are you hurt?"

"I've fallen down and hurt myself. Please help me." The girl sounded as though she might be in distress. He continued walking toward the voice.

"Where are you?"

"Over here." The girl's voice originated from a dense thicket. The scent of flowers hung heavily in the air.

"I'm almost there. Hang on." He pushed his way into the thicket. Despite its thickness, it parted easily. After a yard of foliage, he found himself inside a small clearing surrounded by flowers of all types. He recognized a few—roses, daisies, and other common English cottage flowers he'd seen on the covers of magazines Laura liked to buy—but others looked totally alien to him.

The clearing was deserted.

He looked around, searching for a sign of the girl. "Where are you?"

"We're here," said a chorus of voices all around him. It took him a moment to realize it was the flowers that were talking. The voices were gravelly and much coarser than the first one.

James turned to leave, but he found the path he had pushed through the thicket was closed over. As he tried to force his way back, something wrapped itself around his ankle. Looking down, he saw plant stalks from the surrounding flowers beginning to move and entwine his feet.

He was about to call out when the stalks yanked hard on his feet, pulling them from beneath him. He landed on the ground heavily, letting out a grunt of pain even as the takedown winded him. As he struggled to get his breath back, plant stalks slowly wrapped around his arms and neck.

The plants said, "Time to pull off your petals. Time to feast." He tried to struggle, but the plants held him fast. He couldn't move. The stalks around his neck tightened, and the ones holding his arms and legs began to pull as if trying to dismember him.

Boom!

The area lit up as a large ball of fire passed through the ticket, destroying everything it touched. The plants around him screamed, and the stalks loosened their hold. He rolled onto his stomach and crawled forward, desperate to escape.

"It burns—it burns—it burns!" screamed the flowers, over and over. He started to push through the thicket. Stalks wrapped around his ankles again as the thicket walls resisted. "No! No, we won't let you escape!"

Boom!

The plants screamed a second time as another fireball passed through, and his ankles were again released. As he pushed forward, someone grabbed his arms.

"Come on, you've only got a few moments." Kara desperately pulled on his arms. As his head and shoulders came free of the thicket, he saw Torre standing two yards back and to the side, calmly reloading the strange musket weapon he had been carrying.

James had freed himself to his waist when the plants tightened their grip on him again.

"Get off me, you stupid Chelsea Flower Show rejects!" He attempted to kick away the stalks as Kara continued to tug on his arms, but they were at a stalemate.

Boom!

Torre fired a third shot into the thicket. The plants screamed again, and James was suddenly released. He catapulted out of the thicket, collapsing on the ground beside Kara. Relief that he was alive flooded through him, and he started to laugh. After a slight pause, Kara joined him. They spontaneously hugged, continuing to laugh, then partially separated. Their laughter died as he found himself staring into Kara's eyes.

The sound of Torre slinging his rifle over his shoulder broke the moment. Kara looked away, and James quickly rolled to the side to stare at the thicket.

He coughed awkwardly. "What was that thing?"

"Hellflower." Torre didn't look in his direction. "There are a few of them in Tulgey Wood. They hypnotize their prey, luring them in by mimicking the sound of a creature in distress. Once they've brought in their target, they dismember and dissolve the victim. Not a pleasant way to go."

"And you didn't think of mentioning this before we came in?"

Kara stared at the ground. "I keep forgetting you're not from Wonderland and don't know about the native dangers. I'm sorry. I'm glad you're all right."

James gave her a smile he hoped appeared more confident than he felt. He felt a tinge of sadness when she didn't meet his gaze. "Me, too. Thanks, both of you." James looked at Torre, but he was already moving.

"We should head back to camp. It'll be light in a few hours, and we need to get going as soon as possible so we can cover a good area."

He looked back at Kara. He wanted to say something about the moment they had shared, but her reaction changed his mind. Instead, he decided to focus on Torre. "What's got him all worked up?"

Kara shrugged as she got up, not looking at him. "Who knows? Maybe he doesn't have much ammunition for his gun. We'd best do as he says, though."

James nodded. Eyeing every plant suspiciously, he followed Kara back to camp.

CHAPTER 16

James was beginning to hate Tulgey Wood. It was around midday of their first full day in the wood, and Kara and Torre were helping him out of the fifth hole he'd managed to fall into. The first two occasions they had been worried and sympathetic, and like James, mystified about why they hadn't noticed the hole beforehand, as they had walked in front of him.

The third and fourth times, they began to get annoyed.

The fifth time, they were way past annoyed.

"Do you *have* to find every single hole in the woods to fall into?" Kara wore a look of total exasperation. "I'm sure we've missed a few. Maybe you'd like to go back and find them as well?"

"Like I'm enjoying falling into these holes," snapped James. "Besides, it's not like the two of you are pointing them out to me. If you did, I wouldn't fall into them."

"You have eyes in your head," said Torre. "Use them. Otherwise, the next hole you fall into, you can stay there. It's not like you have anything useful to contribute."

"That's rich, coming from Mr 'I-Mumble-to-Myself-as-I-Walk,'" replied James.

"It's the only way I'm going to get any intelligent conversation around here."

"What the hell is that supposed to mean?" asked Kara.

"The two of you have no clue what you're doing. You'd be dead if it wasn't for me. Him, many times over."

"Well, at least I know what soap is. It's no wonder everything in here has left you alone for so long. They'd die if they came within ten yards of you."

James was about to say something to continue the argument when he noticed a strange feeling at the back of his mind. It felt like an itch that wouldn't go away, no matter how much he scratched it. A noise in the trees behind him made him whirl, but he saw nothing.

"Look at you now," said Kara, pushing him in the back hard enough to make him take a step. "You don't even know which way you're supposed to be going. It's a miracle anyone in your world survives past childhood, let alone gets anything done."

"Wait. Something's not right." All of the annoyance he'd felt toward the others was gone.

"You're right. I should have never rescued you two in the first place. You're slowing me down. I can find Caterpillar quicker on my own."

"Yeah, you've been so successful at that, haven't you? You've only been looking for five years, right? I'm sure you'll find him in another century or two."

"At least I'll be alive in a century or two. You're not going to last five minutes once I'm gone." Torre shouldered his pack and rifle and continued in the direction they had been traveling.

James motioned for them to stay still. "Guys, calm down a second. You're not thinking clearly. Something is affecting our minds."

Kara turned on him. "Oh, so now you're the expert on Wonderland, are you? You know when something is 'affecting our minds.' Know what? To hell with both of you. I don't need any of this. I didn't want any of this. I'm out of here." She began walking back the way they had come.

James was struck by indecision, then moved to follow. "Kara, wait."

He took a step, then found himself falling. He landed heavily on a thick pile of grass and leaves at the bottom of the hole he swore had appeared where Kara had been standing moments before. He stood and quickly dusted himself off.

"Kara? Torre? A little help, please?"

There was no reply.

"Kara? Guys? Hello?"

No response. He was all alone.

He pushed away his first instinct to panic. Something strange was going on, something that affected the other two, but no longer affected him. Hopefully, it was location-based. All he had to do was catch up with Kara, wait for her to settle down, then they could find Torre again.

It was tough work climbing out of the hole. The sides were crumbly, and several times the roots he tried to use to pull himself up ripped out of the loose soil. But after many attempts, he finally managed to leverage himself to the top of the hole, and then drag himself out.

A small sign that hadn't been there before was stuck in the ground. It read, 'Follow Me,' in cursive handwriting and had an arrow at the bottom.

He stared at it in disbelief. "What is it with Wonderland and labeling everything? 'Drink Me' and 'Eat Me' from the books. Now 'Follow Me' here. What's next? Chickens with a tag that says 'Roast Me'?" He looked around to see where the others had gone, but realized he couldn't even tell in what direction they had walked. Falling in the hole and then climbing back out had disoriented him.

He shook his head. "I guess I've got no choice, do I, little sign?" He half-expected it to answer him, but it remained silent.

James walked in the direction the arrow pointed. After about twenty yards, he found a second sign with an arrow and 'Follow Me.' The signs repeated over and over, until he had lost count of the number of signs he passed. As he walked, he noticed that the forest was changing. It was opening up a little and didn't feel as oppressive and foreboding as it had earlier.

After half an hour, a clearing with some sort of camp became visible through the trees ahead. A fire blazed with a pot set over it, and to the side was a separate spit-roast where the carcass of a small animal, perhaps a rabbit, slowly cooked. A rough shanty hut with a pile of chopped wood in front of it stood at the edge of the clearing.

A tall, thin old man dressed in a green suit with horizontal stripes sat next to the fire with his back to James. He was working with the contents of a bucket, although James couldn't see what the bucket contained.

"Well, don't stand there staring," said the old man. "Come make yourself useful. The herbs need to be torn up and put into the soup."

James stepped into the clearing and made his way to the fire. Three cut stumps sat around the fire. He chose the one nearest the bucket of greenery the man indicated.

He was able to get a closer look at the man as he sat opposite him. He looked like he was in his eighties, which probably meant he was many hundreds of years old in Wonderland terms. He had gray stubble on his face and blue eyes that seemed to pierce into James's soul.

The man indicated the bucket again. "Tear up those leaves and throw them in the pot." The man had a similar bucket and was already doing the same thing.

"Are you the one they call Caterpillar?"

"Well done, boy. Perceptive one, aren't you? When you want to be, anyway."

"You were expecting us?" James indicated the other stumps with his head.

"I wouldn't be much of an oracle if I couldn't foresee house guests arriving, would I?"

"You caused the holes and everyone to fight, didn't you?"

Caterpillar shrugged. "The first hole you managed to find yourself. I found it amusing, so decided to repeat the act. Besides, we needed to talk alone for a bit. The other two will find their way here soon enough."

"You're some kind of wizard?"

The man laughed. "Hardly. Wonderland is an old land, much older than the world you grew up in. They both had what you would call 'magic' in the old days, but outsiders have long forgotten it in their world. Most people in Wonderland have forgotten it as well. There are only a few of us left who remember the old ways. The effects are subtle for the most part, but useful."

"So you can see the future? You know what's going to happen?"

Caterpillar shook his head. "No one can see everything of the future. At best, we can see glimpses of the future, images that show us possibilities. For example, I saw you arriving here at my camp, so I put down a bucket of plant leaves for you to tear. They're not going to do it by themselves, you know."

"Sorry." James began tearing the leaves again. "So, I guess I'm supposed to ask you some questions, but Kara was the one who knew what to ask. I was just here for the ride."

"Are you sure about that?"

"How do you mean?"

"Why are you here?"

"Well, Kara and a guy called Gryphon said—"

"No, no, no. Not why have you come to see me. Why are you in Wonderland?"

"I don't know. Not exactly. I ran away from the guy who had murdered my friend—"

"Melvin."

He started at Caterpillar's use of Melvin's name, but chose to ignore it. He was an oracle, after all. "Yes, Melvin. Anyway, I was running away when this guy in a white suit, apparently White Rabbit, knocked me into a hole that brought me here. He said something about keeping a promise."

"And what do you think that means?"

"I don't know. He thinks I'm someone else? I don't know why he decided to kidnap me."

Caterpillar shook his head sadly. "Gryphon suspects part of it, but I don't believe any of your other acquaintances have made the connection yet."

"Do you think you could you be any more mysterious?"

Caterpillar smiled. "Oh, yes. Quite easily."

"Well you're doing a good enough as it is. How about giving me some straight answers?"

"If you wish straight answers, you need to ask the right questions."

James tore up the final leaves and put them into the pot. Caterpillar stirred the pot, then looked at him expectantly.

"What was the promise White Rabbit was keeping?"

"To make sure you were safe from Lahire."

"What?" He stared at Caterpillar in disbelief. "Safe? How does bringing me here keep me safe? And why would Lahire care about me?"

"Lahire would have become interested in you because of the mark you possess. If you are here, at least there are people who can keep you hidden and protect you from Lahire and his henchmen. In the Otherworld, with the death of Melvin, there was no one left to protect you or keep you hidden."

"What do you mean? Why is everyone so worked up over this stupid tattoo? And how was Melvin involved?"

Caterpillar sighed. "For the pedigree you have, you can be distressingly oblivious at times. Waiting for you to ask the right questions will take time we don't have. I see I'm going to have to explain from the beginning.

"You had no way of knowing, but your parents were from Wonderland. They were high-level generals—"

James interrupted in shock. "What? My parents were from Wonderland?"

Caterpillar sighed. "That's what I said. Please don't interrupt. As I was saying, they were high-level generals in their respective kingdoms. Your mother was a general for the White Kingdom, and your father for the Red Kingdom. Because the two kingdoms had been at war for so long, the law prohibited them from getting married, or even associating with each other. But love always finds a way, and they managed to steal time with each other when their two kingdoms weren't otherwise bickering.

"Unfortunately, this was around the time Lahire, the new King of Hearts, began moving his forces on the two kingdoms. Your father wanted to keep your mother and his unborn child safe, so with the help of White Rabbit, they decided on the risky plan of escaping to the Otherworld. Your world.

"They were ambushed by Heart Guard when they reached one of the few portals unaffected by Lahire's barriers. Your father and his men died protecting your mother and her bodyguards as they escaped through the portal. Several months later, your mother died in childbirth giving her life force so you would survive the birth outside of Wonderland. Your parents had hoped that you would live a good life, free from the disaster that had befallen your home. And your mother's former bodyguards were tasked with watching over you."

James stared at Caterpillar, unable to form a coherent sentence. He couldn't believe what he was hearing. His parents were from Wonderland? His father, who he had always assumed was a deadbeat loser for leaving his mother, had died protecting them? And his mother had died so he could live?

No, change that. He had been the cause of his mother's death.

Caterpillar's last sentence finally sunk in. In a small voice, he asked, "Bodyguards?"

"Melvin was the youngest, and the last. The others watched you from afar, but died early of accelerated aging from living in the Otherworld, or by running afoul of Taxard."

"Wait, what? You're saying that not only am I from Wonderland, but Melvin was, too?"

"That is correct. That's why he was killed by Taxard. Lahire doesn't like any Wonderlanders escaping. He's afraid they might find a way to return with an outsider. With Melvin's presence no longer masking you, it would have only been a matter of time before Lahire detected that you were a Wonderlander, and sent Taxard after you. That's why White Rabbit acted to bring you to Wonderland."

James put his head in his hands. "You knew about that?"

"Of course. I was the one who told him to bring you here, if he wanted to honor his promise to keep you safe."

He shook his head in disbelief. "I can't believe this. Not about Melvin. I've known him for most of my life. He never gave any hint that he wasn't from my world."

"Of course he didn't. You would have thought he was insane if he had. Tell me, did he encourage you in chess?"

"Sure. He taught me how to play soon after we met. I was ten at the time. It wasn't long until I could beat him at the game, and pretty much anyone else I played. He encouraged me to enter tournaments and get better."

Caterpillar nodded. "Your parents were from the Knight orders of their kingdoms, which produced all their generals. They were the best generals either kingdom had ever produced. Melvin hoped that you had inherited some of their abilities, and that it would keep you safe when he was gone. That's why you find accounting for all the possibilities easy when you're focused in your planning.

"And then there is the matter of your mark."

James unconsciously touched his left bicep. "It's just a tattoo I got on a whim after winning a big chess tournament and getting drunk."

"Do you remember actually getting the tattoo?"

James paused, then looked uncomfortable. "Well, no. It was there when I woke up the next morning."

"Your mark appeared because you had finally tapped into your natural skills, gained from your parents. It is the combination of your mother's and father's marks. If you had been born in Wonderland, you would have had your father's mark. That's the way it works here. But because your mother gave her life force to you so you could be born in the Otherworld, you have both marks. A blending of Red and White. Something unique in all of Wonderland."

"Is that why Lahire's after me?"

Caterpillar shook his head. "No. Lahire fears *all* outsiders."

"Why?"

"The last outsider to visit, a girl named Alice, changed our land. Her thoughts and dreams formed Wonderland into an echo of your Victorian society. Lahire was one of the few people who noticed it happening, and so was able take advantage of it. People believe

Wonderland changed because he took the throne, but Wonderland would have changed even if he had done nothing. He fears what could happen if another outsider remained long enough to cause new changes."

"But you said I'm a Wonderlander."

"You are both. As I said, something unique. It remains to be seen how Wonderland will react to you. It's already begun to change in small ways."

"What do you mean?"

"The speech patterns of the people in Wonderland. They've shifted to match how people in your world speak today. You haven't wondered why people spoke the same way as you?"

"Wait. Everyone I've met, everyone I've talked to, Torre, Kara, Hatter, Gryphon. They all spoke differently before I got here?"

"That is how Wonderland works."

James shook his head. It was all too much to take in, to even believe. "Assuming I believe a word of what you're telling me, what am I supposed to do now?"

"Only you can decide if you believe me or not, although I fear events in your near future will make it easier for you to know I speak the truth. But your next task is to go to the White Kingdom and find what you will find."

"What will I find?"

Caterpillar looked up, first to one side then the other, ignoring James's question. "Oh, good. I do believe your friends have finally joined us."

James glanced around. After a moment, he could hear, and then see, Kara and Torre approaching the clearing from opposite directions. They paused uncertainly at the edge of the clearing.

"Hurry up, hurry up." Caterpillar waved them in. "We don't have much time. Sit down." He motioned them to the two empty stumps next to James, then ladled soup from the large pot into bowls.

"I'm sorry," said Kara quietly, as she sat down next to James. "I don't know what came over me. I got really angry, and—"

"It's okay." James gave her a reassuring smile. "It wasn't you. He did it." He indicated Caterpillar.

Torre crossed the clearing and knelt in front of Caterpillar. "My lord, it is a great honor to be—"

"Stop that," said Caterpillar, forcing a bowl of soup into his hands and guiding him to the empty stump. "We needn't worry about formalities at a time like this. Eat quickly, and I'll answer your questions." He handed a bowl to Kara and one to James.

They all dutifully ate. It had an unusual flavor. James wasn't sold on the appearance of the food—it looked like wilted weeds steeped in water—but the flavor was pleasant. It had a faint peppery aftertaste.

"Now then, I've already spoken to James. What he chooses to tell you is up to him." He looked at Torre. "You want to know how to avenge the fall of the Red Kingdom and make Taxard pay for assassinating the king. You need to find the real King of Hearts and restore him to the throne. If you plan for that, you will find your assassin."

"What do you mean the *real* king?" asked Torre. "Lahire isn't the real King of Hearts?"

Caterpillar waved dismissively. "In a manner of speaking. It's a simple matter of succession. Son follows father upon the father's death. He turned to Kara. "As for you, you will find your mother one day. Or more accurately, she will find you. But the meeting will not go how you hope."

Kara started to ask a question, but Caterpillar held up his hand. "I'm afraid our time is up. There is another pressing appointment I must attend to, and it is best I don't hold you up any longer. You have a kingdom to visit, and if you don't die, a land to reclaim. I wish you all the best. Do watch out for the wine."

The next instant, everything in the clearing disappeared—the hut, the fire and spit-roast, Caterpillar, the food, and their bowls. All that remained were the three tree stumps where they sat.

Torre stood angrily. "Five years I searched for him. Five long years! And all I get is a bowl of soup and some cryptic remark about finding the *real* king. It was a waste of time."

Kara looked slightly shaken. "You know the stories about Caterpillar. His answers are cryptic and vague, but always correct and helpful in the end." She looked over at James, who sat silently on his stump. "What did he tell you?"

He opened and closed his mouth several times, not sure what to say or where to begin. He didn't want to say anything about his parents. Not yet. "We need to go to the White Kingdom," he said finally.

Torre kicked the stump he had been sitting on. "Why? There's nothing there. I know. I looked for the spineless cowards to find out why they betrayed us."

"What is there?" asked James.

"Empty land. You can see where the roads and buildings once were, but now there's nothing there. It's just grass, slowly being overgrown by the other plant life in the area."

James shrugged. "Either way, that's where Caterpillar said I had to go next. There's something I have to find there."

"What?" asked Kara.

"I have no idea. He didn't say."

Kara slumped. "Even if we wanted to go there, we can't. The flier is destroyed, and the *Nighthawk* gone."

Torre eyed them both. "We can use my ship."

Kara turned. "You have a ship, and you didn't tell us?"

"You never asked. Besides, how else did you think I got here? Walking?"

It was Kara's turn to be speechless. Finally, she simply asked, "Is it far from here?"

Torre looked around for a moment, then frowned. "That's not right."

"What's not right?" asked James.

"We're close. Very close. The ship is about an hour from here."

"That's good," offered Kara. "We don't have far to travel."

Torre turned to look at her. "You don't understand. We've moved over a hundred miles. The ship was at least a week away from where we camped last night."

Kara stood up. "We all know Caterpillar can do some strange things. This is another example of it. Let's get going."

James walked automatically, thoughts about what Caterpillar had told him crashing through his mind. All he wanted to do was sit down and think through everything he had learned, especially about his parents, his *real* parents. But it would have to wait until later.

Kara must have sensed his confusion. After they had been walking for a few minutes, she moved to his side. "Are you okay?"

He tried to hide his feelings. "I think so. I just need some time to think about what Caterpillar told me."

Kara put her hand lightly on his arm. "If you want to talk about it, I'm here."

Grateful for her concern, James nodded and squeezed her hand. They followed Torre through the woods in silence.

CHAPTER 17

Torre's ship was well hidden. James could have walked within five yards of it and not seen it. It sat in a gully on the edge of a small cliff, the perfect naturally hidden docking bay. Torre had pulled a number of saplings, branches, and other vegetation across the end of the gully to hide the entrance from view, while the thick undergrowth in the area hid the rest of the ship.

It only took them a few minutes to clear away the camouflage materials. Unlike the flier they had flown—and the ones they'd been chased by—Torre's vessel was totally enclosed by an outer shell shaped much like the bullet shape he was used to seeing on blimps. It was around twenty yards long and five yards wide, with a large corkscrew propeller at the back for propulsion. It was mostly gray, but had a large red symbol on the side that he assumed marked it as belonging to the Red Kingdom.

"Let's go." Torre opened a hatch in the side and climbed in. Kara followed, with James getting in last.

The inside of the ship was sparse. It definitely looked like a military vessel, with no thought of comfort or decoration. A few benches ran along either side in the main cabin, but nothing else. An open doorway led to the cockpit, while a closed door was located toward the rear of the ship.

Torre turned to Kara. "You said you're good with machinery, right?"

"Yeah. Why?"

He pointed to the closed door. "The engine's that way. It needs lighting and stoking. Let me know when it's ready."

Kara rolled her eyes but said nothing as she stepped through the door to the right. A faint smile played across Torre's face as he watched her leave, then he moved through an open doorway to the left.

Sticking his head through the door, James saw that it had the appearance of a basic cockpit like on a plane, but without the huge array of dials, lights, and switches. "Anything I can do to help?"

Torre didn't bother to turn. "Sit down and don't touch anything. Kara has the engine under control, and the last thing I need up here is someone getting in the way."

James sat on one of the benches as he had been told. After a minute, he got up and looked into the engine room to see if he could help Kara. Seeing that the room was barely large enough for one person, he sat back down and waited, feeling useless.

After about ten minutes, Kara exited the engine room, a look of annoyance on her face. "You're set to go. Although if we don't all get blown up, it will be a miracle. When was the last time you serviced the engine?"

"Do I look like an engineer? Besides, it's Red technology. We built everything to last. Hang on. This isn't the most comfortable of rides."

The ship shuddered, then lurched as it moved out of its hiding place. The uncomfortably loud noise was nothing like that of the *Nighthawk* or the flier, both of which had been relatively quiet. James wondered how people from the Red Kingdom had managed to avoid becoming permanently deaf if they had to ride in such loud ships all the time.

The ship lurched again as it accelerated. Several seconds later, they had left land and were heading out to sea.

"Is the White Kingdom far from here?" he asked Kara, raising his voice to be heard over the noise.

"I don't know. Well, not exactly, anyway. It's at least a few hours, possibly more on this ship."

"What does it look like?"

"The Red and White Kingdoms are on a group of islands, sixty-four in total. The islands are a mixture of all terrains—plains, mountains, lakes, all kinds. Some of the larger islands always belonged to one kingdom or the other, like the islands where the capitals were. Other smaller islands constantly changed sides, depending on who had a use for them."

He shook his head slightly. "I shouldn't be surprised."

"What do you mean?"

"Sixty-four islands. A chessboard has sixty-four squares. The two kingdoms have chess pieces for their marks. It all fits together real... peachy." He let bitterness creep into his voice as he thought back to what Caterpillar had told him.

Kara opened her mouth, then obviously changed her mind. Finally, she asked, "Do you have any idea what you're supposed to do when we get to the White Kingdom?"

"No idea. Caterpillar didn't elaborate on that area."

"Maybe there's some sort of weapon or powerful artifact they hid away that you have to find."

"If that's the case, why didn't they use it themselves? Why did they vanish from Wonderland?"

Kara shrugged. "I don't know."

"Hopefully, we'll find some answers when we get there." He paused for a moment. "I assume Lahire has searched the White Kingdom?"

"Extensively. After the battle with the Red Kingdom, he had his army search the White Kingdom for months, trying to find out what happened to them. As far as I know, he never found anything."

James sighed. "Hopefully, we'll have better luck."

* * *

Lahire slowly made his way up the steps of the tower. He hadn't allowed anyone but a single maid up there for the past hundred years, and tonight was no different. It was his duty, and his duty alone, the burden he had to bear to ensure the future of Wonderland.

He paused to rest on the landing outside the door. It wouldn't be wise to allow his father to see that he was short of breath. He could never show any sign of weakness. Not ever.

Once he had regained his breath, he took the single key from his pocket and unlocked the door. He stepped through into the dimly lit room and closed the door behind him.

His father lay in the bed, as he had for the past century. His eyes were open, and they tracked Lahire as he crossed to room. Lahire had a routine he used every week when he visited, and he fell into it automatically.

"You're looking well, Father." Lahire sat on the edge of the bed. "I hope the cook is providing you with good food. You'll be happy to know the Kingdom is well. I'm taking good care of it. Everyone is happy, and the Heart Kingdom is the crown jewel of Wonderland, as it should be."

He paused. Normally, he would continue talking about how wonderfully the kingdom was doing, but the words slipped away from him. As he was leaving to visit his father, Lahire had received word that the patrol ship that had intercepted the pirate vessel had been located, crashed on the coast with no survivors. The patrol ships in the area had found no further sign of either the pirates or the outsider. It was possible they had crashed into the sea, but Lahire needed proof before he could rest easy.

Images of what it could mean for Wonderland if the outsider was alive slipped into his mind.

"There's been a problem," he began after a pause to collect his thoughts. "An outsider has come through. A man this time. I don't know anything about him, but it seems he has made contact with the terrorists. I don't know what he plans to do to Wonderland, but I'm not going to let him ruin things." Lahire stood and paced in front of his father's bed.

"The Club Kingdom is causing trouble again. Their rulers are trying to undermine my authority and are actively plotting to find the outsider and use him for their own evil purposes. Discipline has begun to fall apart in the Heart Guard, with drinking and dereliction of duty. Even Taxard has failed me."

Lahire smashed his fist into his open palm. "Damn that outsider. All this started because he appeared. I won't let him destroy everything I've worked for, everything I sacrificed to build Wonderland to where it is today."

Lahire took a deep breath and let it out slowly. He sat back on the bed beside his father. "I'm sorry, Father. I don't mean to bore you with these concerns. I will take care of everything. Wonderland is in safe hands. You don't need to worry about a thing. You need your rest." He took a bottle and spoon from the bedside table, removed the stopper, which had an eyedropper attached, and dropped a single drop of liquid into the spoon.

"No..." whispered his father with a weak voice. Lahire looked over. His father's eyes looked rather clear and coherent.

"Shush, now. You need to have your medicine." Lahire moved the spoon toward his father's mouth.

"Please—" began his father, but Lahire took that opportunity to put the spoon in his father's mouth, then he lifted the jaw to close it and ensure the drop of liquid stayed in the mouth. The old man looked at him pleadingly, then his eyes glazed over and finally closed.

"Sleep well, Father." Lahire replaced the stoppered bottle and spoon on the bedside table, then smoothed his father's hair. "When you next awake, the outsider will be gone, and everything will be back to normal."

Lahire stood and left the room, locking the door behind him.

* * *

James looked out at the island as they approached. It was huge, much bigger than he had first thought when Kara had called it an island. It had to be at least twenty miles wide, if not more, and from what he could tell in the fading light, it had a large mixture of plains, woods, and even a small mountain at one end.

However, one thing struck him as details became clearer along the coast. "I thought you said the island had no traces of the White Kingdom left?"

"It doesn't," replied Torre, concentrating on flying.

"Then, what's that?" asked James. He pointed at the village sitting on the edge of the sea.

"What are you pointing at?" asked Kara.

"The village, of course."

"What village?"

"The village right there in front of us, next to the sea."

Kara and Torre exchanged glances, as if he had gone crazy. "We don't see any village," said Kara finally.

James was confused. "But it's right there. Clear as day."

Kara shook her head.

James covered his face with his hands. "Great, now I'm going insane."

"And people say I'm crazy," commented Torre. "At least I don't see imaginary buildings."

They passed over many more buildings and villages, along with roads and other obvious signs of civilization. Examining the structures more closely—as much as he could from high above—he realized the buildings and roads looked slightly translucent, almost as if they were only half there.

Ahead, the huge structures of the capital city became visible. Massive walls with large guard towers surrounded the stone buildings making up the majority of the architecture. It looked a lot like a medieval city from his world, complete with large castle at the center of the city.

Torre began to take the ship down. "Not here," said James in a panic, as the buildings rushed toward them.

"What?"

"Don't land here. Go a little bit further."

Torre shrugged and did as James asked. Up ahead, he could see a large city square clear of obstacles, and he directed Torre to land there. The ship landed on the ground with a loud thump and heavy shudder. The loud hiss of escaping steam followed as vents opened to relieve pressure.

"Well, let's go and see what we can see." Kara headed toward the door. He followed silently.

They climbed out of the ship. James found the view confusing. Ghostly buildings surrounded them, and the streets were paved in translucent well-fitted stone that showed signs of many years of wear. However, grass, shrubs, and saplings also grew around them, sticking up through the stonework as if the structures of the city weren't actually there.

He walked over to one of the ghost buildings and put his hand forward to touch it. His hand passed through the wall with an unpleasant sensation. His hand also took on a slightly faded appearance as it passed into the wall.

Torre and Kara looked on in surprise. "You're touching something?" asked Kara.

He nodded. "One of the walls. My hand can go through it, although it feels strange."

"Why don't you try going inside one of the buildings?"

He moved over to the door of the ghostly building. He was able to grip the door handle enough to make the door turn, and it opened ahead of him. Taking a deep breath, he stepped into the building.

"Wow," said Kara. Even Torre looked surprised.

James looked back in concern. "What is it?"

"You've gone all ghostly. We can still see you, but not clearly."

"I guess there really is something here," said Torre begrudgingly. "Although I don't understand why none of us can see anything."

Kara looked around "Are there any people?"

He stepped out of the building and shook his head. "I don't see any around. Maybe there are some in the buildings, but I'd have to go searching."

"That's something we can do tomorrow, when the light is better. For now, we should set up camp, before it gets totally dark."

They quickly built and lit a fire, then began food preparation. Despite the sun slipping below the horizon, James noticed that the light level didn't change. When Kara grabbed a lantern as she returned to the ship, that he realized he was the only one who could see without a light source. He commented on it to the others.

"So everywhere is all lit up?" asked Kara.

"It seems it to me." He looked around. "Let me do a circuit of the ship, and see if the effect is everywhere."

As he reached the other side, he realized the source of the light. One of the tall towers in the main castle was glowing like a lighthouse, casting its light out as far as he could see. He relayed the information to the others when he returned to the fire.

Kara looked thoughtful. "I wonder what it could be?"

James shrugged. "Maybe it's the reason the city seems to have disappeared. The light somehow hides it all."

"And if we shut down the light, the city will reappear," said Torre.

"I suppose it might. But we don't know how it works."

"Nevertheless, it's something worth looking at," said Kara. "That should probably be the first place we check out tomorrow." She turned to Torre. "Do you have any knowledge of the layout of this city?"

Torre shrugged. "Of course. We studied old maps during training in the hope that one day we would invade the city."

"Sketch out what you can remember. It could help us, or James at least, find the way to the tower light."

Torre nodded and began sketching plans in the dirt. James did his best to memorize what Torre drew, but it was a confusing mess that wasn't helped by Torre obviously overstating what he knew. After an hour of Torre scribbling, scratching out sections, and redrawing, James had to admit defeat. He sat back.

"Maybe it would be best to play it by ear tomorrow. I'm sure it will be pretty obvious as we move around."

Torre also sat back. "Since we can't see anything, it will be all down to you. The White Kingdom wasn't known for building cities in a logical fashion."

"Is that actually true, or are you just dumping on the White Kingdom like you normally do?" asked James testily.

Torre pushed his chest forward. "The White Kingdom was inferior in every way. The Red Kingdom was the jewel of the islands."

James stood angrily. "If the Red Kingdom was so great, why did the White Kingdom keep them at a stalemate for centuries? Face it, the Red Kingdom was no better or worse than the White Kingdom. You've been so conditioned in your beliefs that you can't realize the truth, even when it's right in front of you."

Not waiting for a response, James stormed off to the ship.

CHAPTER 18

A tiny voice timidly called from the door. "Uncle Lahire?"

Lahire sat in his study, going over the reports on the Heart army's progress in its march toward the Club Kingdom. He looked up.

"Now, Lucy, what are you still doing up? I thought I put you in bed already. Can't you sleep?" His voice was light and warm. He noticed Lucy was holding a piece of paper. She stood at the door, obviously unsure if she should come in.

"Come here, little one." He held out his arms. Lucy ran over, and he picked her up and spun her around. She hugged him tightly.

"What do you have there?" he asked gently.

She looked at him, frightened.

"It's okay. You won't get into trouble. Good girls who tell the truth never get in trouble, remember?"

She timidly handed over the paper. Without putting her down, he opened the note.

It was a hand-drawn picture of a small girl—labeled 'Lucy'—holding hands with a person on either side. The other two had been labeled 'Mommy' and 'Daddy.' Love hearts had been drawn to fill the space between the two parents and Lucy, while behind them was a castle with the Club symbol prominently visible.

"Where did you get this, Lucy?"

Lucy hid her face in his shoulder.

"Come on, little one," he said coaxingly. "I'm not mad at you. I just want to know."

"Madeline gave it to me."

"Your nanny?"

Lucy nodded.

"You did the right thing bringing this to me, Lucy. You've been a good girl, and good girls get nice presents. Would you like a nice present?"

Lucy nodded with a smile.

"Then, tomorrow you're going to get a very nice present indeed." He poked her nose, and she giggled. "Now, you need to get some sleep. Otherwise, you'll be too tired to unwrap your present. Let's get you back into bed."

He carried her back up to the bedroom where the children slept and opened the door quietly. The other children were all asleep, and Lucy was starting to nod off in his arms. He carried her over to her bed and tucked her in. Giving her a quick peck on the forehead, he carefully left the children's room.

He waved a guard over once he was far enough away not to disturb them. "I want the children's nanny, Madeline Dowell, arrested and brought to the throne room immediately. Then, search her quarters. Tear it apart if you have to."

"Sire!" The guard saluted and move away quickly.

He made his way to the throne room at a leisurely pace. By the time he had arrived, two guards held the trembling nanny in front of the throne. She had obviously been in bed, as she wore her nightclothes.

He took his seat on the throne. "I'm sorry to get you up so late, Madeline. Only I've run into a minor concern that I believe you may be able to assist me with."

"Y—your Majesty knows I l—live only to serve." Madeline's wide eyes darted around as she spoke.

"I'm glad to hear that. You see, my problem is with the upbringing of the children. After all, it's extremely important that they have a stable upbringing, don't you agree?"

"O—of course, Your M-Majesty."

"And the children need everything to be kept simple for them. The world is a complex place, and they need to be exposed to those complexities slowly in a managed manner, otherwise they can become overwhelmed and confused. Isn't that right?"

"Yes, Y—Your Majesty." Madeline began to shake.

He exploded out of the throne, shoving Lucy's picture in the terrified woman's face. "So, what the hell are you playing at, giving the children pictures like this?"

Madeline sobbed. "P—please, Your Majesty. I was only passing on a note from a mother who missed her child. I didn't think there was any harm."

"Any harm? You agreed that the children need a stable upbringing. To give them strange notes from their parents is going to confuse them. Lucy was distraught by the note you gave her and couldn't sleep this evening. How many other notes have you passed on?"

"It was the only one. I swear, Your Majesty!"

"And how did you come by the note?"

"Your Majesty?"

"It's a simple enough question. How did you get the note to pass on to Lucy?"

Madeline looked uneasy. He stared at her, unblinking.

Finally, she slumped. "The Queen of Clubs gave it to me when we ran into each other in the hallway. My mother was a handmaiden for her for many years, and she knew me when I was young. She begged me to pass on the note, and I couldn't say no."

"I see." He stepped back. He'd suspected the Queen of Clubs, presumably when the queen and her husband had been in the castle to see him. Yet more evidence of their plotting against him. Not that he needed any more.

A guard carrying a small wooden box stepped into the throne room. He moved forward quickly, then kneeled when he neared Lahire.

"Your Majesty. This was found in the woman's quarters. It was hidden in the back of a dresser."

Madeline gasped.

He raised an eyebrow and stepped forward to look inside the box. It contained notes of various observations about the workings of the castle. Guard schedules, notes on prisoners, and even several notes on Taxard's trips to the Otherworld.

He had found his spy.

Shaking his head, he turned to Madeline, and said in an icy voice, "Yet another betrayal. I trusted you. Trusted you with the most valuable resource in Wonderland, the children, and you chose to betray me."

Madeline looked back at him, trembling.

"What was it that made you betray Wonderland. Money? A debt? Or were you confused by the twisted lies spread by the terrorists?"

She started to say something, but he waved his hand. "No matter. You'll tell me everything I want to know about your contacts and activities after a stay in the dungeon. Then you will pay for your treason with the loss of your head. Take her away."

Lahire listened impassively as Madeline was dragged away, her sobs and pleas for mercy nothing he hadn't heard thousands of times before.

* * *

The next morning was slightly awkward between James and Torre, with neither doing more than acknowledging the other's presence.

Finally, Kara threw her hands up in exasperation. "Okay, you two. We've got to work together to find whatever it was that Caterpillar wanted us to find. If you two are going to act like three year olds and not talk to each other, we're never going to get anything done. I want the two of you to shake hands, say you're sorry, and get over it."

Torre looked as uncomfortable as James felt, but under Kara's unwavering stare, they finally shook hands with a mumbled apology.

"Right. Now that you children have decided to behave, we need to get to work. Let's go."

They moved toward the tower James had noticed the night before, with James leading the way along streets visible only to him. They made their way up the gentle slope to the gates of the White Kingdom castle. The gates lay open and appeared inviting from a distance. When they reached the gates, he found the first signs of what had happened to the people of the White Kingdom.

The others apparently realized something was wrong from the expression on his face.

"What is it?" asked Torre.

"Skeletons. Hundreds of skeletons, everywhere." He looked through the gates at the courtyard beyond in horror. The skeletons were arranged haphazardly, as if everyone had been gathered in the courtyard, then collapsed where they stood. Some were slumped against the walls in groups, while others were scattered throughout the courtyard center. The skeletons were clean, and the bones weathered. They had been there for a long time.

He described the scene to Kara and Torre. They looked around uneasily, although they could see nothing.

"Are there any signs of injury?" asked Torre.

James shook his head. "Not that I can see. They all look intact. Remarkably so."

"I guess there hasn't been anything to damage them," said Kara quietly. "What about clothes and equipment?"

"There are some remains of their equipment." He took a closer look at a group of skeletons near the gate. He could see lots of metal items lying on the ground beneath the bones, although most had corroded in some manner. Leather and cloth had disintegrated almost entirely, with only a few odd scraps left.

"Let's keep moving inside," suggested Kara. "I don't like not being able to see dead people around me."

The main entrance to the castle was closed, the double metal doors towering over his head. He put his hand forward to touch them. To his surprise, he found he couldn't push his hand through the doors.

"The doors feel solid." He felt around a bit more. "And cold. Much colder than they should."

Torre stepped forward to touch the air where James could see the doors, but his hand passed through without any problem.

With a shrug, James pushed hard on the doors. One of them shifted slightly, and when he focused all his efforts on that door, it opened wide enough for him to step through.

CHAPTER 19

Surprised at how his surroundings had changed after stepping through the door, James stood inside the main entrance to the castle hall. Instead of being translucent, everything looked as solid and real as any other building.

He turned to tell the others about the change, but they had disappeared. He stepped out of the castle hall and back into the courtyard, but everything remained solid. He saw no sign of Kara or Torre, or of the grass and other plant life that had been visible before. Only the castle he had expected to find.

And a whole lot of skeletons.

For a brief moment, he had the mental image of being in the middle of a horror movie where the skeletons all stood and shambled toward him. To his relief, they remained piles of bones on the ground.

"Hello?" There was no answer.

"Great. Wonderful. Everyone wanted to know what happened to the White Kingdom. Now, I have the answer, since it's happened to me as well." He looked around the courtyard, doing his best to avoid staring at the all-too-solid skeletons lying around him. "I guess I'm heading up to the tower."

He stepped back inside the castle. Taking the time to look properly inside the main entrance, he noticed many more skeletons lying in random positions. Unlike the ones outside, their clothes had survived in relatively good condition. Some wore fine clothes, like those he would expect a noble or court official to wear. Others had been wearing armor when they died, and were positioned around the hall where he would expect guards to be. A few had obviously been servants. Like the ones in the courtyard, none of them showed any signs of physical trauma.

As he moved through the castle, James found every hallway and almost every room held at least one skeleton. He began to get the impression that everyone in the castle and surrounds had simultaneously dropped dead where they stood, with no warning. He passed a skeleton that appeared to be playing a harp, a group that had been doing needlework, and several that had been carrying trays of dishes.

It took a number of false starts and several trips to nearby windows to get his bearings, but he finally managed make his way to the tower that held the shining beacon of light he had seen the previous evening. The heavy doors at the bottom of the stairs opened easily, and he ascended the spiral staircase without any trouble.

Reaching the top, he stepped out into a large open room that overlooked the castle and city. In the center of the room stood a huge white crystal, six feet high and three feet wide. It pulsed like a heartbeat, causing white light to flood the chamber. Arrayed around the crystal was a circle of white-robed skeletons, collapsed on the ground like all the others he had passed.

But the most surprising sight in the room was the thin, pale old woman slumped against the crystal. Like the skeletons around her, she wore a plain white robe. However, unlike the skeletons, she appeared alive and unharmed. As if confirming his thoughts, she twitched slightly.

James hurried over and knelt beside the woman. She had a strong pulse, and her breathing was regular. He gently shook her shoulder.

"Hello? Hello? Can you hear me?"

The woman slowly opened her eyes, seeming to focus on his face with difficulty. She opened and closed her mouth a few times, then finally spoke in a soft voice. "Someone survived. I had prayed that I was not alone, but I dared not hope."

"Who are you? What happened here?"

The woman gave him a look of confusion, then a sad smile as realization struck. "I see. I was wrong. You're not the survivor I had hoped for, but someone from beyond our kingdom who has stumbled upon our greatest mistake." She sighed. "I'm the queen of the White Kingdom, for all that title means anything now, and you are witness to the folly of our pride."

"What do you mean? What happened here? Why is the kingdom invisible? How did everyone die?"

The queen chuckled, then coughed. She waved his concerns away. "So many questions. I will answer as best I can.

"It began when the King of Hearts made it clear that he was going to attack the Island Kingdoms. Our first instinct was to fight. We even put aside our differences with the Red Kingdom to forge an alliance. But many of us were worried that even together, we would not win. At best, we believed the fighting would end in a stalemate, at the cost of thousands of lives. So, we came up with another plan.

"Our intention was to hide the Island Kingdoms from Lahire's eyes, so he could never find us. We hoped this would give us more time to build better defenses, but also to give Lahire a chance to change his mind and abandon his militaristic ways."

"I take it things went wrong?"

The queen nodded sadly. "We should have listened to the warnings of Caterpillar, but we were overconfident and gravely miscalculated. The magic was too unstable. The kingdom was hidden from view, but the magic also froze everyone in place. One by one, everyone died of dehydration or starvation. Over time, they became the skeletons you see. Now the kingdom itself is being absorbed by the magic. In a few more decades, a century at the most, there will be nothing left."

He looked around again, conflicting thoughts running through his mind at the new information. They had done it to themselves. An entire kingdom dead because of their fear of Lahire and his armies.

And now he was trapped, and likely to suffer the same fate as everyone else. He sat down heavily.

Finally, he looked over at the queen. "You said everyone else was frozen in place and died where they were. But what about you? Why are you still alive?"

"I was the focal point of the magic. I will be the last thing to be destroyed, when my kingdom finally disappears." She looked at him with new focus. "Tell me, how have you managed to come here?"

He shrugged. "I don't know really. Caterpillar told me I had to come here, but he didn't say anything else about it. Looks like he was playing a trick on me, since now I'm stuck here."

"Who are you?"

"My name is James Riggs. I was born in what you call the Otherworld. But according to Caterpillar, my mother was from the White Kingdom and my father the Red Kingdom."

"Show me your mark."

He lifted his sleeve to reveal the tattoo. The queen breathed in sharply.

"So, the rumors were true. In the final days, rumors spread that one of our generals had established a relationship with a Red general after she disappeared from the kingdom, but I refused to believe it. Such a thing seemed impossible."

"Caterpillar said my father and his men gave their lives to protect my mother so she could escaped to my world. She died giving birth to me."

The queen closed her eyes. "It's amazing how much time you have to think over past mistakes and prejudices when you're stuck in the same location for twenty-five years with nothing to do. If I could change only one thing from my past, it would be to create a real peace between the White and Red Kingdoms. We were like children, letting the pettiest issue be an excuse for fighting. But now, it is too late. I assume Lahire conquered the Red Kingdom?"

He nodded. "I haven't seen it, but I've heard it was totally destroyed. There were few survivors."

"I'm not surprised. They were ferocious combatants. Even by themselves, they would have given Lahire trouble." The queen sighed again. "If only we hadn't gone ahead with this foolhardy plan, we might have both survived."

"Caterpillar must have sent me here for some reason. I assume it's to find some way of beating Lahire and freeing Wonderland. Do you know what it would be? Some sort of weapon or secret information that we could use?"

The White Queen chuckled. "If we had such a thing, don't you think we would have used it when it became obvious Lahire had his eyes set on the islands? No, I'm afraid there is no such thing here. Maybe Caterpillar sent you here as a final laugh at our folly, as some sort of *I told you so*. But if you hoped to find anything of value here, I'm afraid you're in for disappointment."

He shook his head. "I can't believe he would do something like that."

"You only met him once, briefly, I assume? Then, you don't know him at all. He spent many years in our kingdom. His prophesies may be accurate, but they are almost never the entire story. He chooses what to tell people and twists his words to suit his own ends."

James was about to argue, but stopped. How well did he know Caterpillar? A five-minute conversation and a brief chapter in an old novel were hardly a glowing character reference.

"How do I escape from here?"

The queen looked at him with pity. "You don't, I'm afraid. You'll stay here forever, or until the magic finishes absorbing everything. There is no going back."

"I don't believe it. There has to be a way out."

"If there is, I don't know it. And the only people who might have been able to figure it out died a long time ago." She indicated the dead skeletons around the large crystal.

"This crystal is the key to the whole magic thing, right? What would happen if I smashed it?"

"Then, you, I, and everything in this city would be consumed in a huge explosion."

He stood and paced. "I can't believe I'm trapped. I won't."

The queen shrugged. "Whether you believe in something or not doesn't change the facts. Once upon a time, I would believe up to six impossible things before breakfast. It didn't mean that they were true, just that I believed them."

"So that's it, then? Give up and wait to die?"

"At least you're able to walk around. I've been stuck to this crystal for who-knows-how-long."

"Why don't you move away?"

"I can't. No matter how much I try, a part of me must always be touching the crystal. It seems to be another rule of the magic."

"Show me."

The queen stood, leaning against the crystal for balance. She was able to remove one hand, but when she tried to remove her other hand one finger remained stuck to the crystal.

He tried to help her remove her hand, but it was no use. Her finger would slide around happily, but if she tried to lift it, it acted as if it were somehow glued to the crystal.

"Okay, so that won't work," said James in frustration. The queen gave him a sympathetic smile. A thought occurred to him. "What if we moved the crystal?"

"What?"

"Well, I'm only guessing, but I assume this magic thing is all precise. Could we move the crystal out of position and affect the whole *feng shui* of the area or something?"

The queen took on an expression he couldn't read. "I have no idea what *feng shui* is, but you might be on to something. The crystal had to be precisely positioned in the first place, so moving it should have an effect. It won't be easy, though. The crystal is extremely heavy and was mounted so it wouldn't go anywhere."

He knelt to look at the base of the crystal. A framework of masonry and metal had been built around the base to prop it up. The construction looked solid, but not unbreakable.

"I need to find some tools."

"The various craftsmen had their workshops at the east end of the castle." The queen indicated a particular direction. "You may find what you are looking for there."

"All right, then. I'll be back." He descended the stairs to the main castle. It took him almost two hours to find the various tools he thought he would need—a hammer, a pick, several wedges, and something he could use as a crowbar.

The queen looked up as he re-ascended the stairs to the open room. "I was beginning to think I had imagined your visit."

"No, I'm real." He put his gathered tools down at the base of the crystal. He selected the hammer from his collection.

"Before you begin, I have a request."

"I'd be happy to help. What is it?"

"You see that skeleton over there?" She indicated a skeleton opposite her. "I would like you to place him in a more dignified pose, with his hands clasped on his chest."

"Sure." He moved to carry out her request. It took a few minutes to carefully move the skeleton into the position the queen wanted, but he managed to do so without damaging it.

"Thank you." The queen had tears in her eyes as she looked at the body.

Realization struck him. "He was your husband? The king?"

The queen nodded. He took a step back and bowed his head, not sure what else to do.

Finally, the queen spoke. "His sword, on his side. I gift it to you."

"What? Why?"

"Consider it a belated birthday present. Please, take it and put it on."

James awkwardly unstrapped the sword from around the skeleton's waist and, at the queen's prompting, put it around his own.

"Very good." She pulled herself upright and regained her composure. "You may proceed."

He picked up the hammer again and started to attack the base of the crystal.

After she had watched him strike the base for several minutes, the queen spoke again. "You'll find the pick more effective. That is how you will finally break the base."

"What do you mean?"

"I've finally remembered how you remove the base of the crystal."

"Huh?" He was confused for a moment. Then he remembered the story of Alice meeting the White Queen in *Through The Looking Glass*. The White Queen had been able to remember the future as well as the past, because she lived her life backward.

"Wait. If you're able to remember the future, why didn't you know what was going to happen with the crystal and trying to hide the kingdom? Why didn't you warn people?"

The queen smiled sadly. "I wondered the same thing myself. Why couldn't I remember anything for the past twenty-five years? Why couldn't I remember what would happen when we decided to meddle with magic we didn't properly understand? The only reason I can come up with was that I blocked it out of my mind. I was responsible for the death of my kingdom, and there is nothing I can do to change that. That was something no one would ever want to remember. But now, I remember you, and how you destroy the base of the crystal. You should hurry."

Taking the queen at her word, he took up the pick and attacked the base of the crystal again. Slowly, cracks began to appear, and he began to smash away the supporting structure.

"Now the crowbar. You use the crowbar for the final bit."

"Are you sure? If I break a bit more of the stone, it will probably fall over by itself."

"Trust me, use the crowbar."

He did as she said and worked the crowbar on the opposite side of the crystal. As he applied weight to the bar, the crystal shifted slightly.

The queen spoke encouragingly. "That's it, keep going."

Straining to shift the crystal, he applied his full weight to the bar. Slowly, the crystal began to move, gaining momentum on its own without any extra pressure from him. Time seemed to slow as the crystal toppled. It was like watching a video play frame by frame. Then, everything sped back up again, and the crystal fell out of its base and onto the ground.

The queen let go of the crystal.

She smiled at James. Suddenly, a strong wind blew around him. It picked up the dust and threw it into the air, blinding him and forcing him to close his eyes. He felt the queen touch him on his shoulder as she whispered in his ear.

"Thank you."

The wind disappeared as quickly as it had begun. It was nighttime. He stood on the hill he and the others had walked up earlier, the crowbar he had been using to lever the crystal in his hands. The White Kingdom had disappeared.

It was possible he could just no longer see it, but deep in his heart, he knew that the White Kingdom was gone. The White Queen had obviously known what would happen when he moved the crystal to disrupt the spell. She had sacrificed her life so he could escape.

While he wasn't religious, James spent several moments saying a silent prayer for all the people who had died in the White Kingdom.

CHAPTER 20

Lahire breathed in the scent of the white roses, relishing their perfume. He never understood why his mother had insisted on red roses. The plants she had grown may have been a brilliant red, but they had no scent at all. He had been very happy to rip out her old roses and spread the small white patch that had been mistakenly planted to fill the rest of the garden.

The roses had another benefit. He wasn't the only one who liked to walk through the garden admiring the flowers at that time of day.

He glanced around, making sure no court officials were in sight. Once he was sure they would be undisturbed, he altered his path to intersect with the two ladies ahead of him. They stopped and curtsied as he reached them.

"Your Majesty."

He smiled. "Helen, Nicole. It is lovely to see you both today." The younger girl dropped back as the older woman stepped up to walk beside him, taking his offered arm. They began a circuit of the garden.

"You're looking very beautiful today, Helen. The color of the dress suits your eyes."

Helen blushed. "You are too kind."

"I trust your father is well?"

"He's feeling much better now, thank you. The doctor you recommended was able to treat his illness, and he is recovering quickly. He hopes to be well enough to attend the ball, but I fear he might be pushing himself too hard."

"Yes, he should rest as much as possible. It's always tempting to get back to work too quickly after an illness and make yourself unwell again. Please pass on my best wishes to him."

"I will do so, Your Majesty. I'm sure he will appreciate being in your thoughts."

"Have you decided what color dress you will wear to the ball?"

"Not yet." She looked shyly at Lahire. "Perhaps if I knew what color you are to wear, I could wear something to match."

He chuckled. "I was hoping I could choose a color to match you."

"Maybe we can come to a compromise? You pick the color, and we shall both wear it."

"That sounds like an excellent idea. How about a deep purple? I feel it would match your hair and skin tone."

"If Your Majesty commands it."

"Please, you know you don't have to call me that when we are here, alone."

She put her head on his shoulder. "I know. I was just teasing."

They shared another smile and continued walking.

* * *

The object that hit his leg when he took his first step down the hill momentarily confused James, then he realized the sword the queen had given him was strapped to his waist. He adjusted the belt so the sword didn't get in the way, then resumed walking.

Despite it being nighttime, he could see clearly. The area was lit up, as it had been the previous night. He wasn't sure what allowed him to see with the crystal gone, but he was happy not to be fumbling around in the dark.

As he walked, he looked around the hill trying to find any sign of the others. They were nowhere to be seen. They had probably given up waiting after he had disappeared, and gone back to the ship to get some rest. His stomach rumbled, and he realized he was feeling hungry. Starving, even. He hoped they had made some dinner.

After several hundred yards, he noticed something lying on the ground. As he moved closer, he realized it was Kara's satchel. It lay on the ground, as if it had been discarded. He picked it up with concern. Kara would never leave her satchel out in the middle of nowhere. Not voluntarily at least.

Crouching, he moved forward as quietly as he could. Finding refuge in a patch of bushes, he took the spyglass from the bag and looked toward their camp.

The condition of the ship made his heart sink. It had been damaged beyond repair. Several large holes had been blown in the sides, and the propellers had been removed from the ship and left in pieces on the ground. Of the others, he saw no sign.

Once he was sure they weren't near the camp, he systematically scanned his surroundings with the spyglass, trying to locate any trace of where the others might have gone, or been taken.

After several minutes, he noticed the faint glow of a campfire in the distance. Putting the spyglass away, he moved in that direction, staying as hidden as he could manage. Once close enough to observe, he found another place to hide and pulled out the spyglass.

Five Heart Guard sat around the fire laughing and talking with one another. He noticed another ship, three times the size of Torre's, sitting in a clear area a short distance from the camp. Kara and Torre sat near the edge of the firelight, tied to wooden poles. Torre looked like he had a serious head wound.

It was up to James to somehow rescue the others. A frontal assault was out of the question. He had a sword, but the only experience he'd ever had with one was a brief stage fighting class in college. He doubted he would survive more than a few seconds against one guard in a straight sword fight, let alone the five he could see.

He spent some more time watching, forcing himself to relax and take in everything. He noticed a sixth guard patrolling a regular route that took him away from the camp and around in a large loop. James watched the guard make two passes, scrutinizing carefully to make sure he always followed the same path. He did.

As a plan formed in his mind, he quickly checked the contents of Kara's satchel for the required items. He waited for the guard to reach the far end of his route, then made his way as quietly as he could to the ambush site he had spotted. He was only going to have one chance to take out the guard, and he couldn't afford to make any mistakes.

He held his breath as the patrolling guard made his way toward James's new hiding spot. Firming his grip on the crowbar, he quickly stood as the guard walked past, then swung the crowbar as hard as he could at the back of the guard's head.

It connected with a sickening thud. The guard collapsed silently to the ground.

James paused to listen, but no sound of alarm was raised. He pulled the guard into the bushes, pushing aside his mixed feelings at what he had done, and set about removing his armor and clothing. They weren't a good fit, but he hoped it would give him the time he needed to fool the other guards.

Next, he took the two ball devices out of Kara's satchel, the ones that he had seen Kara use in the city. They looked simple enough to use, like a grenade, except with a button and a dial on them. Leaving behind the crowbar, but taking the sword and the satchel, he traced the route he knew the guard had followed.

His heart pounded loudly as he approached the camp. What if his plan didn't work? He pushed aside his fears. He didn't have a choice. The others were depending on him. He had to try.

As he neared the circle of firelight, he pressed the buttons on the balls and threw them as far away from Kara and Torre as he could. He then continued walking forward.

The balls activated as he entered the firelight. Like the time Kara had used them in the city, it appeared as though the camp was under attack. James collapsed to the ground with a cry, as if he had been shot. Seeing him fall, the guards panicked. They grabbed their weapons and scattered out of the camp firelight. They shouted instructions, then counter instructions as they confused each other.

While the guards were distracted, he quickly crawled along the ground toward Kara and Torre.

Kara had obviously figured out what was going on as soon as the balls had gone off. "James? Is that you?"

"Were you expecting someone else?"

"Where the hell did you go? You've been gone over a day!"

"A day?" James shook his head. "I'll tell you later. First, we need to get out of here."

"Sounds good to me," said Torre.

Up close, he could see the wound on Torre's face wasn't too serious. The blood was dry, and had come from a single cut on his forehead. "Are you all right to move?"

"Of course I am. Just hurry up and get us free!"

James took the sword out of the scabbard and used it to cut their bonds. Torre's eyes went wide with surprise, and even Kara looked shocked, but neither said anything. He had them free in moments.

Kara rubbed her wrists. "They have a ship somewhere nearby. If we can find it, we can use it to escape."

James stood to get his bearings. "I see it. I can lead us there."

The others got to their feet. James and Kara turned in the direction of the ship, but Torre hurried toward the center of the camp and the fire.

"Where are you going?" hissed Kara.

"I'm not leaving without my gun." He moved toward a pile James recognized as their gear from the ship. Realizing that having their supplies would prove useful, James followed. As Torre grabbed his rifle, James picked up the pack and one of the sacks.

They rejoined the impatiently waiting Kara, then quickly moved out of the light thrown by the fire.

"This would be much easier if we could see," muttered Kara. "We don't know where the guards are."

"I can see them." James glanced back. The guards had found the balls and realized they had been tricked. He turned back. "We need to hurry."

James led them to the ship. They reached it as one of the guards shouted the alarm that the prisoners had escaped.

"I hope the ship is ready to go quickly," said James, as they climbed in.

Kara nodded. "Don't worry. These ships are built to get moving straight away. They store a reserve of pressure for use until the furnace is fully heated. It can't move for long with the reserves, but as least we'll be able to get away. Torre, can you take care of firing up the furnace?"

Torre muttered something under his breath, but moved to the back of the ship as asked. Kara headed up to the cockpit.

James locked the main door, then followed her. "Can you fly it?"

Kara sat down confidently in the pilot's seat. "Piece of cake." The way she looked over the control panel suggested she wasn't as confident as she sounded.

Sounds of shouting came from outside, then heavy banging on the door and side of the ship.

He threw a worried glance back at the door. "Any time now would be good."

"Here we go." Kara hit a button.

Nothing happened.

The hammering on the door grew in intensity. He looked back again. He could see it shuddering.

"Hurry up. I don't think the door will hold them much longer."

"Got it!" The ship lurched forward, and he was thrown into the cockpit wall.

"Ow!"

"You were the one who was still standing up."

He watched out the window as the island quickly fell away. He breathed a sigh of relief.

"I can't believe that worked."

"Thank you. When you disappeared, and we couldn't find any sign of you after a day, we thought you were gone for good."

"I'm sorry. It didn't seem that long for me. I thought it was still the same day."

"Where did you go? And how did you manage to get the sword of the White Kingdom?"

James looked down at the sword on his hip. "This? Remind me to ask you about the sword later. But to answer your question, I was in the White Kingdom, the translucent one that I could see. Apparently, they tried to hide the islands from Lahire by using some sort of magic, but something went wrong. Instead of hiding them, the White Kingdom ended up in another place. Everyone in the kingdom was frozen in place and died of starvation. The only person still alive was the White Queen. She was the one who gave me the sword."

"How did you escape?"

He gave a sad smile. "I guess I managed to disrupt the spell. Unfortunately, I think I managed to destroy the White Kingdom in the process."

The air pressure in the ship suddenly dropped as the screech of metal being torn and shredded filled the ship.

James turned to see what was happening and felt his heart skip a beat as he stood face to face with the man—no, *thing*—that had killed Melvin. The twin daggers the giant held in his hands glinted in the low light, the destroyed door of the ship visible beyond.

The *thing* regarded him. "A pity the White Kingdom is gone. My liege would have enjoyed the pleasure of destroying it himself. Still, you've saved him the trouble."

"Taxard!" The fear in Kara's voice was obvious.

James went for his sword, but before his hand had even reached the pommel, Taxard held Kara with a knife at her throat.

"I wouldn't do anything stupid if I were you. Not if you want your young friend here to live another day."

143

James slowly moved his hand away from the sword and raised his hands in the air.

"Very good. Now, I could kill you both, but I think the king would prefer to do that himself. And I'm sure he will be fascinated to hear all the details your young friend here can pass on about the terrorists in the city. So why don't we all sit down, make ourselves comfortable, and enjoy our trip back to the Heart capital."

A loud boom from behind him took James by surprise. A fireball flew past, taking out a section at the front of the ship. He didn't see Taxard move. One moment, he was holding Kara, and the next, he had moved to the side to avoid the shot. But he hadn't been able to completely dodge it. His right arm was a hanging mangled mess of metal and clockwork, and the sudden gust of air from the gaping hole in the side of the ship had unbalanced him.

James didn't hesitate in throwing himself at Taxard to try and grapple with him. The Ace of Spades effortlessly sidestepped, avoiding his lunge. Taxard raised his dagger above James's neck. Suddenly, Torre was between them, knocking James back and crashing into Taxard.

Pure luck allowed James to reach out and grab Torre's armor before the Red Rook toppled over the side. Taxard wasn't so lucky. Without a sound, he fell backward out of the hole in the front of the ship. James and Torre watched him fall away until he was swallowed by the darkness.

Torre had a satisfied look on his face. "The one who killed my king is dead. I have avenged the Brigade." He fell to one knee facing the hole and bowed his head in prayer.

James looked out where Taxard had fallen. "That was also for Melvin, you bastard." He stared silently at the darkness. He thought he saw a brief flash of light, but then it was gone.

Kara recovered quickly and checked the controls. After several moments, she looked over at James. "With the ship the way it is, we won't be able to travel very fast. We should head to the Club Kingdom. We've got a lot of allies there in the resistance. We can figure out what we're going to do next, and you can tell us everything you found out in the White Kingdom."

"Will this thing still fly? The damage looks pretty bad." He looked at the section where the controls had been. Half the panel, and a good portion of the front where the panel had been, was missing.

Kara nodded. "These ships are built tough and with several redundancies. It'll fly."

James shrugged. "You know Wonderland better than me. Take us wherever you think best."

CHAPTER 21

Lahire looked impassively at the kneeling Taxard. The damaged automaton had limped into the throne room with its arm hanging uselessly at its side.

"What do you have to report?" He held the tone of his voice neutral.

"I regret to inform you that the outsider is still alive, and that he and his accomplices—a female from the city and a survivor of the Red Castle Brigade—have escaped."

"Is this the same Castle Brigade member who tried to assassinate me two years ago?"

"I believe so, Your Majesty."

"Explain yourself."

"We tracked Caterpillar through Tulgey Wood and were eventually successful in capturing him. After some resistance, he offered up the information that the outsider had traveled to the White Kingdom. We followed, and my men captured his accomplices. There was no sign of the outsider. As I searched for him, the outsider freed the two prisoners and managed to escape. I was damaged attempting to stop them."

"And Caterpillar?"

Taxard looked uncomfortable. "After giving us the information on the outsider's whereabouts, he disappeared."

"So not only is the outsider still alive, but you allowed him *and* Caterpillar to escape?"

Taxard remained silent.

"You have failed." The words had an air of finality.

Taxard bowed his head. "I am sorry, Your Majesty. I misjudged the enemy. It won't happen again."

"Indeed, it won't."

Taxard continued hurriedly. "If it pleases Your Majesty, the mission wasn't a total loss."

Lahire stared at Taxard. If he didn't know any better, he would have said the automaton was reacting with fear. He kept his expression blank. "Continue."

"I have discovered a lead on the rebels. I recognized the girl in the group. Her father owns a hat shop in the city. He may lead us to the rest of the terrorists, or provide bait to lure his daughter into a trap. That is why I returned so quickly, risking travel via the Otherworld. I knew it was important to bring you this information without delay."

"Hatter." He rubbed his chin. "Yes, I should have known. He caused trouble for my mother as well and was a known associate of the last outsider, the Alice girl. Mother should have executed him when she had the chance. Yet another example of how much her weakness has cost Wonderland. I see it is up to me to remedy another of her mistakes.

"As for you, your failure to carry out my instructions indicates you have reached the end of your operational life. I believe it is time to replace you with a more up-to-date and reliable model."

A figure emerged from the side curtains and stood beside Lahire. It looked identical to the kneeling Taxard, except undamaged and moving with a smoother grace than the other.

"Please, Your Majesty! I can be returned to full working condition with only a few repairs."

Lahire looked at the damaged Taxard. The tone the automaton had taken on confirmed his suspicions. He had kept the current model for too long. It had become defective, learning to feel fear and putting its own life ahead of the sake of Wonderland and its ruler.

He waved a hand dismissively. "If you wish to survive, you must prove you are more worthy than your successor."

The damaged Taxard reached for one of its knives, and then toppled back, hitting the ground with a loud crash as the new Taxard surged forward and planted its own knife in the old model's chest.

Lahire looked at the fallen creation. "A pity. I was expecting it to put up more of a fight." He looked at the new Taxard. "Absorb this one's memories, then put Hatter under observation. We may be able to discover the terrorists' hideout and remove them from Wonderland once and for all."

The new Taxard inclined its head, acknowledging the order. He watched without emotion as the new Taxard effortlessly picked up the old model and carried it from the throne room.

* * *

It had been a slow flight after their escape from the islands, the destroyed front of the ship ensuring their rate of travel was much lower than it could have been. They traveled all through the night and most of the next day, stopping on the far edge of Tulgey Wood as it had begun to get dark again. Torre took charge of setting up camp, and after a limited meal from their few supplies, they settled down for the night.

Despite being exhausted, James found sleep impossible. After tossing and turning for an hour inside the ship, he finally got up and sat by the fire. It flared up again after some poking, and he stared at its flames as he mulled over everything Caterpillar had told him.

His parents were from Wonderland, and they had died trying to protect him. Melvin had been from Wonderland, and had also died trying to protect him. He had learned so much he never knew, never even suspected. So much he wished he could ask them about.

When he had been a kid, after Natalie was born, he had dreamed that one day his real parents would turn up and save him, take him away to a home where he would be loved and have fun again. After he learned that his mother had died in childbirth, he had hoped that his father was out there somewhere, regretting that he had abandoned his child, that one day they would find each other, and he would finally have a father who was proud of him.

That would never happen. He was alone, stuck in a strange place that he knew nothing about, on the run from a homicidal king who wanted him dead.

He was so lost in thought he failed to notice Torre until he sat down beside him. The Red Rook had been quiet since the previous evening. He imagined Torre also had a lot to think about. He gave Torre a nod, then returned to his fire gazing.

They sat in silence for several minutes, staring at the fire, until Torre finally spoke. "I thought it would be different."

"What would be different?"

"Killing the assassin. I thought I would feel satisfied and at peace, perhaps even happy, knowing I had restored the honor of my order. But I am not. The emptiness I feel from the failure to protect my king remains."

James struggled to find the right response. "You can't do anything to change what's happened, no matter how much you wish you could. You were able to kill Taxard, but it won't bring back your king or your friends. Revenge rarely makes us happy, even if we think it will. The best we can do is to find a reason to live, or something to strive for."

"Maybe." Torre glanced down at the sword by James's side. He hadn't even realized he'd carried it with him from his bedroll. "May I?"

"Sure." James unbuckled the sword and handed it over.

Torre examined the hilt, turning the sword over in his hands. His voice had a far-off sound to it. "There's a story—a legend—that says long ago the Red and White Kingdoms were united as one. The Islands Kingdom. The ruler of the Islands Kingdom had two sons, twins. They grew up pampered, having everything given to them. For their eighteenth birthday, he had two swords forged, identical in every way except for the stone in the hilt. One had a ruby, and the other had a diamond." Torre tapped the diamond in the hilt of James's sword.

"The day after their birthday, the king died. The two brothers argued over which was the rightful successor and fought to gain control of the kingdom. Half followed the brother with the red stone, and other half the one with the white. The fighting split the kingdom in two."

"Who was the older brother? The rightful heir?"

Torre stared at the sword. "Several days ago, I would have said the brother with the red sword was the elder one, and his twin with the white sword was the usurper. But the White Kingdom had a similar story that says the brother with the white sword was the rightful ruler. I don't know. I don't think anyone ever did."

"What happened to your king's sword? The red sword?"

Torre had a sad look on his face as he handed his sword back to him. "We destroyed it. There could never be another Red King, and we would never allow Lahire to get his hands on it, so we melted it down. Once that was done, we attacked Lahire's army. The twelve of us who were still alive expected to die, wanted to die, since we had failed our liege. Our sole aim was to take as many of the Heart bastards with us before we fell. I was knocked out during the fighting and woke up under a pile of bodies. I guess that's why they didn't see me. I waited until night, then took one of the undamaged ships and made my escape."

James stared at the diamond in the hilt, watching it glint in the firelight. "Don't take this question the wrong way, but why did you escape? I don't know anything about your order, but from what you've said, I thought your first instinct would have been to keep fighting."

Torre stared into the fire for a few moments before answering. "I had a vision while I was unconscious. The Red King told me I had to survive, that I had to leave the kingdom. He said it was the last order he could give me as my king." Torre opened his mouth as if to say more, then closed it again.

He looked at Torre. "For what it's worth, I'm glad you survived. I would have been dead at least twice already if it wasn't for you."

Torre stood abruptly. "We'll be leaving at first light. Get some sleep." With that, he returned to the ship.

James shook his head, watching the retreating figure. He didn't think he'd ever figure out that guy.

Holding the sword in front of him, he returned to watching the fire.

* * *

The land below had begun to change from the close-knit trees of Tulgey Wood to a more open landscape. After several hours of flight, James began to notice signs of civilization as trees and rough ground gave way to patches of farmland. A strange smoke haze to the left, far off in the distance, also became noticeable.

"Do you get many forest fires around here?" He pointed out the smoke haze to Kara when she looked questioningly at him. Her face went pale as she looked in the direction he indicated.

He asked, "What is it?"

Kara didn't answer straight away. When she did, it was a whisper.

"The Heart army. It's on the move."

"What?" James looked back to the haze. "Why? I thought they'd already conquered Wonderland?"

"I think they're heading toward the Club capital. They must be planning to crush the resistance and get rid of the royal family."

Torre stepped into the cockpit and looked in the direction of the smoke haze. "It's a big force. Not as large as the one that attacked the Red Kingdom, but close. The resistance doesn't stand a chance."

James looked between the smoke haze and Kara. "Aren't we trying to find the resistance?"

She nodded. "The army is still at least a week away from the capital. Their walkers are deadly on the battlefield, but not much faster than a horse, and Lahire never likes to split his army when he's moving it. He always relies on overwhelming force. We still have time to find and warn them, if they don't already know."

Torre looked at Kara. "We should fly over them. Get some intel for the resistance. They'll need all the help they can get."

James looked at Torre in shock. "You can't be serious!"

Torre stared back, his face resolute. "The more info the resistance has, the better they will be able to defend themselves. The Club Kingdom has fierce fighters, almost as strong as the Red Kingdom. With the right information they could do some serious damage to the Heart army."

Kara nodded again. "He's right. The Club Kingdom is the strongest source of resistance in Wonderland. If Lahire eliminates them, it will hurt all the groups left. We have to do everything we can to help them. Besides, we're in a Heart ship. They'll ignore us."

James shook his head slowly. "I think we're going to get killed, but you guys know best. Do what you have to." He swapped positions with Torre to let the Red Rook have a better view. Kara changed the course of the ship to fly toward the haze-filled sky.

As the source of the haze became clear, he couldn't help but gasp. Stretched out below, moving in what looked like a sea of metal, was all manner of strange contraptions. They looked like the strange carriage he had seen the first night he had arrived in Wonderland—weird lattices of metal bars meshed together in a way that suggested function was the primary purpose—but unlike the carriage, the machines walked on six and eight legs. Huge smoke stacks in the middle of the machines belched thick smoke into the air that caused the visible haze, and every larger machine had several gun turrets on its back that wouldn't have looked out of place on a battleship.

Between the larger machines moved smaller ones. From the patches of red he could make out on the surfaces of them, he assumed they acted as some sort of troop transport. Given the number of the machines he could see, thousands of troops were being moved in for the attack.

Kara looked grim. "Lahire's latest war machines. He's not taking any chances."

Torre shared her expression. "The resistance won't stand a chance against this force. Not with the equipment they have available to them."

One of the lead machines effortlessly pushed over a huge tree, allowing the smaller troop transports to move forward past it. James watched the mass of metal moving beneath them. "We have to warn them."

"We've seen what we needed to." Kara altered the ship's course again. "I just don't know what they'll say when we tell them."

* * *

The ship settled down in a small clearing. James shivered, feeling the chill running up and down his spine from the sound the branches had made scraping against the hull.

Torre opened the door of the ship and looked around. "The undergrowth here is fairly thick. We shouldn't need to do anything to ensure the ship remains hidden."

"Unless the army walks over it," muttered James.

Kara shook her head. "They're days away, and we're not in the path they'll be taking. It will be fine."

"And you're sure we'll be able to find the resistance from here?"

Kara picked up her satchel. "I spent a few weeks in a nearby village and know the people. They're all collaborators for the resistance and will be able to direct us to where the main group currently is. With any luck, we'll be able to get transport as well."

"I still say the ship would have been easier."

Kara rolled her eyes. "Even if we'd found them, they would have shot us out of the sky before we could tell them who we were. Stop complaining and start walking."

James sighed and tried to shake himself awake. Kara was right. He had been negative ever since he woke up, the lack of sleep putting him in a bad mood. She didn't deserve that sort of treatment. Neither did Torre, although the Red Rook had paid little attention to him since their talk the night before. He forced himself to smile. He would get over his bad mood, even if he had to plaster a grin on his face to do so.

"What're you so happy about?" asked Torre, as he stepped out of the ship.

James shrugged. "Seems like nice weather for a walk."

Torre looked at him as if he were an idiot.

Kara exited the ship, walking past the two of them. "This way."

They walked in silence. Unlike Tulgey Wood, the forest felt relatively normal. With the sound of birds chirping in the trees and the occasional buzz of insects flying around, he could almost have believed he was back in his world.

After half an hour of walking, they reached a narrow dirt road. It was a nice change to be walking along a clear path, and he began to relax. When no one was trying to kill him, Wonderland could be a nice place.

"We're almost there." Kara picked up the pace.

He interrupted his daydreaming to focus on the road ahead. The road led into another clearing, with a simple stone building visible. As they moved closer, more buildings in the village could be seen.

Only buildings.

"Where are the people?" he asked in confusion.

Kara frowned as Torre unslung his rifle. "I don't know."

They moved forward cautiously, looking all around them. The place was deserted. The buildings were all closed, and no smoke wafted from any of the chimneys.

"They might have left because of the Heart army," suggested James.

"And went where?" asked Kara. "This was their home."

Torre examined the ground. "Heart Guard have been out here recently. Within the last day or so."

A noise behind James made him turn, then raise his hands as the source of the noise became obvious.

"I'd say they've been here much more recently than that."

The three Heart Guard who had appeared pointed their muskets menacingly. He glanced over his shoulder as five more guards stepped out from behind a building. The second group pointed their weapons at Torre and Kara.

"Drop your weapons," yelled one of the guards. Torre had a look of disgust, but moved to comply.

James turned back to face the group of three. They advanced slowly, keeping James and the others covered.

A sudden glint of light appeared in the air ahead. All three guards staggered, then fell, clutching at their chests and throats.

"Down!" James threw himself to the ground at Torre's command. The boom of Torre's gun echoed off the buildings of the village, and James rolled to see what was happening.

Torre's shot had hit two of the Heart Guard, who lay collapsed on the ground. The others in the group had elected to dive for cover.

Torre rolled to be behind cover of his own. Kara crawled toward a closer building that offered shelter, and James followed her. They crouched as the Heart Guard fired several shots in Torre's direction.

"We should help him," whispered James.

"With what?" Kara looked at him. "In case you hadn't noticed, neither of us has a ranged weapon."

A second boom of Torre's weapon firing was followed by a cry of pain. James risked a glance. A third guard from the larger group lay injured and obviously out of the fight, the wall he had hidden behind having provided no protection. He ducked back.

"Besides, Torre can handle himself. It's what he's trained to do. We'd get in his way."

He frowned. "I guess."

He took a second glance. Torre had reloaded and waited for an opportunity for his next shot. A sudden cry of pain erupted from where the remaining Heart Guard had taken cover, then one of them rolled out and collapsed to the ground.

The village was silent, then a voice James recognized called out, "The Heart Guard have been taken care of. Please ask your Red Kingdom friend not to shoot me as I step out."

James stepped out of cover. "Torre, it's all right. He's on our side. I think."

Torre stood slowly, his weapon lowered but held ready. Moments later, White Rabbit stepped out from behind the building the Heart Guard had been hiding behind.

"You're still alive, I see. Good. I knew you'd be safer here."

"Safer? Safer?" James strode forward to where White Rabbit stood. "I've got some lunatic king sending people to kill me, I'm in the middle of what's about to be a war zone, half the people I meet are trying to shoot me, and you're saying I'm safer here?"

White Rabbit paid no attention to the outburst as he retrieved his knives from the bodies of the guards. He wiped them on their coats to clean them before putting them away under his jacket.

"Of course you're safer. If you'd remained in your world, you'd be dead by now. Lahire would have sent Taxard after you, and there would have been no one left to protect you. You spoke with Caterpillar. You know that."

Kara moved to stand beside James. "Wait, you brought James here because you thought he'd be safe? Why?"

White Rabbit looked from Kara to James and back. "You haven't told them then, I see."

Kara looked at James. "Told us what?"

He winced. "What Caterpillar told me. I'll tell you later, I promise."

Kara looked away. For a moment, he thought she wore a hurt expression on her face.

"It doesn't matter what he does or doesn't tell us." Torre slung his rifle over his shoulder. "The question is, what do you know about the people disappearing from this village?"

"Don't worry. They're safe." White Rabbit moved over to the group of three to collect his knives. "Ariston found out that the local Heart Guard were going to start raiding suspected collaborator villages around the capital ahead of the attack. We were able to move them to a safer location before the guards arrived."

The contempt in Kara's voice was obvious. "So, you're working with the resistance now? How much did Ariston have to pay you to manage that?"

White Rabbit regarded Kara dismissively. "Who I work for, and on what terms, are none of your business."

"Can you get us to Ariston?" asked James quickly, hoping to deflect the conversation. "We flew over the Heart army and have details on their makeup and position. I imagine it's information Ariston would like to have."

White Rabbit motioned in the direction they had been walking. "I've got transport ahead. You'll be able to fit in if you're willing to squeeze together."

CHAPTER 22

White Rabbit's transport was a contraption that looked like a weird cross between a flatbed truck and a carriage, with a narrow smoke stack sticking up between the two sections. The carriage part was only large enough for one person. White Rabbit motioned to the tray on the back.

"You'll have to ride in there. It won't be comfortable, but it beats walking."

The three sat in the tray as best they could. It was cramped, but James suspected the tight fit might help with the rough roads they were likely to pass over.

With a loud hiss, the vehicle began to move. The first twenty minutes was torture, as they traveled over the rough dirt track. The tight fit meant they didn't have far to shift when they hit the bumps, but it also meant they were constantly crashing in to one another.

Thankfully, they eventually reached roads that were better maintained, and the journey became slightly more pleasant. Trees gave way to cleared farmland, which showed signs of habitation. In the far distance, the city lay against the horizon.

After another half an hour, the carriage slowed, turned down a dirt driveway, and drew to a stop in a small courtyard. The courtyard, like the buildings around it, looked like it hadn't had any maintenance in decades, but the place was obviously in use. The courtyard was clear of vegetation, and fires burned inside.

Kara slid out of the back. "They've gone up in the world. The last time I was here, they were hiding in a leaky basement beneath an old warehouse."

James supported himself on the side of the tray as feeling slowly returned to his legs. "Do they have to move often?"

"Two or three times a year. Usually, they let the Heart Guard find the hideout to make them think they're making some sort of progress on eliminating the resistance. After they've had a chance to remove anything of importance, of course."

A door opened across from them, and a man who looked to be in his late fifties emerged. He had several scars on his face and walked with a slight limp. Something about his manner suggested to James that he was a military man, or had been earlier in his life. He certainly had an air of command about him.

He walked over to White Rabbit, who had stepped out of the vehicle. "I wasn't expecting you back until tomorrow. I assume you have news?"

White Rabbit motioned to the group. "They do."

The man looked at the group, then grinned when he saw Kara. "I don't believe it. Kara! Of all the times you pick to visit, you had to choose now. It's good to see you again."

"It's nice to see you again, too." Kara returned his smile and gave him a hug. "Allow me to introduce my friends, James and Torre." She indicated each in turn. "James, Torre, this is Ariston Bachrach."

Torre looked surprised. "The famed Club Army general who outmaneuvered the Spade armies and tied up several divisions for a week without losing a single man?"

Ariston chuckled. "That was a long time ago. These days, I do what I can to fight from the shadows. Anonymity is the key to our survival."

"Until now." Kara's face had a look of concern. "We saw the army approaching."

Ariston's expression became serious. "It's dark times for the Club Kingdom. We don't stand a chance if we fight the army head on. While I have people who are willing to fight, we don't have enough weapons. Our only choice at the moment is to go to ground and fight a guerrilla action against the army once they've moved in. Which will be difficult. They've sealed off the city, and the king and queen have been detained in their castle."

"We flew over the army. We can give you the details on the makeup of their army, and how they're moving."

Ariston looked surprised. "How did you manage to fly that close? They should have shot you out of the sky."

"We managed to acquire a Heart ship. It's damaged, but it still works."

Ariston smiled. "It seems you have some stories to tell. Come, you can tell me all about it over lunch." Ariston led them inside the house. The interior was extremely plain. No attempt had been made to make it feel like a home. It was obviously only a place to sleep, eat, and plan. But it was warm, and the smell of fresh cooking filled the air.

James' stomach growled in complaint.

Ariston chuckled. "I'll have some food brought in to us."

"Ariston? About White Rabbit."

Ariston glanced at Kara. "What about him?"

"You can't trust him. He's a mercenary. As soon as the money runs out, he'll be gone."

"A few months ago, I would have agreed with you. But the situation has changed. I'm convinced he will stick with us until the end."

Kara looked about to argue, but he held up a hand. "Trust me, Kara. I wouldn't have him here unless I was one hundred percent sure it was safe. Now, take a seat through there. I'll join you in a moment."

The room he indicated was cramped, furnished with a large table that took up almost the entire space, and several chairs. Kara shook her head in obvious disagreement, but took her seat with the others.

Ariston returned after a minute. "Food will be with us shortly. Now, what trouble have you gotten yourself into this time, Kara?"

Kara explained their story, starting with James's arrival in the Heart Capital and their escape from the city.

When she finished, and the three had finished their meal, Ariston said, "Impressive. No one could have guessed the White Kingdom was still there, hidden from view. But I guess that was the point. I had always hoped the White Kingdom would return one day to help us fight Lahire. It's too bad."

He turned to Kara. "I do have one piece of news that will make you happy. The *Nighthawk* survived."

"It did?" Kara's face had a look of surprise, then happiness. "How do you know?"

"It landed at one of our villages two days ago, badly damaged. They stayed long enough to make some basic repairs and take on supplies, but left late last night. I don't know where they were going."

Kara grinned. "So they made it after all."

Matching her smile, James patted her on the arm. "I told you they would."

Kara allowed herself to smile for a few more moments, then a look of seriousness returned. "We don't have time to think about them now. Not with Lahire's army on the march."

Ariston nodded. He spread a map on the table showing the terrain surrounding the Club capital. "We can use this to mark what you saw." Kara and Torre spent several minutes marking out the positions of the army.

Ariston looked on with growing concern. "It's worse than I thought. With that makeup and those numbers, they don't just intend to occupy the city. They can destroy any part of the city that tries to resist. Hell, they could destroy the entire city. It would be a repeat of what happened to the Red Kingdom."

Kara asked, "What are you going to do?"

Ariston shook his head. "There's not a lot we can do. As I said before, our main problem is weapons. We have firearms and some explosives, but only five walkers left from the original war. We had more, but lost them three years ago when the Heart Guard stumbled upon one of our depots. Not only did we lose the equipment, but Lahire used that as an excuse to take the royal children. The king and queen have been limited in the support they can provide us ever since.

"But your arrival with a Heart ship has given me an idea. I need to spend some time working out the details. I'll have the ship brought here so we can repair it, and we can discuss plans further tomorrow morning. For now, I have matters to attend to, and you would probably enjoy a chance to rest and get cleaned up properly."

"A bath would be fantastic," said Kara.

Ariston scribbled a quick note, folded it in half, and handed it to Kara. "I'll have a coach take all of you to Lady Joyce Baultin. Give her this when you arrive. She will put you up for the night and ensure you have everything you need."

"Thank you, Ariston." Kara leaned over the table and gave him a quick hug.

He led them back out to the courtyard. White Rabbit's vehicle was gone, but in its place was a coach. It at least looked like a normal coach with an engine on the back, unlike the one James had seen the night of his first arrival. A short man leaned against it, smoking a cigarette. He dropped it on the ground as they approached, and climbed up into the driver's position.

Ariston opened the door to the coach and helped Kara get in. Torre and James climbed in behind her.

"Try not to get into any more trouble."

"I can't promise anything," said Kara, returning his smile. The coach lurched to a start. In moments, they were out of the courtyard and back on the road.

"Who is Lady Baultin?" asked James.

Kara shrugged. "I have no idea. Nobility, obviously, but I don't know what relation she is to the royal family. The nobles of the Club Kingdom have had it tough since Lahire took over. Many of them lost land or wealth. Some of them lost both. Almost every noble in the Club Kingdom is at least a collaborator for the resistance."

* * *

Riding around the outskirts of the city, it took an hour to get to their destination. Unlike the farmhouse where they had met Ariston, Lady Baultin's residence was large, extravagant, and well maintained. Neatly manicured lawns and perfectly kept gardens lined the drive leading to a mansion James wouldn't have found out of place in a Jane Austen novel.

The coach drew up to the front door. Stiff from the journey in the confined space, they slowly climbed out of the cabin. After a brief stretch, Kara led them to the front door.

A butler answered the doorbell. "Yes?" He eyed them with suspicion.

Kara handed over the note. "We're here to see Lady Baultin. This is our letter of introduction."

The butler took the letter. "Very good. You may wait in the entrance hall and put your bags..." He glanced at their weapons. "And other belongings in the corner. Please don't touch anything." He stood to one side to allow the three of them to enter, then headed deeper into the house. Several moments later, a young man entered the entrance hall from where the butler had exited. He stood awkwardly next to the door, glancing in their direction repeatedly, while trying to pretend that he wasn't observing them.

"Looks like we're not trusted," commented Torre.

"Are you surprised?" asked James. "Considering the state we're in, I wouldn't trust us either."

Torre made a face. "People care too much about outward appearances. Fancy clothes and nice belongings don't make you any better than someone who only has the clothes on their back."

James shrugged, not sure how to respond. They waited in silence. He took the time to examine their surroundings.

The hall was large, with many doors off both sides and a large staircase sweeping its way down from the second floor. The polished marble floor gleamed, matched perfectly by the intricate carved-wood paneling and metallic-tinted wallpaper. Paintings, a mixture of landscapes and portraits, dotted the walls at intervals around the room. The style of the paintings was similar to many he had seen, but they all had Wonderland twists with the inclusion of strange plant life and unusual backdrops.

After a ten-minute wait, footsteps approached. A woman who looked to be in her mid-thirties appeared at the top of the landing.

Beautiful was the only word James had to describe her. She looked like a supermodel with the way her hair, makeup, and clothes had been done. She wore a blue and silver brocade dress that glittered in the light, and which somehow matched her blond hair and pale skin tone perfectly. She moved with a grace he had never seen, and he found himself mesmerized.

She paused at the top of the stairs to regard them with a welcoming smile, then glided down to meet them.

"Welcome to my house. I am Lady Joyce Baultin. Please, make yourself at home here. Henry will prepare rooms for you for your stay, but I would be honored if you would join me for some tea, so we can get to know each other."

He took a step forward, speaking before Kara could respond. "Thank you. That would be delightful."

Lady Baultin nodded slightly, giving him a secretive smile, then turned and glided down the hall. She entered a room on her left.

"That would be *delightful*," mimicked Kara quietly as they followed.

"What? I was being polite."

"Uh huh." Kara had an unreadable expression on her face.

The room they entered contained extravagant paintings, gilded and intricately carved wood pieces, fancy rugs, and plush furniture. Every furnishing spoke of money. Lady Baultin sat as they entered. The table had been set with fine china, and a selection of cakes and biscuits lay in the center.

"Please, sit." Lady Baultin indicated the seats. "I would love to hear your tale. Ariston gave few details in his note."

He started to speak, but Kara cut in quickly. "There's not a lot to tell. Lahire has been cracking down on the resistance in the Heart capital, so we had to flee the city. We had a run-in with the Heart patrol, and the ship we were on was damaged. We managed to make it here, and Ariston was kind enough to take us in."

He took a bite of one of the biscuits. "Well, there was a bit more to it than that. We—"

"Did almost crash in Tulgey Wood," cut in Kara. "Luckily we managed to avoid that. I'm sure Lady Baultin doesn't want to hear the details about all the people who were hurt in the fight, or how the ship had to limp back here."

"I see." Lady Baultin glanced at him before turning to Torre. "I'm surprised to see a member of the Castle Brigade here. How did you end up joining the group?"

Torre shrugged. "Near Tulgey Wood." He put his fifth biscuit into his mouth, not bothering to elaborate.

"We saw his camp when we almost crashed, and took him on board." Kara glanced at James with an expression that told him to shut up.

He smiled uneasily at Lady Baultin, who sat back and gave them all her welcoming smile again.

"Well, I am happy to help Ariston, or his friends, any time he has need to call on me. He has done a lot for my family over the years, and I do everything I can to repay him."

Kara gave her a fixed smile. "If you don't mind my asking, how are you able to keep such a place as untouched as it is? I thought Lahire was taking everything he could out of the kingdom."

"Indeed, he has taken much. Appearances can be deceiving. We have lost a lot over the years, to Lahire or whatever crony he has decided to appoint as local governor at the time. However, my family has been more fortunate than many. We had ties with Lahire's father from the happier times. Those ties have limited how hard we have been hit. We have been able to put forward a convincing face of supporting Lahire, while providing aid to the resistance.

"There have been a few close situations in the past, true, but so far we have managed to stay ahead of Lahire and his Heart Guard. There are many hidden areas on this estate that we can secrete you in if need be. They won't find you here."

"We certainly appreciate all your help," said James.

"It is my pleasure. Now, I expect you would all appreciate a bath and a chance to change into some fresh clothes. I have had my servants prepare baths for you in your rooms. Oh…" She stopped, as if something had occurred to her. "I'm sorry, I didn't think to ask if you two were together. I've had separate rooms prepared." She indicated Kara and James.

He managed to stammer out his reply first. "What? No—"

Kara's reply cut in. "Why do you ask?"

Covering her mouth, Lady Baultin gave Kara a horrified look. "Oh dear, I'm sorry. I didn't mean to embarrass the two of you. It's just that you were answering for each other, and that's when I realized that I should have asked if you were a couple. And now I've gone and made the situation more uncomfortable. Please forgive me. I want you all to feel relaxed during your stay here. My home is your home. Now, if you'll excuse me, I have matters to attend to. Henry will show you upstairs once you've finished your afternoon tea. We can talk more at dinner this evening." She gave everyone a parting smile, then left.

Kara muttered something under her breath, but he was unable to make it out. They continued their tea in silence. He wanted to ask Kara about her reaction to Lady Baultin, but seeing her expression, decided better of it.

Once they had finished, the butler led them out of the room, up the stairs, and down the hallway opposite to where Lady Baultin had emerged. He stopped at a door halfway along.

"This is the young lady's room." He opened the door and motioned for Kara to enter.

"It will be nice to have a real bath," said Kara, somewhat distantly. She stepped through quickly, closing the door without a glance back.

The butler led James and Torre further down the hall, stopped at opposite doors at the end of the corridor, and motioned to them.

"These are your rooms." He indicated James. "Yours is the one to my right."

Torre said nothing, simply entering his room and closing the door behind him. "Thank you," said James to the retreating butler, then he entered his own room.

The bedroom was huge. The large four-poster bed on the wall was the largest he had seen, but it looked small in comparison to the room. His bag and the bundle he had wrapped the sword rested in a far corner, as if whoever had placed them had tried to minimize the impact they would have on the décor of the room. Clean clothes, perfectly pressed and obviously of fine quality, had been laid out on the bed. A door led off the side of the room into a bathroom. The bathtub was full of steaming hot water, and James had to admit the idea of a bath was appealing.

He quickly discarded his dirty clothes and settled down for a long soak.

* * *

Lahire fought to keep his expression neutral as the commander finished her report. For the first time in almost two weeks, events were finally going right. He hoped it was an omen for the evening.

"How many of the terrorists were you able to capture in the raid?"

"We captured thirty trying to flee their underground base. Another fifty collaborators had houses connected to the tunnel network, and they are now in custody."

"And their leader? Gryphon?"

The commander's confident expression cracked slightly. "Unfortunately, we were unable to apprehend him alive. He triggered an explosive device soon after our men entered their hideout. He perished in the explosion, along with fifty Heart Guard."

"How can you be sure he died? Have you found a body?"

"We had men positioned in all the tunnels leading out of their base. Gryphon didn't leave via any of them, nor did he try to leave via any of the collaborator houses. I have men digging through the rubble now, but it will take weeks. However, given the size of the explosion, I am confident that he is dead."

Lahire nodded. "Good work, Commander. Once the terrorists and collaborators have been interrogated, hand them over to the head executioner. I want a public display, so the citizens will know they can now sleep safe in their beds at night. I trust everything is in place for this evening?"

"Yes, Your Majesty. I have assigned triple guards to ensure there are no problems. Nothing will ruin the event."

"Excellent. Your efforts today have made up for your earlier mistakes. I expect you to continue at the same level."

"Of course, Your Majesty. Thank you, Your Majesty."

He waved his hand in dismissal, and the commander quickly left. He stood and made his way to his study, closing the door behind him.

Only when he was alone did he allow himself a smile. It was a good day.

"I must congratulate you on your success, Your Majesty."

Despite himself, Lahire jumped at the voice.

"Shireche! How many times have I asked you not to surprise me like that?" Lahire strode over to sit at his desk.

"My apologies, Your Majesty. I was overwhelmed by the news of your success and forgot myself."

"Yes, well, it has been a good day for the kingdom."

"Indeed. I am sure the citizens will feel much safer knowing the terrorists have finally been caught. They will never forget this day. And soon, you will have the Club Kingdom brought into hand. The only thing left to worry about is the outsider."

Lahire frowned slightly. "Yes, him. There has been no sign of him since he left the White Kingdom."

"I am sure he will turn up in due course, Your Majesty. Then, you will be able to deal with him, and the safety of Wonderland will be assured. Enjoy your party this evening."

He waited to see if Shireche had anything else to say, but the voice was silent. He allowed himself a faint smile. His gaze wandered across his desk to fall on the ring box. He picked it up, and his smile grew.

It was a good day, but it would be a fantastic evening.

CHAPTER 23

James planned to lie down only for a moment, but he found himself woken from a deep sleep by a knock on the door. Getting off the bed and shaking himself awake, he went to answer.

A young maid curtsied as he opened the door. "Forgive the interruption sir, but Lady Baultin has invited you to join her for a walk in the gardens."

"Oh, of course." He looked back in his room, then realized he didn't need anything else. "Um, when and where?"

"I can take you to her now, if you are ready."

"Certainly. Lead on."

As they passed the other doors in the hall, he looked at the maid curiously. "The others aren't coming?"

The maid shook her head. "The invitation was only for you."

"Oh." James felt a mix of nervousness and excitement at the news.

The maid led him through a conservatory then onto a back patio. A large garden lay before him, with flowers and trees arranged in pleasing patterns on the green and well-tended lawn. Lady Baultin had changed into a pink and yellow dress with matching parasol. She stood at the edge of the stairs leading from the patio. She was as mesmerizing as before.

She smiled when she saw him.

"You're looking very handsome, if you don't mind me saying. The clothes suit you."

He looked down at the clothes that had been provided. He wore a finely tailored suit with waistcoat and shirt, much nicer and more expensive than the clothes Gryphon had given him all that time ago. He looked every part a Victorian gentleman.

James returned her smile warmly.

"Thank you, I feel much better after the bath. Everything has been rather hectic the past week."

"Indeed." Lady Baultin offered her arm. "Why don't we walk for a while, and you can tell me all about it? I'm ever so curious to hear the details about your adventures."

He took her arm. He noticed the maid following them, although remaining at a discreet distance.

"So, you come from the Heart Kingdom, I presume?"

"Well, not exactly."

"Oh? I thought that's where you were running from Lahire?"

"Yes, that's where we started from. But I'm not sure I should talk about it."

Lady Baultin leaned close. "I'm an expert at keeping secrets. I won't tell a soul. I won't even let Kara know that you've told me."

He smiled. "Well, you're part of the resistance, so I guess it's all right. I'm an outsider."

Lady Baultin looked surprised. "An outsider? There hasn't been an outsider in Wonderland for over a century. No wonder you had to leave the Heart Kingdom. Lahire has standing orders for all outsiders to be caught on sight."

"So I found out. I only spent a few hours in the Heart city, and for pretty much the whole time, I was either running or hiding."

"That must have been terrible for you. But how did you manage to end up in Wonderland?"

"It was White Rabbit. He brought me here, although I still don't really understand the reason. I mean, I know the reason. But I don't understand it."

"And what was the reason?"

He thought back to his meeting with Caterpillar, then shook his head. "I'd rather not talk about it."

"Of course." Lady Baultin patted his arm. "It must have been difficult for you, being taken from your own world, losing all your friends and family, and being thrown into one that was alien to you."

"Alien is right," agreed James. "Everything is familiar, but different. And then there are places like Tulgey Wood, which are just plain evil."

Lady Baultin nodded. "Yes, I have heard that Tulgey Wood is a strange place. I'm glad I've never been there. Did you spend long there?"

"Only a day or so." He thought about expanding his answer, then remembered how Kara had seemed determined not to elaborate. "Torre helped us out and kept us safe until we could leave."

"And did you meet Caterpillar?" His expression must have shown shock, as Lady Baultin laughed and added, "Don't be so surprised. Everyone knows Caterpillar is supposed to be hiding in Tulgey Wood."

"No, we didn't see him." He looked away.

"A pity. I would like to meet him one day. I hear he is quite wise, and that he can even see the future."

When he didn't respond, she asked, "So, what do you plan to do next?"

"I don't know. Ariston said he had some ideas, but he needed some time to think. I guess he has a lot on his mind right now, with the invasion and everything. I hope your Kingdom will be all right."

"We will endure, I'm sure."

They had completed a circuit of the garden. Lady Baultin disengaged her arm from his. "Thank you for a wonderful walk, James. I enjoyed our talk."

"Oh, you have to leave?"

"I'm afraid so. Hopefully, we can talk some more at dinner, but once again, there are matters I must deal with."

He smiled. "Of course, I understand. I look forward to dinner."

Lady Baultin gave her secretive smile, then turned and made her way back into the house.

* * *

James smelled food as soon as he left his room. The aroma was fantastic, especially after the simple food they had eaten the past few days. Stepping into the dining hall, he found the table laden with a huge selection of lavish dishes. Torre was already seated, looking uncomfortable in the suit he wore, but eying the food hungrily.

Lady Baultin, changed once again into a new dress, sat at the head of the table. The forest-green dress with gold embroidery was her most elaborate one yet, and made her look every part the noblewoman her title indicated. She motioned to the seat nearest her for James. "I wasn't sure what each of you liked to eat, so I had the chef prepare a selection of dishes for you to try. Please, eat as much as you like. I hope you enjoy."

James sat and was about to ask about Kara when she finally entered the room.

For the second time that day, he couldn't stop staring. Kara had undergone a complete transformation. No longer was she wearing the dirty jacket and trousers she had acquired on the *Nighthawk*. Instead, she wore a fine white and silver dress that fit her perfectly. Her hair had been styled to give it a lifted, full look, and she wore a faint trace of makeup that evened her complexion and shaded her eyes.

She looked stunning. More than stunning. She was breathtaking.

Kara smiled politely as she took her seat on the same side as Torre, but otherwise said nothing.

He forced himself to look away and focus on the food. From the glances he took, he could see Kara was determined to maintain a level of dignity, putting only small portions on her plate. He tried to limit the amount of food he put on his plate, but the enticing aromas got the better of him and his plate was soon piled high. Opposite, Torre did the same.

The conversation over the meal was light, with Lady Baultin talking about life in the Club Kingdom. The Heart Guard maintained a tight grip on society, but he learned that the citizens were able to steal moments of happiness and joy. The descriptions she gave of the festivals and social events sounded fascinating, and he idly found himself hoping he could attend such an event one day.

To his surprise, he also found himself hoping that Kara would be there to join him. Glancing at her again, he thought he caught her looking in his direction before quickly turning away. He mentally shook his head. He was imagining things.

Once the meal was finished, Lady Baultin motioned the butler over. He carried a crystal carafe containing a dark amber liquid. "I believe this is the perfect end to a lovely meal. It's a rather rare wine from before the war. I was lucky enough to have it hidden away in a separate cellar on the estate, so it wasn't lost when Lahire's troops raided our property. It's sweet, but the flavor is unbelievable. I hope you all enjoy."

The butler finished pouring all four glasses. Lady Baultin raised her glass to everyone. "To freedom."

"To freedom," echoed everyone. He took a sip. It was delicious, like honey, but with a complex aftertaste like nothing he had ever tasted before.

Torre looked at his glass strangely, his head tilted slightly to one side. James was about to ask him what the matter was when a sudden wave of dizziness hit him. He dropped the glass and was dimly aware that Kara had done the same. After a slight pause, Torre dropped his glass as well.

Lady Baultin spoke again, her voice containing the same light tone she had used before. "To freedom, which can only come through sacrifice and knowing how to pick the winning side. Long live King Lahire."

James turned to look at her. She stared at the three of them coldly. He tried to say something, but the world began to spin, then everything went black.

* * *

The hall was full of guests by the time Lahire made his entrance. His tailor had done a superb job, as he had demanded. The trousers and tails were made out of a deep purple silk, and the top hat was made to match. He wore a silver waistcoat over his light purple shirt and carried a dress cane with his silver gloves. It was his tailor's best work yet, and further evidence that it was going to be a perfect day.

The nobles of Wonderland were all dressed in various degrees of outlandishness. It was slow going, moving through the crowd as various nobles tried to compliment him or engage him in small talk in an attempt to gain his favor, but he was in no mood for them tonight. He had only one person he wanted to find.

He felt his heart skip a beat when he spotted her. Helen wore a dress that perfectly matched his suit. The deep purple fabric was shot with red, and it shimmered in the light. Gold trim ran throughout the dress and along the edges, giving it a look of sophistication that made all the other dresses in the room pale in comparison. Her hair had been curled slightly, but otherwise allowed to fall free at the back. Like many of the noblewomen, she had painted tiny symbols of her home kingdom on her face; they ran from the corner of her right eye down to the base of her neck. Lahire had always thought the practice pointless, but seeing the gold diamonds cascade off the curves of her cheek, he realized it was intoxicating.

Helen curtsied as he reached her. "Your Majesty. You look dashing this evening."

He bowed slightly in return, aware of the eyes all around watching his every move. "Helen, it is wonderful to see you this evening. You are looking more radiant than ever. The belle of the ball."

Helen bowed her head again, but he caught sight of her blush. "Your words humble me, Your Majesty."

He turned to Helen's parents, who stood to one side. Her father looked pale but beamed with happiness. His wife, her expression unreadable, supported him slightly with a hand on his arm.

"Lord Chadwick, I am glad to see that you were well enough to make this event. I was concerned when I heard of your ill health."

Helen's father bowed his head. "I am humbled by your concern, Your Majesty. The doctor assures me I will recover fully."

"I am glad to hear it. I hope we may have a chance to talk later this evening. I feel there are several matters we should discuss."

Her father smiled slightly and bowed his head again. Several nearby nobles tittered at his remark, but Lahire paid them no heed.

"I would be delighted, Your Majesty. I am your loyal servant."

He turned his attention back to Helen. "My lady, the musicians are playing a lively tune, and it seems a waste to spend it standing at the side. Would you care to dance?"

Helen curtsied again. "I would be honored, Your Majesty."

He led her into the central area of the hall, joining the couples already dancing.

She kept her eyes lowered as they began to dance.

"You can look at me, you know," said Lahire lightly.

"Everyone is watching us, Your Majesty. I don't wish to be improper."

"Let them watch. I don't care."

She raised her head and smiled.

They danced. Couples entered and left the dance floor, but they continued to dance. Helen's smile mesmerized him, and he wanted the moment to never end. He wished the two of them could stay where they were forever. Wonderland could go to ruin as far as he was concerned, as long as Helen kept smiling.

But the moment had to end. He sensed that she was tiring, and, truth be told, he was tiring too. He also had the matter to discuss with her father, as tradition demanded. While Helen rested was the perfect opportunity.

He led her back to her mother and father, who sat talking with another diamond couple. The second couple quickly excused themselves as he helped Helen into her chair.

"Lord Chadwick, I wonder if I could have a moment of your time. Perhaps in five minutes, out on the balcony?"

Helen's father beamed. "Of course, Your Majesty. I will be there."

Lahire made his way to the balcony. The people outside quickly got the hint that he wanted privacy and returned to the ballroom. He looked out on the city and sighed in contentment.

He was disturbed from his reverie by Shireche's voice.

"Your Majesty, I come with urgent news."

"Not now, Shireche," said Lahire, unable to keep the annoyance out of his voice. "Whatever it is can wait."

"I'm afraid it can't, Your Majesty. There is a plot on your life!"

"What?" He stood looking around the deserted balcony. "When? How?"

"A noble family from the Diamond Kingdom is in league with the terrorists. They had planned to merely act as spies, but with your magnificent coup earlier today, they have decided to take drastic action. I only found evidence of their plot this evening, and rushed to inform you. They hope to get you alone, where they will carry out their evil plans."

"Who is this traitorous family?"

"It is the Chadwick family, Your Majesty. I believe you are familiar with the father and daughter?"

He straightened his shoulders. "Impossible! Whatever evidence you have found, it is obviously a forgery. That family has my complete trust. Helen... The Chadwicks would never act against me. I won't hear another bad word said about them."

Two eyes glowed in the shadows where Shireche's voice emanated. "Are you sure, Your Majesty? Think of how they have been manipulating you, trying to get close to you."

He thought back over his encounters with them the past six months. Of course, it all made sense. He had thought meeting Helen in the gardens had been an accident; she had claimed to be unaware of the time he had the garden to himself, and her embarrassment had seemed so enticing. Her sob stories, of her father falling ill and their doctor not knowing what to do, had been so convincing. The trickery used to gain his sympathy was so obvious on reflection.

Lies. It had all been lies! Once again, he had almost been fooled. Only Shireche's constant vigilance had saved him.

"You wished to see me, Your Majesty?" Helen's father stood at the door. He smiled warmly, but Lahire saw the cold, calculating look in his eyes.

"Indeed, I did, Lord Chadwick." Lahire motioned him toward him. Once he had moved away from the doors, Lahire shouted, "Guards, to me! An assassin is present!"

Within moments, ten Heart Guard had surged onto the balcony. Six of them surrounded Lahire protectively, while the others grabbed Lord Chadwick. Fear filled the man's face.

"Your Majesty? What's going on?"

"You don't fool me, Lord Chadwick." Lahire strode forward, poking him hard in the chest. "I'm onto your plot. You and the rest of your family will join your terrorist friends in the dungeon. You will be tortured until you have revealed everything about your plot and accomplices, and then you will be executed. Take him away, and arrest his wife and daughter as well."

Lord Chadwick feebly protested as he was dragged away. "Your Majesty, please, there must be some mistake, I swear..."

Inside the hall, the guards arresting the mother and daughter caused a commotion. He turned to the guard in charge. "The ball is canceled. I want everyone removed from here within five minutes. Leave me. I will be safe here."

The guard saluted, and he and his men moved to carry out Lahire's order. From inside, he thought he heard Helen's voice screaming for Lahire to save her. He closed his eyes tightly, fighting back tears and the feeling of betrayal. His hands brushed against the ring box in his pocket. He pulled it out, opening it to view the elaborate engagement ring inside.

With a surge of anger, he threw the box into the darkness.

CHAPTER 24

James slowly opened his eyes. His head throbbed, he felt nauseous, and he was cold. He lay on some sort of hard surface that smelled like the men's toilets late Saturday night down at his local pub. As his eyes focused, he realized he was in serious trouble.

He lay in a jail cell.

He shakily pushed himself up and looked around. The cell obviously hadn't been cleaned in, well, ever, and all sorts of things that he didn't want to think about covered the floor. Against the side wall sat a small bed that didn't look much cleaner. The back wall had a tiny window in it that let in sunlight a foot above his head, while the front of the cell had a heavy wooden door, with another opening at head height. Both windows had thick metal bars over them.

He looked out the window in the door. The only thing visible was a cell opposite, although it was impossible to tell if someone was in there or not. He moved to the back wall and managed to pull himself up to look out. The building stood on the edge of a cliff. What little of the ground he could see was hundreds of yards below.

He wondered what had happened to the others. Presumably, they were in cells like his own, although he had no idea if they were close by or not.

James moved over to the window in the cell door and yelled out, "Kara? Torre?" He heard no response.

"Kara? Torre? Can you hear me?"

Heavy footsteps moved along the corridor toward him, and a gruff voice spoke. "Pipe down in there." A large Heart Guard stepped into view. His uniform looked grubby compared to the guards he had seen before, but the large club he carried suggested he wasn't someone be messed with. "One more word out of you, and I'll break your teeth."

"What about my friends? I only want to know if they're alive."

"I said shut it." The man struck the club against the bars. James took a step back in alarm. "The way I hear it, you're being shipped out of here this evening to the Heart capital. The governor wants to present you in person to the king as a surprise gift and get all sorts of rewards for heroically organizing your capture. That means we have to keep you alive. But our orders don't say anything about what other injuries you may have. And I hear outsider blood is good for all sorts of goodies. Love potions, for one. Got my eye on a girlie down in the tavern, and I might test that story out for myself, if you catch my meaning. So don't make me come in there."

James raised his arms in surrender. The guard looked at him for a moment, then spat through the window. Without a word, he turned and walked back the way he had come.

James wiped the spit off his face and dejectedly sat down on the edge of the bed.

Food was brought in several hours later. Well, *food* was a loose term for what he was given. The contents of the bowl looked like water with floating bits of fat in it.

"Eat up." The toothless guard who handed him the bowl gave him a leering grin. The guard with the club stood watching, ready if James caused any trouble.

He watched the fat and gristle bob in the bowl. "It looks... lovely."

The other guard waved his club in James's face. "You're lucky you're getting anything at all. So no more bellyaching from you."

"What about my friends? Are they being fed? Where are they?"

He didn't see it coming. One moment the toothless guard was motionless, the next he backhanded him across the face. The bowl went flying, and James crumpled to the floor.

The guard with the club stood menacingly over him. "I warned you earlier. Shut it. It looks like some people are slow learners and need to learn the hard way."

The toothless guard kicked him hard in the stomach, then stomped down hard for good measure. James curled up in the fetal position, clutching his torso. "Don't make us give you another lesson." The toothless guard gave him a grin, then both guards laughed and left the cell.

After several minutes, the pain abated enough for him to pull himself up onto the edge of the bed. He glanced over to where the bowl had landed, but it was upside down with the contents spread across the floor. It was probably for the best.

"What an unfortunate situation you find yourself in." The Cheshire Cat was perched on the ledge of the window. "Things are certainly looking bleak."

"Can you help me?" asked James hopefully.

The Cheshire Cat shook his head. "I'm afraid not. I can't do anything directly to be involved. I can talk, suggest, even hint or charm, but action isn't really my thing. I'm afraid you're on your own here."

James looked down to the floor dejectedly.

"I must say, I'm a little disappointed."

"What do you mean, disappointed?" He looked back up at the cat.

"I'd rather hoped you would last longer than you have and provide more entertainment and excitement. Instead, you had to go and be deceived by a pretty face, then get yourself drugged and put in prison. That's very tiresome, you know."

"You make it all sound like a game."

"Everything is a game, my boy. Life is a game. You just have to know how to play it. I mean, look at this land." The cat waved its paw around as if encompassing all of Wonderland. "It changed from small villages and isolated castles to huge cities and lots of people, all in a hundred and fifty years. That's exciting. Massive battles and diplomatic maneuvering to take over kingdoms without a fight, that's exciting. An outsider, feared by many for the change he can bring, running across Wonderland visiting oracles and lost kingdoms, that's exciting. A dead outsider who finds himself a foot shorter? That's boring."

"Hang on." He got painfully to his feet. "You mean you've been watching what's happening in Wonderland the whole time? Following Lahire as he took over Wonderland and enslaved everyone?"

"Watching?" The cat laughed. "My dear boy, who do you think it was who put the idea in his head in the first place? A whisper here, a subtle suggestion there, an occasional charming voice when he was being stubborn. It was all too easy. He's like a puppet, dancing to my tune."

James lunged at the cat, but grabbed only air as its body disappeared, leaving just its head. The head floated up to the center of the room, out of James's reach, and grinned down at him.

"Of course, no one is ever going to believe the word of an outsider, especially not the king, who fears all outsiders for what they can do to Wonderland."

"And what is it that outsiders can do to Wonderland?" asked James bitterly.

"I would have thought Caterpillar had told you. They change it. They bring with them ideas and possibilities. And if there's one thing the current King of Hearts fears, it's change. But you can't change anything when you're dead."

The Cheshire Cat began to fade away.

"You won't get away with this!"

The cat's grin only grew bigger, and then it was gone. James kicked his bed in frustration and paced his cell. He had to get out. He had to tell people.

* * *

By late afternoon, James had given up pacing his cell and was sitting down trying to think. Several ideas occurred to him, but he rejected all of them. He wasn't a fighter, so he couldn't overpower the guards. He didn't have the skill to pick the locks on the door, or the equipment to take out the bars in the window and climb down, or up, the outside wall. And there didn't appear to be any hidden escape tunnel that someone else had already made in his cell—he'd checked.

And more importantly, he didn't know where Kara and Torre were being held. He couldn't possibly leave without them.

He had to face facts. He was stuck.

Then, the faint but unmistakable sound of an explosion sounded off in the distance.

Feeling a faint sense of hope, he leapt to his feet. Maybe Ariston and the resistance were coming to rescue them.

His flash of hope faded as silence followed. Then, two more explosions, louder and closer, caused the bed to shake slightly. Shouts echoed from somewhere in the building, but they were some distance from his cell.

A strange sound originated from outside his window. He pulled himself up by the bars to see out as best he could.

He could see nothing.

A grappling hook suddenly arced up and latched onto the ledge of the window on the outside. He let go of the bars in surprise. By the time he had pulled himself back up, he could see the rope attached to the hook vibrating, as if someone were climbing it. A strange metal device slid into view on the rope. He soon saw a hand and finally a face he recognized outside his window.

Kara said, "James! Thank goodness, we got the right cell. Stand back from the wall. I'll have you out of there in a few moments."

"I thought you'd been captured as well!"

"Torre saved me. I'll explain more in a moment. Please, step back. I've got to take out the wall so you can get out."

He had a sudden sense of panic. "Wait! I saw this on *Mythbusters*. An explosion in a confined space like this will kill me."

Kara rolled her eyes. "I'm not going to all this effort to do something that will kill you. Trust me."

He nodded and stepped back. Kara hammered something into the wall, then disappeared from sight.

A strange humming sound radiated from the wall. To his disbelief, the stonework between the floor and the window began to crumble. After thirty seconds, it had fallen away, leaving a two-foot hole in the wall. Through the hole, he could see the rope Kara was using. She returned into view, holding onto loops of rope attached to a strange device about the size of a small plate. He recognized it from when she had been packing the backpack back in the Heart city. She held a second device that looked like a large flashlight, although it had a spike in one end—another item from her backpack.

"Come on, we don't have long. Grab a hold of this loop, and put your foot down here." She indicated two loops in the rope. He eased himself out of the hole and put his foot in the loop. Several more explosions sounded nearby. "Here we go, hold on tight."

He suddenly found that they were descending at a heart-stopping rate. With his free hand, he grabbed Kara's waist to keep himself steady. She glanced at him but said nothing. The ground at the base of the building approached much too fast, and his stomach knotted in fear. Just as he thought they would crash into the ground, their descent slowed dramatically. They finally stopped a foot or so above the ground.

Once James and Kara had stepped off the loops, Kara pulled a lever on the device connected to the rope, releasing it. She then carried the machine over to a second rope attached to the top of the cliff.

The process of descending was repeated, although the distance down the cliff was much further than the tower. He tried not to think about how he was holding Kara close, and how much he enjoyed holding her close, and instead focused on trying not to fall off.

After a minute of descent, they reached the bottom of the cliff safely.

"Now what?"

"Now, we hope our ride has survived and arrives here in the next minute or two."

"How did you manage to escape from the prison?"

"We never came here. Torre wasn't affected by the drug Lady Baultin put in the wine. Something about poison-immunity training from the Castle Brigade; he didn't go into it. He played along with being drugged so he could find out what was going on. When we were briefly left alone, he grabbed me and escaped. He tried to go back for you, but the Heart Guard were already there. He was only able to get our gear from our rooms.

"We managed to steal a ride and warned Ariston as soon as we could. His people evacuated the farmhouse before the Heart Guard arrived. We convinced him to help us rescue you when we pointed out it could be a distraction to help him to rescue the King and Queen of Clubs. There are only three of us here. The rest of them are going after the king and queen. Torre insisted on leading the distraction at the front of the jail. I hope he's all right."

"I hope so, too. Thanks for coming to get me."

Kara gave him a smile. She looked like she was about to say something, then looked away quickly. "It's nothing. You rescued us earlier, remember? We had to repay the favor. Besides, Torre was rather upset that you had been caught. It was all I could do to stop him from launching a frontal assault on this place by himself."

The sound of a ship approaching gradually got louder, followed by a Heart ship coming into view. James recognized it as the ship they had stolen from the guards in the White Kingdom. It looked like the front of the ship had been repaired, but it had also been altered. Instead of the usual rounded front, a large number of tubes had been attached. They reminded him of a bank of rocket tubes.

The ship flew in fast and settled down twenty yards from the face of the cliff.

"Come on." Kara ran toward the ship. He followed. The side door opened, and a man he didn't recognize waved for them to hurry. Next to the man lay several muskets and a number of bundles of what James recognized as explosives. As soon as they were on board, the ship took to the air.

James sat down heavily on one of the benches. "Thanks, guys. I thought it was all over."

The man in the cabin nodded and sat down next to the door. Kara sat on the bench opposite James.

Torre called back from the cockpit. "Bernard, can you take over?"

"Sure." The man stood and moved to the front.

Torre entered the cabin. He carried the sword James had retrieved from the White Kingdom. He stopped in front of Kara. "I need you to witness this."

She looked confused. "Witness what?"

Ignoring her question, he turned to James and handed him the White Kingdom sword.

James took it awkwardly. "Thank you for coming back for me. I owe you my life. Again."

Torre knelt on one knee in front of James and bowed his head as he placed the tips of his fingers to his forehead. Kara gasped.

"What—" began James.

"I pledge my life to you as a member of the Castle Brigade. Where you walk, I walk. Where you fight, I fight. Your enemies are my enemies. No matter what, I will stand by your side and do all I can to protect you. Even if it should cost me my own life. This, I so swear."

He looked at Torre with confusion. "Torre? What's going on?"

Torre stood. "You hold the sword of the White Kingdom. It was given to you freely by the ruler of the White Kingdom, which makes you the new ruler. The Red Kingdom is no more, and the sword of the Red Kingdom is destroyed. The war of the Island Kingdoms is over. You are now the ruler of the reunited Islands Kingdom. The Castle Brigade was originally made to protect the life of the King of the Islands Kingdom, many centuries ago. I pledge my services to you."

"You don't have to do this—"

"It isn't a matter of choice. We are what we are. I told you about the vision I had when I was unconscious on the battlefield. The Red King told me that I had to escape, I had to survive. But he also told me the reason. He said I had to survive because one day there would be a new king, one that would rebuild the kingdom. I had to live so I could protect the new king."

He tried to wrap his head around what Torre was saying. "How long have you thought this?"

Torre bowed his head. "I apologize, Your Majesty. I had a suspicion after we encountered Taxard, when I moved to intercept Taxard's attack on you. That move can only be used when a Castle Brigade member is protecting their king, but I didn't want to believe it. It was after I was unaffected by the drug Lady Baultin put in the drink that I came to realize I couldn't deny the truth. You are my king. I apologize for my failure to protect you and understand if you wish to dismiss me from your service. "

"Failure? You saved Kara. And the two of you came to save me. How can that be a failure?"

"My first duty is to you, Your Majesty. I should never have left you behind."

James shook his head. "I don't know what to make of any of this. What you're saying is unbelievable. I can't be a king. I've never even wanted to be a king."

"Whether you wanted it or not, you are now the King of the Islands Kingdom. My entire life has been devoted to protecting the king. I failed in that duty once. I won't do so again."

James noticed a burning sensation on his left bicep. The burning suddenly became intense, making him wince in pain, before fading away.

"What on earth..." He grabbed at his arm, trying to see if something was biting or stinging him.

Kara's expression had been one of stunned silence as Torre made his announcement, but she looked even more shocked at James's reaction to his arm. "It's your mark. Take off your jacket, and look at your arm."

He took off his soiled suit jacket and rolled up the sleeve of his shirt. His tattoo became visible, but it wasn't the tattoo he was familiar with.

Instead of the two knights crossed, it depicted red and white King chess pieces crossed, exactly like the pictures he had seen in Gryphon's book.

He didn't know what to say. Him, a king? It had to be a misunderstanding of some sort. He couldn't possibly be a king. Until a week ago, he had thought Wonderland was a fictional place in a children's storybook. Telling him he was a king of Wonderland had to be some sort of joke.

He looked at Torre. With fear, dread, and shock, he realized Torre would never joke about something like that.

After opening and closing his mouth several times, he finally found his voice.

"Thank you." He stopped, not sure what else to say as he looked between Kara and Torre. Kara's expression had turned unreadable, while Torre didn't look surprised in the slightest.

Finally, he managed to find his voice. "I don't want this to come between any of us. You're both my friends, and I don't want that to change. I owe you my life."

Torre answered, "Of course, Your Majesty."

"And you can cut that 'majesty' bit out right away." James gave him a smile.

Torre returned his smile. "As you command, Your Majesty."

CHAPTER 25

"Then it grinned some more and disappeared."

The others sat back after listening to his description of his conversation with the Cheshire Cat. Torre scowled. Kara looked surprised.

Ariston had a thoughtful expression. "So, this cat has manipulated Lahire into doing everything he's done to Wonderland? Invading and taking control of the other kingdoms, sending people off to work in mines and factories, it was all the work of this Cheshire Cat?"

James nodded. "That's what the cat claimed. It didn't have any reason to lie to me, since it thought I was going to be taken away and executed. But I don't know how much it can be trusted."

Kara shook her head. "I've heard tales about the cat from my father. Never anything positive, it was always a trickster. But the stories also said it tended to be reclusive, and rarely interacted with people."

James shrugged. "It could be another change that Alice's visit caused? The cat decided to interact more with the rest of the world."

"And invade the whole of Wonderland while doing so," said Torre. James nodded.

Torre continued, "So, now we know the real power behind the throne. We just need a way to track it down, and capture or eliminate it."

Ariston shook his head slowly. "That won't change anything. The cat might have influenced Lahire, but with the cat gone, he will still be in his current position. I doubt he's going to change all his policies to free the other kingdoms or support the people."

"So what do you suggest?" asked Kara.

Ariston shrugged. "I don't know."

Thoughts and images swirled in James's mind, snippets of what he had seen and heard since he had come to Wonderland.

Kara noticed his thoughtful expression. "What is it?"

"I'm thinking back to what Caterpillar said to Torre. 'Find the real King of Hearts and restore him to the throne.' Those were Caterpillar's words."

Torre shrugged. "So? He also said I'd find the assassin if we did that, but we found Taxard when we were escaping the White Kingdom."

James looked at Kara. "Gryphon said Lahire took over as king permanently when his father was on his deathbed, but he didn't say anything about when his father died. When Torre asked about the *real* King of Hearts, Caterpillar said a son succeeds his father once the father is dead."

Kara scrunched her face up in thought. "Well, Lahire's father stepped back from the throne when the queen was killed, and he became ill soon after. I don't know of the details after that. It was a huge time of mourning, and the people in the kingdom acted as if they had lost both the king and the queen. Lahire was seen as the new light that would lead the kingdom into a bright future. Everyone thought he was putting on a brave face after losing so much."

Ariston nodded. "I never heard of a funeral for Lahire's father. With all the invasions and other events that took place soon after Lahire came into power, it wasn't something anyone thought about. We had too many other things on our mind."

James looked around. "Then he might still be alive."

Kara looked doubtful. "It's a weak premise on which to base a plan."

"Caterpillar was right about the wine. That was how Lady Baultin drugged us. And he did say we'd find something if we went to the White Kingdom."

"I guess…" It was Kara's turn to look thoughtful.

"You've got an idea?"

"Maybe. We've been gathering intelligence on the castle for years from servants willing to spy for us, hoping the information would be useful one day. The castle itself is heavily guarded, but there is one tower in the northeast corner that only Lahire and a single maid are allowed in. Not even guards are allowed in, on pain of death. The maid lives in rooms at the base of the tower and isn't allowed to leave or see anyone. She even had her tongue cut out when she was given the job. We had no idea what was up there, but if Lahire's father is alive anywhere, he would be up there."

"That's it. We need to go there."

"And do what?" asked Torre.

"If we can find the old king and rescue him, Lahire can be removed from power. Right?"

"If the old king is deemed fit to rule, some of the nobles in the Heart Kingdom might be willing to support you," said Ariston. "But you would still need to gain the support of the Heart Guard. Otherwise, Lahire would simply order them to throw you and the real king in prison."

James looked at Kara. "You said only Lahire visits the tower. How often does he do so?"

"Once a week. Every Tuesday night at seven o'clock, without fail. He's even left feasts and balls to make the trip."

James tried to remember what day it had been when he had arrived in Wonderland, and how long he had been here. Then he realized he didn't even know if Wonderland days were the same as the ones he was used to. "What day is it today, and how far away is that?"

Ariston answered, "It's Sunday today. So we have two days."

"And it never varies?"

Kara shook her head. "Never."

James smiled as he looked around the table. "Don't you see? Since he's alone when he visits, it would be the perfect time to ambush him. If we have Lahire as well as his father, he can't order his men to attack without risking injury to himself."

Ariston nodded slowly. The look on his face suggested he was impressed with James's idea.

Kara shook her head again. "We'd never get to it. Between the tower and the main area of the castle are the Heart Guard barracks, training grounds, and main port."

"Do Heart ships land in the castle itself?"

"Of course. Near the barracks."

James smiled again. "We have the Heart ship we stole in the White Kingdom. It will let us get to the castle without being stopped."

"You'll need papers for the ship to indicate why you've landed," said Ariston. "I can organize that. We're well-practiced in forging papers. They won't pass a detailed inspection, but they should be good enough to get you inside."

"How about a distraction outside the castle? To take men and attention away from what's going on inside?" He turned to Kara. "Do you think Gryphon and the resistance would be able to do that?"

"Sure. We've got a few ideas on various locations we could hit to cause a lot of damage. We just never had a reason to, since Lahire would have taken it out on the citizens."

"I could send several men with you," said Ariston. "They could provide distractions at other points within the castle to give you a clear run at the tower."

Kara chimed in, "And I could rig something up so the ship explodes shortly after we land. We won't be able to leave on it anyway, and an explosion would cause more chaos."

James nodded. "So, that's it. With all the distractions going on, with any luck, the guards won't be watching the tower too closely. We get into the tower and wait for Lahire to arrive. Even if he's delayed because of the commotion, he's sure to go to the tower sometime that evening."

Torre cracked his knuckles. "And we'll be waiting for him."

* * *

James found Kara sitting on the fence outside the shed the resistance called their 'headquarters' and staring at the sky. He moved to stand beside her.

"Mind if I join you?"

Kara glanced over, then returned to staring at the stars.

"The Club King and Queen loved you."

He pulled a face. "Yeah, that was awkward. I didn't know how to act around them. It's not like I've ever met a real king or queen. Then, they kept calling me 'Your Majesty' and acting like I was like them."

"You are. Your mark says so."

"But it's only a mark on my arm. How can it say whether I'm a king or not? I'm just an IT consultant who works for a crappy boss in a job he really hates."

Kara turned to look at him. "It's how Wonderland works. It's like Torre described. You were given the Kingdom sword. Therefore, you became King. Your mark changed when it was officially recognized. It still doesn't explain why you have a mark in the first place, though."

He gave her an embarrassed smile. "Actually, Caterpillar explained that to me. He said my parents were from Wonderland—generals from the Red and White Kingdoms who escaped before Lahire's final invasion. White Rabbit knew them both and helped them escape. My father died protecting my mother when she escaped to my world. She died when she gave birth to me. Apparently, even Melvin, my friend who Taxard murdered, was from Wonderland. I had no idea about any of it."

Kara touched his arm. "I'm sorry."

He smiled sadly. "It's okay. It's hard to mourn people you've never met. I'm sorry I didn't say something sooner. It took a while to process." Glancing at the night sky, he tried to pluck up the courage to tell her how he felt. "I never got a chance to say it, but I thought you looked amazing in that dress."

Kara blushed. "You did?"

He nodded. "You were stunning."

"What about Lady Joyce Baultin? You couldn't take your eyes off her earlier."

He winced. "Okay, I admit she seemed nice at first. But she was nothing compared to you at the dinner. She might as well not have been there."

Kara looked happy with the answer. He stepped up onto the fence, staring into her eyes for a moment, then moved to kiss her. Kara leaned forward to meet him, then abruptly pulled away and jumped down so the fence was between them.

"What is it?"

Kara looked back at him. He couldn't read the expression on her face. "It won't work. It can't work. You're from the Otherworld. And you're a king. The Club Kingdom is about to be invaded. We have a crazy plan to kidnap Lahire and hopefully find his father alive. It's too complicated."

"It doesn't have to be complicated. I have feelings for you. You seem to have feelings for me. How hard can it be?"

Tears ran down Kara's face. "But what about when this is over? If we win, then what? You'll run off and be king, or run back to your own world. Either way, you'll leave, just like everyone else."

James shook his head and began to protest, but Kara ran through the gate and back to the shed. He watched her go, wanting to run after her, but knowing it wasn't the right time. He leaned back against the fence and stared at the night sky.

CHAPTER 26

The final repairs to the Heart ship took the rest of the night, but by morning, the vessel had been restored and showed no signs of ever having been damaged. Kara had taken charge of the repairs, ignoring him when he returned inside, so he had left her alone to get on with her work.

Ariston arranged for Heart Guard uniforms to be acquired for their group. It was a process made both more difficult and easier with almost the entire Heart Guard garrison combing the city looking for them. After making sure everyone's uniforms fit properly, they loaded the ship with supplies. Four of Ariston's men had volunteered to join the trip to the castle, and after some final quiet words with them, Ariston pulled James aside.

"They're good men. They'll do everything they can to ensure the mission is a success, including give their lives. I place them in your care."

He tried to hide his nervousness. "I hope I can bring them all back safely."

Ariston shook his hand, clasping his shoulder with his other hand. "We're counting on you. Take care of Lahire, and you not only save the Club Kingdom, but all of Wonderland."

James nodded, feeling the weight of responsibility he was being handed.

Kara's raised voice near the ship caught his attention.

"Where the hell do you think you're going?"

She stood in front of White Rabbit, stopping him from boarding the ship.

"I'm coming with you. You're going to need all the help you can get. Seven people against a castle full of guards doesn't sound like good odds."

"And eight is any better? How do we know you won't sell us out to someone offering you a large sum of cash? You've never given a damn about fighting Lahire in the past, unless someone gave you a lot of money first."

White Rabbit's expression flickered, but he didn't rise to the bait. "For what it's worth, I'm not going to betray you. You have my word."

"Your word? And how exactly can I trust your word?"

James stepped up. "An extra person who can fight would be useful. And he is good at sneaking around."

Kara looked at James, then let out a sigh of exasperation and stormed into the ship.

He looked at White Rabbit apologetically. "Thanks for your help. I appreciate it."

White Rabbit shrugged and boarded without further comment. James shook his head. The trip was going to be a blast.

With everyone on board, the door was sealed. Torre piloted the ship out of the shed and into the air toward the Heart Kingdom.

They made good time. By late morning the next day, the Heart capital was visible on the horizon. To his relief, Kara and White Rabbit had managed to avoid any further fights during the trip, with Kara remaining in the engine room of the ship for almost the entire journey.

Kara directed Torre to land on the outskirts of the city in an area that reminded James of a bomb crater.

"It was, in a way," said Kara, when he asked about it. "This area used to be a fireworks factory, making fireworks solely for Lahire's celebratory events. They had an accident a few years ago, and the whole place blew up. It took out all the nearby houses, as you can see. Not many people come here these days, which is handy for us. We can keep the ship out of sight until later."

"Is it far to the hideout from here?"

"A bit under an hour. We'll be back in plenty of time."

Ariston's men were to stay behind to deal with any Heart Guard who investigated. To James's surprise, White Rabbit offered to stay behind as well. Following Kara, James and Torre set off into the city.

As she had done the first night they met, Kara led them quickly through a maze of streets. He soon lost track of where they were, relying on Kara knowing the way. After they had been walking for twenty minutes, she suddenly stopped.

He almost ran into her, but managed to stop in time. "What is it?"

"Something's wrong."

"What?"

"I'm not sure. Keep walking."

Kara led them around the corner, then stopped again. She spoke in a hushed tone.

"I think the house has been raided. We have a system where the homeowners put a yellow towel in their window if they are unable to help us for whatever reason, or a white towel to indicate all is fine. The house has no towel up."

"You don't think it just fell down?"

Kara rolled her eyes. "Now, why didn't I think of that? Of course not. Come on. Let's go to the next house."

She led them further into the city. It was the same story at the next house, with no towel visible. Kara decided to lead them to a third house. He noticed her pick up speed, and she appeared to be upset. After she turned the next corner, she stopped. He realized she was trying not to cry.

"What's wrong?"

Kara wiped away a tear that had escaped the corner of her eye. "A red towel in the window."

"Red is bad?"

Kara nodded. "It means, 'Danger. Stay away.' Lahire probably knows about the tunnels by now. He's probably raided the hideout."

"Is there another meeting location? Another place we could go to try and contact them, see if they're all right?"

Torre stepped forward. "It's too dangerous. If Lahire found the base of the resistance, he probably has all their locations under surveillance."

James shook his head. "We don't have a choice. We need the help of the resistance to do this. Without them, the plan won't work." He turned to Kara. "Is there anywhere else we could look?"

Kara shrugged. "Maybe. It's a long shot, but there's a pub we used a few years ago. We stopped after Lahire started poking around there. Gryphon knew the owner. He could be hiding there."

"Let's check it out."

They made their way through the city to what James could only call the slums. The streets were narrower, garbage lay everywhere, and the houses were small, in poor repair, and looked like they each contained several families. People watched them from windows or in doorways as they passed, but no one approached or spoke with them.

He looked at Kara in concern. "Are we safe here?"

"They're not going to mug or kill us, if that's what you're asking. This is a poor area of the city, but, for the most part, these people are honest individuals. They refused to work in the factories Lahire built and tried to make their own way in life. These are the common people that Lahire doesn't want to know about and doesn't care about. There are some streets around here I wouldn't go near at night, but during the day we'll be fine."

"And the meeting place is in here?"

"Over there." Kara indicated a large building at the end of the street.

They entered the pub. James had expected it to be as rough, rundown, and filthy inside as the streets had been, but he was pleasantly surprised. The inside of the pub looked old and worn, and the lighting level was dim at best, but the owner of the pub obviously took pride in his business.

Kara led them up to the bar. The barkeep stared at Kara without expression.

"I'm looking for a special drink," said Kara.

"What you see is what we have."

"Are you sure you don't have something special out back? Something a bit stronger than usual?"

"I might. What are you looking for?"

"Something old. At least a century old."

"Let me go check." The barkeep stepped through a door at the side of the bar. He returned after half a minute.

"Looks like I do have something out back. I put out a few options. Have a look for yourself." He motioned toward the door. They went through with Kara leading the way.

The door opened into a narrow, dimly lit corridor with a closed door at the end. The room behind the door was dark. The limited light from the corridor illuminated the edge of a table, but little else.

"We're friends," said Kara to the darkness. A match was struck, revealing Gryphon sitting heavily in a chair behind the table, a gun not unlike the one Kara had used held unsteadily in his hand. He looked badly injured.

"Gryphon!" Kara rushed over to him as he put the gun down on the table. He gave her a half smile and lit the lamp on the table. A number of empty spirits bottles sat on the table.

He spoke quietly. "I'm glad to see you're alive. Both of you. I knew if anyone could survive going to Tulgey Wood, it would be you."

Kara fussed over his wounds. "What happened? Have you seen a doctor? I can go and get help—"

Gryphon waved his hand. "I've already seen a doctor. It looks worse than it is. I'll be fine, don't worry. Did you find him? Did you find Caterpillar?"

Kara nodded. "We did. And we found the White Kingdom. We have a plan to deal with Lahire. We have a chance to stop him."

Gryphon leaned back, a look of satisfaction on his face. "That's good. That's good to hear."

James stepped forward. "We need help. We need a distraction in the city, one large enough to get a lot of Heart Guard out of the castle. Is that possible? Do you have many people left?"

Gryphon gave them a grin. "There are still a few of us left. We can create a distraction; don't you worry about that. Tell me a time, and it will happen."

"Six o'clock tonight. And it needs to be big."

Gryphon chuckled. "Don't worry. I've been planning something the last day or so that would be perfect. It will be big."

He was silent for a moment, then he reached out and gripped Kara's hand. "Kara, I'm sorry. I'm so sorry."

"Don't be silly. You don't have anything to be sorry about. I'm the one who needs to apologize. If I'd been here, I could have—"

"It's your father."

"What about my father?" The fear in Kara's voice was obvious.

"They somehow found out he was involved with the resistance. They rounded him up, along with most of our allies in the city."

Kara grabbed Gryphon's arm. "Is he alive? Is my father alive?"

"For now. They've started executing members of the resistance and collaborators, but they haven't executed him yet."

Kara turned to James. "We have to rescue him. We have to get him out." He could see she fought to hold back tears.

"We will." He put his hands on her shoulders and forced her to look at him. "Don't worry, we'll save him. I promise."

She nodded silently, unwilling to look him in the eyes.

"You'd better go," said Gryphon. "It's too dangerous here. And I need to make some preparations."

Kara gave Gryphon a hug. A wince of pain crossed Gryphon's face. Once she let him go, he handed her the pistol.

"Take this."

Kara shook her head. "It's yours. I made it for you."

He pushed it into her hands. "I won't need it this time. I'd rather you had it when you go into the castle."

She took it without further protest, then quickly left the room. James turned to follow.

"James…"

He looked back at Gryphon. "Look after her. After I've gone, make sure she's all right."

James looked into Gryphon's eyes. "I will, always."

Gryphon bowed his head, and James left, followed by Torre.

CHAPTER 27

The trip back to the ship was uneventful. Several times, they passed Heart Guard patrols, but the guards appeared to be more interested in acting as a show of force than looking for anyone, and they ignored the group.

Kara didn't speak for most of the trip back. After they had been walking for fifteen minutes, James tried to break the silence.

"We'll rescue him. He'll be all right."

"I should never have left him. He's an old man and not the most sensible at the best of times. He probably didn't realize what was happening until it was too late. God knows how they treated him. He could be dead for all I know. Just because they haven't executed him, doesn't mean he isn't dead. He might have died from their mistreatment."

"He's tougher than that. We will get him out. I promise."

"You promise? You promise?" Kara turned on him, stabbing her finger into his chest. "It's because of you that he's been taken."

"What?" He stepped back, surprised at her sudden attack.

"If you'd never turned up, I would have been with him. He'd be safe. It's your fault he's in prison!"

"He was always a target," said Torre. "As long as you were with the resistance, he was always in danger."

Kara looked as if she was about to either start throwing punches or burst into tears. After a moment of indecision, she chose a third option, turning abruptly and resuming the trip at a much faster pace.

James had to almost jog to keep up with her, not willing to risk letting her out of his sight in case they became lost in the maze of streets.

The ship was where they had left it. White Rabbit sat in the doorway.

"How did it go?"

"Piss off." Kara pushed past him, moving to the engine room of the ship and closing the door.

White Rabbit looked questioningly at James.

"The news isn't good. The resistance has basically been destroyed in the city. A few made it out, but not many. On the plus side, Gryphon is still alive, and he has promised the distraction we need."

White Rabbit raised an eyebrow. "And the walking thunderstorm?"

He gave him a hard look. "Her father has been captured."

White Rabbit's face softened. "It always hits you hard when Lahire captures someone you care about."

"We're going to rescue him when we go to the castle."

White Rabbit shook his head. "Impossible. We can't let anything distract us from our main goal. We don't want to be taking a non-combatant with us when we're moving through the castle, especially an old man. To be honest, he'd be safer where he is until this is all over, one way or the other."

"I don't think we have a choice," said Torre. "Kara won't agree to anything that doesn't include saving her father."

James nodded in agreement. "Kara will try to rescue her father, whether we help her or not. So I'm altering the plans to include getting him out. Where are the castle floor plans Kara drew?"

White Rabbit slowly shook his head again in obvious disagreement. "We're only going to get one chance at this. I hope you know what you're doing."

* * *

It was a frantic two hours of planning, but James was finally confident that the new plans he had created would work. Kara had softened a little by the time he was ready to tell her the changes and even rejoined the group while they waited. However, she remained uncommunicative, and he didn't want to risk upsetting her further by pushing the issue.

He spent most of the remaining time talking with Torre and trying to learn everything he could about the Red and White Kingdoms.

Constant war was the theme of their history, but he learned the two kingdoms hadn't always been actively fighting each other. There had been long periods of tense posturing, broken up by brief skirmishes on one or more of the border islands. Active warfare between the two kingdoms had been rare.

As six o'clock arrived, an enormous explosion could be heard off in the distance, large enough that they felt it through the base of the ship. Several smaller explosions followed in quick succession. Stepping out, they saw a huge smoke cloud rising into the air.

Kara broke her silence, amazement in her voice. "That was the ammunitions factory! We always talked about targeting it, but never did for fear of the level of retaliation Lahire would inflict on the people. Plus, the place was heavily defended, with guards everywhere. Attacking it would have been suicide…"

Kara's voice trailed off, and she put her hand on the pistol Gryphon had given her. James said nothing, remembering Gryphon's final words to him.

"Gryphon has sacrificed everything to give us this chance," said Torre. "We must not waste it."

James looked up. "He's right. It's time to move."

Everyone returned to the ship. Torre carefully piloted it into the air and turned toward the Heart castle.

He hadn't seen the castle before, as it had been too dark when they had fled on the *Nighthawk*. In the evening light, he could see the huge building in full detail.

It was impressive, towering over the surrounding buildings. The original structure may have once been stone, but it had been added to over the years with huge metal sections built on and up from the original. The castle had two walls, an older inner wall and a much newer wall several hundred yards out from the castle. The space between the walls showed signs of once being part of the city, but the buildings had all been demolished and removed.

They flew over the outer structures of the castle until the Heart Guard barracks became visible. Next to the large buildings was a landing area large enough for five ships the size of theirs. Two ships were currently on the ground. Many guards could be seen running between the buildings of the barracks, probably moving to respond to the explosion at the ammunitions factory.

James looked at Kara. "You've sabotaged the engines?"

She nodded. "The pressure will continue to build once we land. It should be between ten and fifteen minutes before it explodes."

Torre brought the ship in to land. As soon as the ship was stationary, White Rabbit opened the door and led them out. James and Torre lifted the box, supposedly full of equipment to be delivered to the castle lab but actually containing their sabotage supplies, and followed.

A harassed-looking guard hurried over. "Order papers." White Rabbit handed over the forged papers. The guard barely glanced at them before adding them to the folder he carried. "Fine, fine. Take the shipment through to the labs, then report to the sergeant for deployment to the city. You'll be helping secure the site of the terrorist attack."

"Sir." White Rabbit saluted the guard, who was already running to deal with his next crisis.

James and Torres carried the box through the chaos with White Rabbit leading as if they were on an urgent mission with no time for distractions. Once out of sight of the landing area, they diverted course toward the castle. Stepping inside, they found an unoccupied room and closed the door.

James opened the box and handed out the contents. Two of the Club Kingdom rebels took the explosive packages, as Kara, James, and Torre took the wrapped bundles holding their personal weapons.

James looked at the men with the explosives.

"Be careful. Plant the explosives, but don't take any risks. You know what you have to do."

The two men saluted him. "We won't let you down, Your Majesty. For the Club Kingdom!"

James nodded awkwardly, then turned to Kara. "Let's go get your father."

CHAPTER 28

Kara led the group from the room. To James's relief, no one paid them any attention as they moved through the castle. Servants moved to the opposite side of the corridor as they walked past, while the few other guards they encountered didn't give them a second glance.

Kara led them to an ominous-looking door. "The dungeons are at the bottom of these stairs."

White Rabbit moved to the front. "I'll do the talking. On my signal, we hit them hard and fast. Try not to get any blood on your disguises."

He opened the door. James moved to the rear of the group and pulled the door closed behind them.

The stairs were wide, but unlike the rest of the castle, the illumination was poor. The smell wasn't pleasant, reminding James of his brief time in the prison in the Club Kingdom, and the sound of people moaning and sobbing echoed in the distance. They descended in silence.

In the room at the bottom of the stairs, four guards sat around a table playing a game. One of them looked up as the group entered.

"What do you want?" he asked gruffly.

"Prisoner transfer," answered White Rabbit.

"Ain't heard about no prisoner transfer. Where's your paperwork?"

"I've got it right here." White Rabbit took two steps forward, then lunged, drawing his sword to strike with the pummel at the man who had been talking. Torre and the remaining two men Ariston had given them also leapt forward as Kara covered the exits with her gun. James stood back, feeling helpless.

It was over almost as soon as it had begun. One of the guards managed a brief yelp, but in moments all four of the guards were beaten unconscious.

"Here." White Rabbit pulled a set of keys off the wall and handed them to Kara. She hurried forward, pausing to look in each cell as she passed. James and the rest, wary of trouble, followed at a slower pace.

The dungeon was huge with many branching corridors. Unlike the prison James had been held in, the castle cells had metal bars for the front walls instead of stone and a wooden door. Every cell was occupied; a mixture of men in rags, women in what had once been fine clothes, and all manner of people in between filled them. Most were silent, but they did pass one young woman who sobbed inconsolably in a fine purple dress. No one looked their direction as they searched for Kara's father, with most flinching away to the far corner of their cells as they drew near.

James was horrified by what he saw. "My God, what is Lahire doing to these people?"

"Torture, mainly," answered White Rabbit quietly. "Lahire throws anyone he feels threatened by into his dungeons. Slave, commoner, or noble, it doesn't matter to him. They will be tortured, supposedly to extract details on what they have been doing and who they are working with, then executed. Some people are lucky and only stay here a short time. Others can be here for months, or even years."

A side corridor to the left caught James's attention. Unlike the other paths so far, it had only a single wooden door with a small window at the end. Almost dreading what he would find, he turned down the corridor and looked inside.

As he had feared, it was a torture room. Traces of dried blood were visible on the walls and floor, and hideous torture devices hung on pegs and racks. A figure lying unrestrained on the table in the center of the room drew his attention.

It was Taxard. At least, it looked like Taxard. He had been stripped of his clothes, revealing a metal covering over his body. The damaged arm was present, but in addition the legs were bowed and buckled, and a large gash ran through the center of the torso. Then, he noticed the head.

The mask had been removed and half the top of the head crudely cut off to reveal what looked like a human brain. Several metal rods had been pushed into the brain, causing a strange blue liquid to drip onto the table and flow off the side onto the floor. He could see cogs and gears whirring within the exposed part of Taxard's head.

James tried the door. It was unlocked. He opened it and slowly stepped forward, horrified by what he saw on the table, but unable to look away. As he got closer, he realized Taxard's eyes were in constant motion, flicking around in all directions. One of the eyes rotated to stare at him, then the head jerkily turned to face him.

James stumbled back from the table in shock, pulling the door closed behind him.

Kara's voice carried to him. "Father! You're alive!"

He turned and hurried to catch up, trying to put what he had seen out of his mind.

Kara was fumbling at a cell door as he caught up with her and the others. Hatter sat in the middle of the floor, rocking back and forth. He muttered to himself constantly with a far-off expression in his eyes. As he moved closer, James finally made out what he was saying.

"Why is a raven like a writing desk? Why is a raven like a writing desk? Why is a raven like a writing desk?"

Kara finally found the right key and threw open the door. "Father? Father, it's me." She knelt down in front of Hatter and gently touched the side of his face. He didn't seem to notice, simply repeating his phrase over and over as he rocked.

"We can't move him like this," warned White Rabbit from the doorway. "If he can't walk out, we're going to have to leave him here until we're done."

"Why is a raven like a writing desk? Why is a raven like a writing desk?"

"Because they both have inky quills," said James.

Kara looked at him in confusion. Hatter ignored him.

"What? It's an answer I read on *Wikipedia* once."

Kara turned back to her father as he rocked. "Because they're both covered in fur and go moo." It was James's turn to look confused. She noticed his expression. "It's something he would tell me when I was young."

Hatter stopped his rocking and lifted his head to focus on Kara.

"Kara? Is that you?"

"Yes, Father." She hugged him tightly. "I was so worried when I heard you'd been captured. Are you all right? Did they hurt you?"

"I'm fine. But what are you doing here? It's not safe."

"Rescuing you, silly." Kara let go of him and wiped a tear from her cheek.

White Rabbit looked around in concern. "We're on a time limit here. We need to move."

Something thudded in the distance.

"That was the ship," said Torre. "If we want to take advantage of the distraction, we need to go now."

Kara nodded and turned back to the Hatter. "We're going to get you out of here, Father. Can you walk?"

"I think so." Hatter gave his hands to Kara, and she helped lift him to his feet. Hatter noticed everyone else for the first time. "Kara, look out! Heart Guard!"

"No, Father, it's okay. These are my friends." She indicated Ariston's two men, who had moved to stand in the doorway of the cell. "These two will get you out of the castle. Just pretend that they're normal guards taking you somewhere. I'll come find you after we're finished here."

James turned to leave. He barely had a chance to notice the figure moving impossibly fast toward him when he was suddenly knocked back a step, and Torre was standing in front of him. Torre met the attack, blocking the two blades with his rifle.

The masked face of Taxard stared back at Torre, as if mocking him. "Hello again. Miss me?"

"You!" James couldn't keep the shock from his voice. "But I saw you on the table!"

"Ah, so you've seen my little pet. I thought I was only coming down here to have a little fun with my toy. Imagine my surprise when I found a group of rats scurrying around. No matter, I'll soon exterminate you."

Torre gritted his teeth. "I don't know how you survived the first time, but this time I'll kill you with my own hands."

Taxard laughed. Torre roared in anger and swung his rifle, but the automaton sidestepped and again moved toward James. White Rabbit leapt to his defense as James ducked back.

"My, protective of the outsider, aren't we?" Taxard effortlessly avoided the blows from White Rabbit and the turning Torre.

"You'll pay for everything you've done," said White Rabbit, then grunted in pain as one of Taxard's knives sliced his arm. Kara brought her gun up to shoot, but Taxard darted around so she was unable to get a clear shot. Ariston's men moved to flank the assassin, only to fall to quick slashes from Taxard's blades.

James drew his sword and moved forward, hoping to provide a distraction for one of the others if nothing else. Without warning, Taxard was in front of him, swinging his blade at James's neck. Again, Torre managed to step between him and Taxard, blocking the blow and knocking James back from the fight.

Taxard sneered at Torre. "I killed hundreds of your kind when we smashed your kingdom, but none were as pathetic as your king. He begged for his life before I killed him, like a little baby. And his precious Castle Brigade wasn't even there to save him."

"Shut up and *die!*" Torre launched a flurry of blows. Taxard batted them away effortlessly. White Rabbit threw several knives at Taxard, but they bounced off his body and clattered to the ground.

"Is that the best you've got? I'm disappointed. I thought you'd all be much more of a challenge. Oh, well, time to end this."

Taxard ducked low, avoiding Torre's attack as he pivoted to sweep Torre's legs out from under him. As Torre fell, Taxard launched himself toward White Rabbit, neatly avoiding his attempt at defense and slashing him in the chest.

Taxard continued his movement toward James. Kara screamed as he frantically tried to bring his sword up to block the attack, but even as he did, he knew he would never be able to protect himself.

He was going to die.

Time slowed for James as the blade moved toward him, Taxard's certainty of triumph clear in his eyes. Then, Taxard's eyes registered shock. Time sped up again as a figure flew itself past James and crashed into Taxard.

Staggering back, he realized the second Taxard, the one he had seen lying on the table, had saved him.

"I. AM. TAXARD," buzzed the damaged Taxard, as it struggled with the new Taxard. James took several steps back. Torre got to his feet, and in one smooth movement, raised his rifle and fired at the two automatons. The ball of fire struck with a direct hit.

James looked away in time to shield his face from the explosion of stone and metal fragments. The new Taxard was unmoving when he turned back, its head and the upper third of its body gone. The damaged Taxard had lost most of its chest and other arm, but the head full of clockwork and gears turned unsteadily to stare at the group.

"I. Survived. I. Am. Taxard." Its head then drooped, and it stopped moving.

James took a step toward the two bodies.

"Stand back." Torre reloaded the rifle. James moved back and looked away as Torre fired the second shot. When the dust settled, both Taxards had been blown to a pile of broken mechanical parts.

A groan of pain reminded James that White Rabbit had been injured. He lay on the ground to one side. James knelt beside him. "How bad is it? Can you walk?"

White Rabbit pushed his hand away and clenched his teeth. "I'll survive. I've had worse."

He gave White Rabbit a nervous smile. "I thought you said no blood on the uniform?"

White Rabbit grimaced at him. "Plans change."

"Is it safe now?" Hatter was kneeling in the middle of his cell with his hands over his ears and his eyes squeezed tightly shut. Kara moved over to him and gently lifted his hands away from his ears.

"It's safe now, Father."

"Good, good. Very good."

Kara helped Hatter get back to his feet again, and let him out of the cell. Hatter noticed James, and a flash of recognition lit up his face.

"It's you! You're the one who wanted to buy my hat!"

James groaned inwardly but smiled as best he could. "Yes, that's right. But we need to get out of here first."

Torre helped White Rabbit to his feet.

Kara looked at James. "What are we going to do now? White Rabbit is injured, and the two who were going to take my father out of here are dead."

"I'll take him out," said White Rabbit. "I'm in no condition to go on with you. Find me a clean jacket so I can cover the wound and leave me."

"Are you sure?" asked James.

White Rabbit nodded. He looked at Kara. "Don't worry. I'll get your father out safely."

She hesitated for a moment. "Thank you."

They moved back to the guardroom at the entrance of the dungeon. James took a jacket from one of the unconscious guards and handed it to White Rabbit, who roughly bandaged his wound before putting on the new jacket.

"There we go, good as new," he said through gritted teeth.

Kara gave her father a quick hug. "I'll see you soon."

They climbed back up the stairs and stepped through the door. With a final glance at Hatter and White Rabbit, James followed Kara and Torre deeper into the castle.

CHAPTER 29

Kara took the lead again, moving with purpose through the hallways as if on official business. People were running around in a panic, lost in the confusion from the ship explosion. After many twists and turns down passageways that he quickly lost track of, Kara waved them to a stop near the end of a corridor that looked exactly like the last five they had traveled along.

"The guard post is around this corner."

James nodded. "Excellent. Let's hope Ariston's men were able to plant their explosives without being seen."

They stepped into a nearby room and waited, standing at attention as if they had been ordered to guard the room for some reason. They didn't have to wait long. Less than a minute later, explosions triggered in four different areas of the castle. Shouts of alarm went up, along with increased sounds of confusion. Several people ran from the guard post around the corner, and continued past the room and down the hall. After a few moments, they were gone.

James looked at Torre. "You're up."

They moved out of the room and purposefully set off down the corridor the way the footsteps had come from. Rounding the corner, only two guards remained guarding the hallway. They regarded the group with suspicion.

"What are you doing here?" said the one on the right. "You're not cleared for this guard duty."

Torre moved forward, with Kara and James behind. "The castle is under attack. We were ordered to come here." Both guards moved their hands toward their weapons.

"Ordered by who?" asked the guard suspiciously. His hand hovered at the hilt of his sword. The second guard began to unsling the rifle from his shoulder.

Before the guards could make any further move, Torre charged the one with the sword, knocking the man back and off his feet before he could draw the weapon. The second guard started to bring his rifle down as Torre threw his own rifle butt-first into the man's head, knocking him out. Torre then leapt on the first guard lying on the ground, and put him in a chokehold. After several moments of struggling, he finally fell unconscious.

Kara stood watch as he and Torre tied the guards and carried them to the nearby room. The path clear, the three made their way up the stairs beyond the guard post.

The group moved quickly and quietly. James constantly scanned forward and back, worried that additional guards would appear, or that they would run into some other obstacle. After several minutes, they reached the top of the tower. A heavy wooden door stood on the far side of the landing.

Kara knelt in front of the door and took a device the size of a corncob out of her bag. She put it up against the lock and began turning a small crank on the side.

After a minute, James asked worriedly, "Will you be able to open it?"

She didn't look away from the door. "Give me a few minutes. It's a complex lock, but we should be through in a few moments."

They waited anxiously as she continued turning the crank on her device. Finally, the lock emitted an audible click. Kara beamed with success.

Readying their weapons, they carefully opened the door and stepped in.

He had no idea what he had expected to find at the top of the tower, but a lavish bedroom with marble, gold, silk, and fine art was certainly not it. The room was large, at least thirty yards wide, and furnished for someone important. As he took in the room, his eyes finally ended on the large bed to one side that contained the room's occupant.

The man was old. In his world, James would have put him in his seventies or eighties, although what that was in Wonderland years, he didn't know. He was clean-shaven with balding gray hair. At first, James thought he was asleep, then he noticed the man's eyes were open and staring in their direction. He had made no movement or sound of alarm, although James realized he was trying to say something. Kara gasped when she saw him.

"Your Majesty." Kara bowed. "Please forgive our intrusion, but we're here to save you."

James looked at her. "This is the king? The real King of Hearts?"

"It certainly is," said Torre. "I saw him once, many years ago, when the Red King traveled here. This is King Charles Heart, the King of Hearts. And like Caterpillar said, the *true* King of Hearts. This proves that Lahire isn't the real king."

The king made as if to speak again. He managed to say something, but all that could be heard was a mumbled garble. He was obviously frustrated at his inability to communicate.

Kara sat on the edge of his bed and took his hand.

"It's okay. We mean you no harm, I swear. Take your time. What is it you're trying to tell us?"

Standing at the foot of the bed, James noticed the nightstand and the bottle with the spoon next to it. "What's that medicine there?"

Kara looked at it, then frowned. "Strange, the bottle isn't marked. Usually chemists like to put labels on their creations."

Torre moved over and picked up the bottle. He took off the cap and carefully sniffed it. His eyes went wide in surprise.

"It's *wicksia*."

"What's wicksia?" asked James.

Torre looked grave. "If you chew the leaves, it gives a calming effect. But when you distill wicksia like this, it becomes extremely dangerous, even on the skin. Give someone the right dosage, and it turns them into a vegetable. It would explain why the king is in his current state, if Lahire has been giving him this on a weekly basis."

"How strong is it?"

"A drop is all you'd need to put someone to sleep."

"Stop him." The king spoke in a whisper, moving his head slightly to look at first Kara, then the others.

"Stop your son, Lahire?" asked Kara.

King Heart nodded. "Unfit. Mad. Stop him." The strain of speaking was obviously great, and Kara squeezed his hand.

"We will. We're here to stop him tonight. But we need you to pretend we're not here. Can you do that?"

King Heart nodded again.

Torre bowed. "Thank you, Your Majesty. On the honor of the Castle Brigade, I swear your son's tyranny will be brought to an end this evening, and you will be restored to your rightful place on the throne."

James looked around the room. "We'd better find somewhere to hide. Kara, make sure the door is locked. We don't want to give Lahire any more reason to suspect something is up."

James moved to a floor-to-ceiling silk curtain that hung at the back of the room near the only window. Moving the curtain aside, he found a painting showing a younger version of the king, a woman, and several children. He assumed it was a picture of the Heart royal family in happier times.

Pulling the curtain back around him, James settled down to wait.

* * *

The sound of a key turning the lock of the door echoed in the room. The door opened slowly, then someone moved into the room, closing the door behind them. The unknown visitor moved across the floor toward the bed in the room.

"You're looking well, Father," said an unfamiliar male voice.

"Now!" yelled Torre.

Drawing his sword, James threw the silk curtain aside. Torre and Kara burst out of their hiding places at the same time. All three leveled their weapons at the man who stood near the bedridden king. The man turned as if to run toward the door, but then realized it was blocked by Torre. He slowly raised his hands.

"So, you're the terrorists who have been killing my people inside the castle."

Kara almost spat at him. "It ends tonight, Lahire. Your reign of terror is at an end."

"Terror? Terror? I've made Wonderland great again. You are the ones going around blowing everything up and killing people."

"And how many hundreds of thousands have you killed?" asked Torre, angrily. "What about what you did to the Red Kingdom? You massacred everyone. Men, women, children. You didn't care. They all died on your orders."

"What I've done has been solely to build up Wonderland. Your lack of vision is unfortunate, but typical of your people." Lahire stared at each of them, stopping on James. "And so I was right. The outsider has been the cause of all this trouble."

"My name is James."

"It doesn't matter what your name is. Wonderland will fall into chaos because of you. Everything I've worked toward will be destroyed."

"No, Wonderland will be returned to the people, as it should be," said Kara. "And it will happen because the people never gave up during your reign of terror, no matter how many injustices you inflicted on them."

A voice spoke from the window. "Oh, nicely said. Very nice, indeed. I'm sure that stung him." James recognized the voice and turned toward it.

Lahire took a step toward the window. "Shireche! Help me!"

James looked at Lahire. "Shireche? That's the Cheshire Cat. He's been tricking you, lying to you the entire time. He can't be trusted."

A large grin appeared in the window space, followed by a head. Slowly, the rest of the body appeared as well.

"Can't be trusted? I'm hurt. What does it matter what I am called? They are merely names, and ultimately pointless. But I must say this is playing out nicely. Tension, drama, accusations, and counter-accusations. I couldn't have hoped for a more exciting climax." The cat looked at James. "I had my doubts when you were in prison. I thought you'd failed me, like all the others. But I see I abandoned you too soon. You've come through admirably. I can't remember the last time I had this much fun."

Lahire had a look of confusion. "Shireche? What are you talking about?"

The cat grinned. "Shireche? No, the outsider is right. To everyone else I am known as the Cheshire Cat. You may call me Chesh for short, if you like. As for what's going on, why, my own entertainment, of course."

Torre waved his gun angrily at the cat. "You killed hundreds of thousands of people for entertainment?"

"Of course not. I didn't kill anyone. You people did all the killing. I merely suggested. Hinted. Passed on advice or pieces of news. Offered a voice with an opinion, nothing more. True, sometimes I may have used a little mental charm to ensure my message was believed. But can

I help it if one of the people who listened was a homicidal maniac with delusions of grandeur and a god complex?"

Lahire's expression changed to one of realization. "You used me."

Chesh grinned again. "Maybe I did. But it's not like you ever complained. You were always more than happy to slaughter a few more commoners, or send a group of people to the mines or factories because they wore blue instead of red one day. You even imprisoned the girl you loved, Helen, on my word alone. I never did any of that."

"Everything I did, I did—"

"For Wonderland. Yes, yes, I know the routine. I *gave* you the routine. Without me, you'd still be a nobody-prince waiting to inherit a decaying kingdom when your parents finally kicked the bucket. I made you, gave you purpose."

"You used me," repeated Lahire.

Chesh simply grinned… again.

Lahire lunged at the floating Chesh, drawing the dagger on his belt to slash wildly.

Chesh disappeared, then reappeared moments later to the side.

"Temper, temper. Is that any way to treat a close friend? Oh, wait. You don't have any friends, do you? You had them all arrested for treason because they were plotting against you."

Lahire lunged a second time at Chesh, who again disappeared only to reappear in a new location.

"I trusted you!" Lahire slashed wildly at Chesh a third time. "I believed everything you told me." *Slash.* "Did everything you suggested." *Slash.* "Carried out all your ideas." *Slash.* "You betrayed me." *Slash.*

Kara aimed her gun at Chesh. "He's right. You're the real threat to Wonderland. You're the one who has to pay."

Chesh grinned at Kara. "You want to hurt me, too? Tsk, tsk. That's no way to treat a friend, now, is it? After all, he's the one who's attacking poor defenseless me." Chesh's eyes glowed briefly.

Kara pointed the gun at Lahire. "Leave him alone!"

James leapt at her, managing to knock her hand to the side as she fired. The arc of electricity just missed Lahire.

Struggling to keep the gun pointed away from anyone, James stared into Kara's eyes. "Kara, the cat is messing with your mind." Her pupils were slightly dilated and her eyes unfocused. "Fight it. Think! The cat is the real enemy, not Lahire."

Torre aimed his rifle at Chesh. "What trickery are you using?"

The cat looked at Torre, its eyes glowing again. "None at all. These people are trying to hurt me. Are you going to let them hurt your dear friend? Especially that outsider?"

Torre seemed to waver, then swung his rifle toward James. He barely had time to throw himself out of the way before a ball of fire flew past his head, impacting the wall opposite and sending shards of stone flying.

Kara again turned her gun on Lahire, who dove for cover behind his father's bed as she fired a second shot.

James rolled clumsily to his feet, then staggered back as Torre charged him. Torre swung the barrel of the rifle toward his head. He managed to parry the blow with his sword.

"Torre, stop this. He's messing with your mind. You need to concentrate."

The cat began to laugh manically. "This is such fun! I should have done it years ago. I think I'll do it every decade from now on."

He backtracked around the room to keep away from Torre, who advanced menacingly. To his side, the old king struggled to get up. Lahire had climbed under the bed, sliding to the other side to avoid being shot, and looked like he might launch himself toward Chesh again. Then, James saw the bottle of wicksia sitting on the side table.

As Lahire threw himself toward Chesh, James lunged for the table. Grabbing the bottle, he mentally played out all the locations Chesh had teleported to so far, and threw it toward the ceiling in the direction his intuition told him the cat would reappear.

Chesh reappeared, having avoided Lahire's attack, as the bottle smashed against the ceiling. A rain of liquid fell, splashing onto Chesh before he could react. Chesh fell face first to the floor, landing in more of the liquid.

Kara and Torre stumbled, stopping their attacks and grabbing their heads in pain. James breathed a sigh of relief. He carefully helped them sit on the edge of the bed.

"Rest a moment. Take a minute to gather your thoughts."

"What happened?" asked Kara.

"The cat? Where is it?" asked Torre in alarm.

"It's dealt with, at least for the moment." James pointed over to where the cat lay on the floor. It was breathing, but was otherwise motionless. Then, he noticed the collapsed figure of Lahire to the side.

"Oh, no." He crossed to where Lahire lay. Splash marks from the wicksia had landed on the floor and wall around him, obviously hitting him as well.

He looked back at Torre. "Will he be all right?"

Torre shrugged, rubbing his head. "I don't know. It depends how much landed on him. It can be nasty in large doses. He could be out a few hours, or he might never wake up. A doctor would have to examine him to know more."

James turned to the King of Hearts. Relief and sadness were visible in his wrinkled face.

Kara slid over to the king and put her hand on his again. "You'll be safe now. You can rule your kingdom again."

The king struggled to form words. "Thank you."

CHAPTER 30

James looked over Heart City from the castle balcony. It was an impressive view with the gas streetlights twinkling in the night sky. He could almost believe it was a city back in his own world if he squinted hard enough.

"You look lost." He turned to see Caterpillar standing beside him.

"You."

Caterpillar chuckled. "That's not what people usually say when they see me."

"I mean, what are you doing here?"

"Dropping by to see how it all turned out. There's a difference between seeing the future and living it. Sometimes I need to remind myself of that."

"I didn't think I'd see you again after the woods."

Caterpillar looked out into the night, a far-off look on his face. "This isn't the last time we'll meet. Whether that is a good thing or a bad thing remains to be seen."

James raised an eyebrow but said nothing.

"You seem unusually silent for a man who just saved Wonderland."

"I was thinking about home, and how little any of it means to me now. Laura, my boss, my family. It doesn't worry me if I never see them again. It feels right to stay here."

Caterpillar nodded. "That is probably a wise thing. After all, if you returned, you would have to figure out what you would say to the police."

"The police?"

"A man was found dead, you were seen running from the scene, and you've been gone for two weeks. I imagine they would have a few questions for you. And I equally expect that coming up with answers they would believe would be rather difficult."

James smiled. "True. I can hardly tell them what I've been doing." He paused. "Am I really the King of the Islands Kingdom? I mean, I know about the mark and all. But it seems almost impossible. I'm just a normal guy. I don't know the first thing about being a king."

Caterpillar chuckled again. "The title is yours. You are king, if only in name at the moment. It's up to you to decide if it becomes more than a name. Besides, didn't your predecessor used to imagine six impossible things each day before she ate her breakfast?"

James smiled slightly at the memory of his brief encounter with the White Queen.

"And now, I must be going."

"It was nice to see you again." He turned, but realized he was talking to empty air.

"Why is it you're always talking to the air whenever I find you?" asked Kara, as she walked onto the balcony.

He grinned at her. "Caterpillar was here."

"He was here?" Kara looked around. "I didn't see him leave."

"Neither did I."

She joined him in staring out over the city. "The doctors finished examining Lahire. And the king."

"What was their verdict?"

"The king needs some rest, real rest, but he'll be fine. As for Lahire, they don't hold much hope. At best, they think it will be many years before he recovers. He might not recover at all."

He sighed. "I didn't mean to get him with the wicksia. I didn't even think about him, to be honest. That's what makes it worse."

"No one blames you. And at least the cat has been caught. He won't be causing any more problems for us." She was silent for a few moments. "I've been looking everywhere for you. No one knew where you were. I was afraid that…" She looked away.

"I'd gone back to my world?"

Kara nodded slowly.

He smiled. "I'm not going back. There's nothing there for me. I belong here now. And besides, even if I were going back, do you think I'd leave without saying goodbye?"

Kara shook her head, a grin breaking out on her face. "Torre will be happy. I think the reason he's been moping the last day, besides finding out that he tried to kill you, was that he thought you were going to go back to the Otherworld. He was probably trying to psych himself up to follow you."

He laughed. "Torre in my world would be... interesting. But it's probably safer for everyone if he stays here."

"He's hoping you'll rebuild the Islands Kingdom."

The smile fell from his face. "I think one day I will, but not right now. I need to learn more about Wonderland."

Kara fidgeted with the rail in front of her. "I'm going to start searching for my mother again. And track down the *Nighthawk* so I can give Uncle a piece of my mind for scaring me like that. Once I'm sure Father is okay and settled back in the shop. It would be a good way to see more of Wonderland." Kara paused, then continued awkwardly, "I'd like it if you came with me. That's if you want to."

James smiled again, turning to face Kara and taking her hands into his own. "I'd like that. I'd like that a lot."

THE END

ABOUT THE AUTHOR

Jason G. Anderson lives in Hobart, Tasmania with his wife and several cats. During the day, he helps Antarctic scientists manage the vast quantities of data they collect. At night, he dreams of other worlds and realities much different to our own. His writing interests include sci-fi, urban fantasy, post-apocalyptic and steampunk.

You can find him online at www.jasonga.com, along with links to his Twitter and Facebook pages, and a contact form for sending email.

92367661R00132

Made in the USA
Middletown, DE
08 October 2018